THE USUAL WITCHSPECTS

A WICKED WITCHES OF THE MIDWEST
MYSTERY BOOK 25

AMANDA M. LEE

WINCHESTERSHAW PUBLICATIONS

PROLOGUE
EIGHTEEN YEARS AGO

"I don't think this is a good idea," my cousin Clove whined as she wrung her hands and looked out from behind the bush that hid us from Mrs. Little's big bay window.

"Nobody asked your opinion," Aunt Tillie replied. She cuffed the back of Clove's head for good measure. "In fact, I never want your opinion. *Capiche?*"

Clove might've been a whiner—okay, she was definitely a whiner—but she wasn't a pushover. That's why, when she glared at Aunt Tillie and planted her hands on her hips—at ten she didn't really have hips, but she did her best—she meant business.

"I'm going to tell Aunt Winnie," she announced.

I slapped my hand over my face. Leave it to Clove to go straight into tattletale mode. That wasn't out of the ordinary for her. Me, on the other hand? I tended to try to escape when Aunt Tillie forced us to embark on a revenge adventure. It was easier to flee than to fight.

Yes, I, Bay Winchester, was more than willing to take the path of least resistance if I thought the situation warranted it. I wasn't going to apologize for it either.

"You're going to tell Winnie what?" Aunt Tillie challenged.

"I'm going to tell her that you didn't really take us into town for hot chocolate and doughnuts, and instead you made us camp outside Mrs.

Little's house so you can use magic to wrap it in Saran Wrap and lock her in."

"It's not Saran Wrap," Aunt Tillie argued. "It's a gooey transparent substance that will trap her inside her house."

"You said it was like plastic wrap and wouldn't hurt her," Clove argued.

"You did say that," my other cousin Thistle offered. She wasn't interested in hiding behind the bush—it wasn't as if Mrs. Little wouldn't know who had tortured her yet again—and was instead chewing on a licorice piece as she hopped from one foot to the other to amuse herself. Unlike me, who avoided conflict whenever possible, and Clove, who whined until we all wanted to gag her, Thistle attacked things head on. Even if the thing that needed attacking was Aunt Tillie.

"Nobody asked you, Mouth," Aunt Tillie barked.

Inside the house, Mrs. Little stirred. She'd been sitting in the living room watching television, her crochet hook going a mile a minute, seemingly oblivious to our presence. Aunt Tillie had a voice that carried under normal circumstances, however. When she was excited—like now—it was double the volume but half the fun.

Thistle was blasé in the face of Aunt Tillie's annoyance. "I'm just saying."

"Well, don't say." Aunt Tillie looked at me for help. "I thought you were supposed to keep them in line."

I snorted. "Since when have I ever been able to keep them in line?"

"You're the oldest, Bay." Aunt Tillie's tone brooked no nonsense. "You have to keep them on the straight and narrow."

"The straight and narrow what?" I asked.

"The straight and narrow path to 'Do what I say or I'll make you cry!'"

"Why would I be the one in charge? They're both louder."

"Ain't that the truth?" Aunt Tillie glared at my cousins. Thistle shot her a cheeky smile in return, which didn't seem to do anything to alleviate Aunt Tillie's irritation. When she turned back to me, I knew I was in for a lecture. "You're the oldest, Bay. You're supposed to be in charge."

"I don't believe that's an actual rule," I argued.

"And I'm not listening to her just because she's older," Thistle argued.

"You're fourteen, Bay," Aunt Tillie insisted. "You're a woman now. You have to start doing womanly things."

Thistle snorted. "Did you hear that, Bay? Start popping out some babies. Aunt Tillie says it's okay."

Aunt Tillie aimed her hand for the back of Thistle's head, but my cousin was too fast.

"You snooze, you lose, old lady," Thistle taunted.

Aunt Tillie extended a warning finger in Thistle's direction. "You want to be very careful, Mouth," she warned. "If you're as bored as you sound—and you do indeed sound bored—I can make things more exciting for you."

Thistle didn't look worried or impressed. "I'm not afraid of you."

"I am," Clove supplied. "Last week when I told her I wasn't going to do this stuff anymore—I really need my beauty sleep—she hexed my feet so they looked like hobbit feet. I couldn't wear dress shoes to the dance. I had to wear boots and pretend I was making a statement."

"What sort of statement do you make with boots?"

She shrugged. "I don't know. I think it had something to do with feminism. At least that's what I told people."

"Did your feet return to normal when you stopped being a kvetch?" Aunt Tillie challenged.

Clove nodded solemnly. "Yes, but I had to shave a few remaining strands of hair the other day."

"Keep them as a reminder that I'm the boss." Aunt Tillie puffed herself out. Then she deflated a bit. "What was I saying again?"

"That Bay is the boss, but she's not," Thistle replied. "I'm the boss."

"You're not the boss of anything." Aunt Tillie's look of derision might've hurt a mere mortal's feelings. Thistle didn't care in the least.

"Oh, but I am. I'm the boss of you." The smile Thistle shot Aunt Tillie meant trouble.

"Is that so?" Aunt Tillie folded her arms over her chest. She wasn't even paying attention to Mrs. Little any longer, which begged the question of why we were here in the first place.

"I said it," Thistle replied. "I meant it." She did a little dance. "I. Am. The. Boss." She wiggled her hips. "You're too old to stop me."

I opened my mouth to defuse the tension, but it was already too late. Aunt Tillie let loose her magic and it blew Thistle back a good seven or eight feet. My cousin hit the ground with enough force that I cringed. She landed in a mud puddle and rolled to her knees sputtering.

"I lost my licorice," she announced.

Aunt Tillie smiled. "You're the boss. Find it." She turned to me. "Let's get back to the important stuff, shall we?"

I didn't see that I had a choice. If I argued, I would end up in the mud pit right next to Thistle. Clove seemed to have come to that conclusion too, because she was suddenly the picture of cooperation.

"I certainly want to help you, Aunt Tillie," she said. "I'm here to serve."

Aunt Tillie shook her head. "You're such a suck-up." She turned to me. "Are you going to give me lip?"

"Nope." My response was out before Thistle could make a derogatory butt-kissing sound. "I'm all in."

"Lovely." Aunt Tillie's expression projected serenity, but I knew better. She was revved. "You go to the back of the house, Bay. I'm going to throw some magic your way and I expect you to keep it tight to the house and then send it this way. I want it to go around like a circle."

I could picture what she had planned. That didn't mean I thought it would work.

"What's the goal?" I asked. "She's going to try to leave and walk into a wall of magic that ... what?"

"That doesn't allow her to leave."

"Okay, but why not just ward the house so she's trapped?" That was the part I couldn't wrap my head around.

"It's more fun if she gets slimed when she tries to escape."

"Oh," I said in unison with Thistle and Clover.

"You should've led with that part," Thistle said as she tried to deal with the mud. "We would've been much more open to that."

"Just go around back," Aunt Tillie ordered me. "I don't want to be out here all night. I have television to watch."

"Yes, we wouldn't want to get in the way of Aunt Tillie watching *Charmed*."

"Hey!" Aunt Tillie's eyes fired. "I have to get my laughs somewhere. Those girls are out there fighting made-up demons in bras, for crying out loud. If that's not comedy, I don't know what is."

Because I was anxious to put this night behind me, I took off in the direction Aunt Tillie had indicated. I wasn't afraid to walk behind Mrs. Little's house even though it was in the middle of nowhere and the only thing to see besides the house was trees. We'd been out here so many times that I knew this property as well as I did our own.

Once I was in position, I waited. I didn't think it would take long for Aunt Tillie to start funneling me magic. She had zero patience and would lose interest in our task soon if she didn't get moving.

Sure enough, the magic rocketed around the house within seconds of me getting into position. I redirected it so it banked around the house and back to the front. A low hum filled the air as the magic built, and as the wall of slime—why she referred to it as plastic wrap was beyond me—built, I watched, impressed despite my determination not to be.

"Wow," was all I could say as the magic pulsed. Mrs. Little was going to have a rough go of it tomorrow morning.

I watched for a few more seconds and then headed back to where I'd left the others. The area was empty.

My heart leapt as I increased my pace. Aunt Tillie was big on annoying us—she said she had to get her jollies somewhere—but she didn't often leave us to our own devices in the middle of the night. I was old enough to figure out a way home, but that wasn't how I wanted to spend the rest of my night.

I was halfway up Mrs. Little's driveway when a figure appeared. It had broad shoulders and was a good foot and a half taller than Aunt Tillie.

"Officer Terry," I said when his eyes landed on me. Now I was worried for a different reason. Terry Davenport was the lead detective with the Walkerville Police Department. Most people said he would be the next chief. He was a constant presence in my life because Aunt Tillie was always getting us in trouble. He was something of a surrogate father for my cousins and me after our fathers had moved downstate.

"Bay." Officer Terry's tone was grave. "What are you doing out here alone in the middle of the night?"

It was then that I realized what had happened. I had to crane my neck to get a glimpse of the road and, sure enough, his cruiser was parked behind Aunt Tillie's truck. The others would've seen him park and hide. I didn't know he was here, so I hadn't had that opportunity.

"Um ... I was taking a walk," I lied lamely.

"Really?" Officer Terry's eyebrows winged up. "You were walking by Margaret Little's house at midnight? By yourself?"

I was a pretty good liar thanks to Aunt Tillie. She'd given us all lying lessons when we were younger. Clove had excelled compared to the rest of us. Lying didn't make me feel guilty, but for some reason I could never lie to

Officer Terry. It wasn't just that he knew, but that I felt sick to my stomach whenever I tried.

"Um..." I rubbed my cheek.

"Don't give yourself a stroke, Bay," he chided when my cheeks began to burn under his steady gaze. "Come here." He motioned for me to get closer, so I did. He stroked his hand down my hair, then sighed. "Tillie, can you not sacrifice your great-niece and actually take responsibility for once?" he called out.

I didn't hold my breath for her response.

Officer Terry had dealt with Aunt Tillie enough that he wasn't about to fall victim to her silence. "I have cupcakes, Clove," he sang out.

To the right, the bushes rustled.

"He's messing with you," Aunt Tillie hissed in a voice that carried. "Don't listen to him."

"I want a cupcake," Clove replied. She was all smiles as she appeared from behind the bush. "Are they chocolate?"

"I don't actually have a cupcake," Officer Terry replied.

Clove's mouth dropped open as abject horror washed over her face. "You lied to me?"

"I'll take you for cupcakes tomorrow," he promised. "You can get hot chocolate and a cupcake."

"Two cupcakes," Clove negotiated.

He rolled his eyes. "Fine. Two cupcakes." His gaze moved back to the bushes. "You're only getting one if you don't come out right now, Thistle."

Thistle was not having fun. The mud had already started to dry, and it gave her a weird ashy look that reminded me of photos I've seen of refugees after a bombing.

Officer Terry's mouth fell open when he saw her. "What happened to you?"

"What do you think?" Thistle jerked her thumb toward the bushes. "You should lock her up."

"Oh, if only." Officer Terry shook his head. "Tillie, don't you think you should come out?" he prodded.

"No Tillies here, aye," Aunt Tillie replied in a thick accent. I couldn't decide what accent she was trying to adopt. It was a mixture of Mexican, Russian, and maybe even a little Canadian thrown in for good measure.

"Fine." Officer Terry prodded us toward his vehicle. "Since that's Tillie

Winchester's truck, I'm going to have it towed. She's not here and all. Then I'll take her great-nieces home. That's the best I can do this evening."

Aunt Tillie's head popped up from behind the bush. "Don't even think about taking my truck."

Officer Terry didn't jolt at her appearance. "What are you doing out here?" he complained.

"I have no idea what you're talking about," Aunt Tillie replied. "We were out for a walk. Bay told you."

"Bay is the worst liar known to man," Officer Terry replied. His gaze moved to Mrs. Little's house. I had no idea if he could see the magic—he didn't like talking about our witchy abilities—but he wasn't stupid enough to believe we'd just been spying. "How bad is this going to be?" he asked.

"Worse than the time I made her shoes sound like farts when she walked, but better than the time I made her plumbing explode. I really had no idea how bad that one was going to get."

Officer Terry looked caught between annoyance and amusement. "Why won't you leave her alone?"

"You know why."

"She's a pain, yes," Officer Terry acknowledged, "but she's not the Devil."

"You don't know her well enough."

He kept one hand on my shoulder. "Tillie, one of these days you'll push her too far. She'll retaliate in a big way, and it won't be pretty."

"I'm not afraid of her," Aunt Tillie countered.

"Maybe you should be. If she's pushed far enough, she could be dangerous."

"I'm not worried about that." Aunt Tillie was firm. "She'll never be strong enough to take me on."

Officer Terry wouldn't let it go. "What if she figures out a way to ruin your life? If you keep pushing her, that'll be her main focus."

"She'll never beat me."

Officer Terry switched his gaze to me. He looked worried. "Come on, girls. I'm taking you home. I want to talk to your mothers."

Aunt Tillie's mouth dropped open "Are you going to narc on me?"

"You bet."

"And here I was starting to like you," Aunt Tillie lamented.

"I think I'll survive." He sent me an encouraging smile.

"We still get our cupcakes tomorrow, right?" Clove demanded.

"Yes, Clove." Officer Terry sounded tired. "A promise is a promise."

"I just don't want this whole night to be for nothing."

"I'll get you your cupcakes. Give it a rest."

As I walked with him, I thought about what he'd said. Would there come a time when Mrs. Little stopped being a victim and became a real threat? What would that even look like?

1

ONE

PRESENT DAY

"Just where do you think you're going?"

My mother could freeze the testicles off a polar bear when she used that specific tone.

I looked up at the front desk of The Overlook, the inn she ran with my aunts in Hemlock Cove, a small hamlet in northern Lower Michigan that had once been known as Walkerville. Years ago, realizing the industrial base was dying, the town had been rebranded into a witch town. We were real witches, so now we had to pretend to be humans putting on a show. Somehow, we made it work.

"I don't know what you're talking about," I lied.

My husband, Landon Michaels, strolled into the lobby with a cupcake in his hand and his dog Winchester trailing at his heels. The puppy knew that Landon was a softie when it came to food and almost always stuck to him.

"I don't believe you," Mom said.

"That was a pretty weak lie," Landon agreed before biting into his cupcake. He got chocolate frosting all over his cheek but didn't seem to care. When he spoke again, it was with a mouth full of cake. "Did you ever fall for her lies when she was a kid?" he asked my mother.

"When she was a teenager, she was a better liar," Mom replied. "As a child, she folded under pressure. As an adult, it depends on how much effort she puts into it."

I rolled my eyes. "We're not doing anything. Why do you assume we're doing something?"

The question was barely out of my mouth when an enchanted porcelain clown doll strolled into the room and looked around at us.

"Oh, holy hell!" Landon jumped and raced toward my mother. "What's that doing down here?"

I pursed my lips as my mother's gaze sharpened.

"Hi-ho, hi-ho, it's off to stalk we go," the clown sang.

Mom's mouth was a flat line as she regarded me. "Do you want to try answering my question again?"

"Not really," I replied. "It's probably best you don't know."

Mom crossed her arms over her chest and waited.

"Fine. We're taking the clowns out of the attic. You want that space for Chief Terry so he can have an office. You're the one who told us to get the clowns out."

Aunt Tillie had been collecting ugly and creepy—oh, so very creepy—clowns for months. She'd been doing it on the sly and discovering them had been traumatic for everybody. Now we were moving her enchanted collection elsewhere.

"Why are they walking and talking?" Landon demanded. He'd crawled on top of the lobby desk. He still had a firm grip on his cupcake.

"There are too many to carry."

"Where are you moving them to?" Mom asked in her prim and proper voice.

"Tell me about the wedding plans," I asked. "Is everything set? Are you excited?"

Mom was engaged to Chief Terry—something I'd been hoping and dreaming for since I was a child—and their wedding wasn't far off. Mom didn't want a big to-do, but I'd insisted there be a party.

"The wedding is on schedule, and I have everything handled," Mom replied. "I want to know where you plan on taking those clowns."

Her tone told me there was no getting out of this. "We're taking them to Mrs. Little's house. They're going to sing and dance."

Mom scowled. "Bay—"

I cut her off. "Have you forgotten that she was trying to buy up property to become the queen of Hemlock Cove?" I demanded.

In truth, there had been a time when I thought easing up on Mrs. Little was in our best interests. That time had passed. Mrs. Little had allied herself with a djinn to hurt us. Then she'd gone behind everyone's back with a crooked and diabolical real estate agent to purchase huge swathes of town property. I was done playing nice with the woman. If Aunt Tillie wanted to make her cry, I was going to be part of the team that made her cry.

"Of course I haven't forgotten." Some of Mom's irritation waned. "When you do things like this, however, it sets her off."

"She's got it coming." I was grim.

"I have to agree with Bay," Landon said. His cupcake had disappeared, but he was still eyeing the clown with a great deal of dislike. "She does have it coming."

"I can't believe you're for this," Mom argued, her attention moving to Landon. "You're a duly sworn police officer."

"FBI agent," he corrected.

"Doesn't that make it worse?"

He shrugged. "She's got it coming."

"We already told everyone in town what she had planned," Mom argued. "She's the town pariah. This will make things worse."

"Can they get worse?" I challenged.

"Things can always get worse."

"Blah, blah, blah." The clown waved its porcelain hand. "Let's do something," he complained.

I glared at him. The clown dolls weren't a favorite, but they were a necessary evil. "We're going." I moved closer to Landon. "Once we're gone, you can take Winchester home. Take some cupcakes. I'll want a snack."

Landon shook his head. "You know I can't promise those cupcakes will last until you get home."

"There had better be two cupcakes waiting for me. I'll be mad otherwise. That means you'll be sad." I kissed the corner of his mouth, which still tasted of frosting. "Wait up if you want a little treat of your own. I'm betting I'll be feeling pretty good about life when we're done."

Landon's eyes gleamed. "That might convince me to save some

cupcakes." His grin was wide. "Don't get in too much trouble and try not to be late."

With one more look at Mom, who appeared to be resigned, I grinned. "I'll do my best."

WE LOADED THE CLOWNS INTO THE BACK OF Aunt Tillie's truck and then drove to Mrs. Little's house. We had a special spot where we parked—it was hidden behind several big trees—and that's where we unloaded the clowns.

"Listen up," Aunt Tillie commanded her small army. She was dressed in black and had donned her camouflage helmet. "Tonight is the night we take back this town. No longer will we let obnoxious usurpers rule us. We are going to rule." She shook her fist. "We shall be victorious!"

The clowns didn't look impressed.

"Can we just get going?" one of them asked. It was a rag doll clown, and I couldn't understand how it was walking on fabric legs. "I have to sing, or I'll lose my mind."

A murmur of agreement went through the other clowns, which only made them creepier.

"We must sing," one of the other clowns yelled.

"We must sing!" they all raged.

"We must dance," the same clown bellowed.

"We must dance!"

I had to press my lips together to keep from laughing. The clowns might've been creepy, but they were energetic. Who didn't love an energetic clown? Right, me. I didn't love clowns in the slightest. I was making an exception.

My attention was drawn to a car pulling to a stop behind Aunt Tillie's truck. For a moment I thought we were in real trouble. Once the driver killed the engine, however, I realized it was Thistle's car.

"I didn't know you were coming," I said as she exited the vehicle.

"I'm not missing this." She grinned as she took in the clowns. "This feels like a Winchester rite of passage. No self-respecting Winchester would miss this."

"Is Clove coming?" I asked.

"No, she's afraid of the clowns."

"So one self-respecting Winchester is missing this."

She lifted one shoulder. "She'll regret it when all we do is talk about it tomorrow." She clapped her hands together. "Okay, how are we doing this?"

I looked to Aunt Tillie for an answer.

"They're already trained," Aunt Tillie replied. "All we have to do is give them the most innocent of commands."

I was suddenly suspicious. "What ... like are you asking them to trim her bushes?"

Thistle burst out laughing.

"I didn't mean it in a dirty way," I complained.

"She's going to ask them to fluff her pillows," Thistle said.

"Listen, little gutter brains, it's nothing like that." Aunt Tillie looked frustrated. She turned to the clowns, which were practically frothing at the mouth. "Are you guys ready?"

"Hi-ho," they all sang out, dragging out the final syllable.

"Great." Aunt Tillie's smile was serene. "Kill."

I thought for a moment I'd misheard her. The clowns raised their fists and took off into the night at the one-word command.

"Are you kidding me?"

"They're not actually going to kill her," Aunt Tillie replied. We followed her to the driveway "They're going to wreak havoc on her yard."

It wasn't hard to make out the clowns because of the lights in the flowerbeds. Most of the clowns were short—less than sixteen inches—but a few were taller. One, in fact, was four feet tall. I hadn't seen it in the back of the truck, but it was here now. It looked like the clown from *It*. The movie, not the miniseries.

"Where did that come from?" I asked.

"What?" Aunt Tillie looked anywhere but at the tall clown.

"The Pennywise." I pointed.

Aunt Tillie slapped my hand down and hissed. "Don't say his name."

The trepidation I'd felt when I'd first heard about Aunt Tillie's revenge scheme roared back with a vengeance. "What did you do?" I demanded.

"Just don't say his name." Aunt Tillie's eyes flashed. "Ignore him. He only gets worked up if you pay him too much attention."

"What's his deal?"

"He's excitable. His name is Burt, by the way."

"Burt the Clown?" Thistle challenged.

"That's what I said."

I shifted my gaze away from her—although I was still suspicious—and watched as Pennywise—er, Burt—took long strides toward the front of Mrs. Little's house. Compared to the other clowns, he was gigantic. Even though I had more than a foot on him, he made me incredibly nervous.

"Does he have a knife?" Thistle asked.

She had a better vantage point, so I moved closer to her. Sure enough, the clown gripped a huge butcher knife. "Aunt Tillie," I growled.

"It's not my fault," she complained, slapping her hands to her cheeks. "I was just trying to give him a little extra oomph. I think he's sentient."

"What?" I practically roared the question.

"He was supposed to spout horror lines from the movie. At first it was fine, but he was a little dull. Then I revved him up and ... well ... he escaped from the greenhouse."

"Escaped?" I didn't even know they'd been locked up.

"He's got a mean streak. I don't know what to tell you. I'm not even sure how he found us tonight. He's been missing for three days."

My heart caught in my throat when the four-foot doll strolled to the front door to ring the bell. The next part happened in slow motion. Mrs. Little—clearly realizing she was being invaded thanks to the singing clowns—kicked open the screen door, the shotgun in her hands aimed at the big clown.

"Oh," Thistle started.

"My," I muttered.

"Goddess," Aunt Tillie finished.

Mrs. Little leveled the gun at the clown's chest and pulled the trigger before I could manage a single breath. The clown was propelled backward, stuffing flying everywhere, and knocked down the steps. The knife clattered on the walkway.

All the while, the clowns sang and danced.

To my utter horror, the doll got back on its feet. It looked even more evil than it had moments before.

"What did you fuel that thing with?" I shrieked.

"Tillie!" Mrs. Little screamed as she racked the shotgun.

The clown took deliberate steps toward her, all the while cackling like something straight out of a horror movie.

My instinct was to protect Mrs. Little. It was one thing to let the clowns sing until she wanted to scream and to tear up her yard. It was quite another to allow the tall clown to rip her to shreds and use her intestines as a necklace. I tried to throw magic at the clown, but it shrugged off the effort as if it was nothing.

Slowly, I tracked my gaze to Aunt Tillie. "What did you do?"

"This isn't my fault," Aunt Tillie complained. "It was just a little spell. It somehow took on a life of its own."

"Oh, right," Thistle said. "Because that's never happened to us before."

"Not us," I barked. "Her! It's always her!"

"Oh, take it down a notch." Aunt Tillie looked perplexed. "It's fine. I just have to talk to him."

"Talk to him?" Thistle challenged.

"That's what I said."

"Good grief." Thistle slapped her hands over her eyes as Mrs. Little took aim yet again. "I can't look."

Mrs. Little pulled the trigger without any hesitation. The clown was thrown back a second time. This time it didn't get up, which allowed me to breathe again. The relief didn't last long, because Mrs. Little was reloading again.

"I'm going to kill you, Tillie," she screeched. "You've finally gone too far. I'm going to kill you and there's no jury in the world that will convict me."

All around her yard, the clowns sang and danced. She ignored them. I glanced at the fallen Burt and to my horror realized he was no longer on the ground where he'd landed. "Where did he go?" I darted my eyes left and right, horrified at what I might find.

The sound of Mrs. Little snapping the barrel in place drew my eyes back to her.

"I'm going to end you, Tillie! Now!"

I grabbed Aunt Tillie's arm and pushed her back toward the road. Her little legs couldn't move very fast, so I used my magic to push her along.

"I can do it myself," she barked.

I ignored her, and risked a look over my shoulder at Thistle, who had her head down and was passing Aunt Tillie. I slowed enough to meet Mrs. Little's gaze. All I saw was a lot of crazy.

"You've messed with me for the last time!" she yelled before aiming the shotgun in my direction.

I started running again. I made it only a few feet before I tripped over something in the ditch and pitched forward. The deafening roar of the gun had me checking myself for injuries. I'd read stories about people being shot and the adrenaline carrying them for a long time before they fell.

Once I was assured I was fine, I lifted my head to make sure Thistle and Aunt Tillie had made it to safety. I saw them crouching behind Aunt Tillie's truck.

I stayed low in the ditch and swiveled back to gauge Mrs. Little's location. That's when I saw what I'd tripped over.

We'd missed the body on our approach because we'd taken the driveway.

With shaky hands, I pulled out my phone. The only thing I could make out with absolute certainty was that we were dealing with a man. A very dead man. I hit the flashlight app and aimed it at his face.

I heard Mrs. Little screeching at the clowns as she tried to stomp them. At least she'd run out of ammunition. When I finally managed to focus on the body, my blood ran cold.

I recognized him.

He wasn't a resident.

He wasn't a tourist.

It was Brad Childs, the man who had been stalking me for weeks because he knew I was magical and wanted a favor I wasn't willing to give.

My breath snaked out and I briefly closed my eyes. Then I got it together and hit Landon's name on my contact list.

"I need you at Mrs. Little's house," I said.

"I'm on my way, Bay. Sit tight. I'll be there in five minutes."

2
TWO

Mrs. Little's screaming at the clowns turned into background noise as I waited for Landon. He arrived quickly, and he wasn't alone. Chief Terry was with him when he parked on the road and ran to us.

"We can't fix that," Chief Terry warned, pointing at the mayhem.

I glanced in that direction and shrugged. "Nobody can. The Pennywise clown has been shot twice and is now missing."

"The what?" Landon looked caught between hugging me and running. Panic filled his eyes whenever he looked at the clowns.

"Burt," Aunt Tillie insisted. "He's not Pennywise. Calling him that makes him diabolical. He's just Burt."

"I don't like this." Landon shook his head. "Make them stop."

Aunt Tillie glanced up at the clowns, and I swear a smirk washed over her face. Then she collected herself. "I will in a second."

"Bay." Landon said my name with a soupçon of emotion. When he looked at me again, though—I mean really looked—he seemed to realize that it wasn't the clowns getting me going.

"There's a body," I replied to his unasked question. "I tripped over it when Mrs. Little aimed the shotgun at me."

"She shot at you?" Chief Terry's eyebrows practically flew off his forehead.

"To be fair, she shot Burt twice, but he kept getting up," Thistle offered. "In her position, I would've started shooting at us too." She darted a dark glare to Aunt Tillie. "Someone left a few details out of her retelling of the specifics of her animation spell."

"Well, first things first." Landon ran his hand over my shoulder. He could tell I was upset. "Where's the body?"

I led them to it. Landon had his flashlight out and was looking before we even reached our destination. When the beam swept over Childs's face, his body went rigid.

"Bay, that's Brad Childs," Chief Terry said in a tight voice.

"I know."

"Oh, man." Landon moved into the ditch and hunkered down for a look at the body. "I don't see any obvious wounds. His neck might be broken."

Chief Terry looked as if he was about to start yelling. When his eyes moved to me his expression softened. Then Mrs. Little screamed at the clowns again and his face filled with fury. "Make those go away," he barked at Aunt Tillie.

"They're not doing anything but singing," Aunt Tillie argued.

"Burt is out there with a knife," Thistle added.

Aunt Tillie murdered Thistle with a single glare. "Do you want me to send him after you?"

"You can't control him," Thistle shot back. "It's out there—looking like the ghost of horror clowns past—and it's been shot twice and still has a huge butcher knife. You didn't plan for it to do that."

Chief Terry slapped a hand over his face.

Thistle looked at me. "Why does he always spoil you, but I get yelled at?" she complained.

"Because you like to push everybody's buttons," Chief Terry replied. Despite his harsh words, he gave her a soft smile. "I'm just ... concerned ... about this situation. I don't mean to take it out on you."

"It's fine." Thistle waved him off. "I'm kind of numb to it. Bay has always been your favorite."

"That's not true," Chief Terry protested.

Multiple snorts went up, including from Landon and me.

Chief Terry protested. "I always treated you all equally," he insisted.

"Not even close," Aunt Tillie replied. "Bay was your little angel. You treated the rest of us like lepers."

"You can't include yourself in that statement because you weren't a child when I started spending time with you," Chief Terry countered.

"My feelings were still hurt," Aunt Tillie replied. It was obvious to everybody that she was trying to manipulate the situation because the clowns were out of control.

"You'll get over it." Chief Terry planted his hands on his hips and looked out at the clowns. "They have to go before the other investigators get here. We cannot explain those things."

"What other investigators?" My forehead wrinkled.

"The ones we're going to have to call in," Landon replied. He was careful not to get anywhere near the body. "Bay, did you touch him?"

"I tripped over him," I replied. "I think it was only his arm. Why do you have to call in other investigators?"

"Are you kidding?" Landon was incredulous. "This is Brad Childs."

"If you ask me, this is good for us," Aunt Tillie interjected. "He's been stalking Bay for weeks. It's always good to get rid of stalkers."

The look Landon shot her promised retribution. "Nobody asked you."

"I'm just saying!"

Landon stared at her hard, then shook his head. When he turned back to me, it was clear his patience was wearing thin. "We filed a report to cover ourselves, Bay. Remember? We wanted the higher-ups to be aware that Childs was harassing you in case ... well, in case he made a move on the family, and we had to kill him."

"You mentioned doing it, but I didn't think it was that big of a deal," I argued.

"It wasn't a big deal," Landon assured me. "I just sat down with my boss, explained the situation—"

"You explained that Bay used her magic to catch a bunch of escaped prisoners and Childs found out about it and stalked her because he wanted her to cast a spell to get his job as warden back?" Thistle challenged.

Landon's cool glare moved to her. "Not exactly."

"We came up with the story together," Chief Terry volunteered. "We said Childs seemed unhinged after losing his job and embraced the Hemlock Cove mystique. This town having the witch theme was helpful. We told the FBI local director that we were worried because he was demonstrating unhinged behavior toward Bay."

"Unlike the unhinged behavior you deal with on a daily basis at family dinner?" Thistle offered.

Chief Terry narrowed his eyes. "This is why Bay is my favorite, Thistle. We have a serious problem and limited time to deal with it."

"I always knew she was your favorite. At least you finally admitted it." Despite being a constant agitator, Thistle held up her hands in supplication when Chief Terry snarled. "I'm really not trying to be difficult. I'm just thrown."

That seemed to be enough of an apology to placate Chief Terry. "We said that Childs was making demands for potions and spells, and stalking Bay. We needed it on the record just in case."

"In case of what?" I asked.

"In case he broke into our home or ended up dead on the family property," Landon replied.

"What was he doing here?" Aunt Tillie asked. Her face screwed up in concentration and when she lifted her finger in a "eureka" moment, I knew I was going to hate her answer. "I bet he was working with Margaret to bring about the end of the world."

"Or he was working with Margaret to try to get one over on you guys," Landon countered. When the clowns started singing another refrain of their song, he exploded. "Stop them right now!"

Aunt Tillie looked taken aback by his anger. "I was just getting to it. There's no reason to be a whiner." She lifted her hands and started waving them about like some sort of voodoo queen performing a dance. When she finished, the dolls fell motionless in the yard.

"That's something at least." Landon rubbed his cheek. "We have to get them out of here before they send a team from my office."

"Why would it be a team from your office?" I was still trying to figure that part out. "Why not the Michigan State Police?"

"Because they have a history with Childs from the search," Chief Terry replied. "We want Landon's team to do the investigating. That's why we filed the report with them."

If Landon and Chief Terry thought this was the best option, I was right there with them. "Okay, what do we do?"

"Get rid of the clowns," Chief Terry replied.

"What about the clowns that ran off into the woods?" Thistle asked. "Did you turn them off, too?"

Aunt Tillie nodded. "Of course."

I stared at her. "Are you just saying that, or did you really turn them off?"

"Well..." Aunt Tillie tilted her head and scratched her cheek. "The thing is, Burt wasn't the only one showing signs of sentience. It's possible they're in the woods sleeping it off."

"What else is it possible they're doing?" Landon demanded.

"Putting together a hit squad to kill Margaret." Aunt Tillie held out her hands. "What? It was just supposed to be a fun little game. I couldn't know that a body was going to end up in the ditch."

"What body?" a craggy voice demanded. Mrs. Little, her eyes lined with fury and still clutching her shotgun, gave us all dark looks in turn. "I have the legal right to shoot all of you for being on my property without invitation."

Chief Terry made an impatient clucking sound with his tongue. "You're not shooting anybody."

"Besides," Thistle said. "There's already a body." She gestured to Childs, whose wide sightless eyes were pointed at the moon. "What did you do to him?"

I watched Mrs. Little closely as she stared at the body. She looked perplexed. "I don't know him but ... why does he look familiar? He's not a resident."

"He's been hanging around," Chief Terry replied. "You didn't kill him, did you?"

Mrs. Little was incensed. "I've been harassed to the point of no return by clowns tonight and you're blaming me for this?"

"It's your property," Landon added.

"And your wife, her cousin, and her crazy great-aunt invaded my property to terrorize me. Why aren't they your primary suspects?"

"We're not going to have primary suspects," Chief Terry replied grimly. He pulled out his phone. "This isn't going to be our investigation."

"Why not?" Mrs. Little looked a little more than confused.

"Because this man has been hanging around town acting strangely for weeks," Landon replied. "He was the warden at the Antrim Correctional Facility."

"Why was he hanging around here?" Mrs. Little asked.

"That's going to be for the other team to ascertain. We can't investigate this." Landon was resigned. "We need to clean up the clowns. That's one thing we don't need to explain when the team gets here."

"I'm fine explaining what happened with the clowns," Mrs. Little challenged. "I am the victim in all of this."

"Sure," Landon replied in his most reasonable voice. "What are you going to tell the investigators?"

"I'm going to tell them that Tillie Winchester has mounted a campaign of harassment that would've left a lesser woman bereft," Mrs. Little replied without hesitation. "I'm going to tell them that Tillie sent killer clowns after me."

"How do you think they're going to react to that?" Chief Terry demanded.

"Look around." Mrs. Little gestured toward her yard. To her surprise—and mine—the clowns were gone.

I slid my eyes to Aunt Tillie. "What did you do?" I hissed.

"Don't worry about it." Aunt Tillie was the picture of nonchalance. "I've got everything under control."

"Is anybody else terrified?" Thistle asked.

Landon raised his hand. Then he shook his head. "We have to call for help. You guys need to go to the inn. You can't be here when they get here."

I didn't like it, but I understood it. "Are you going to be okay?" I asked him. "Do you need me?"

Landon stroked my hair. "I always need you. Right now, you can't be here."

I nodded. "We'll be back at the inn."

"Don't eat all the cupcakes without me," he warned.

"I promise I'll save you a cupcake."

"Two," he corrected. "Wait ... five."

"Just do what you need to do," I said. "We'll do the same."

"I'm on it," Chief Terry said as he pressed the button. "This isn't going to be pretty."

MOM AND MY AUNTS WERE IN THE FAMILY LIVING quarters when we returned to the inn. Thistle beat a hasty retreat to the converted barn she lived in with her boyfriend Marcus. I didn't blame her for wanting to escape.

That left me to explain things.

"How did it go?" my Aunt Twila asked.

"It could've gone better." I sank into one of the chairs and launched into the tale. It hadn't escaped my attention that Graham Stratton, Hawthorne Hollow's police chief, was on the couch next to my Aunt Marnie. They'd been dating a few weeks, and he was becoming a regular fixture at meals ... both at night and in the morning.

When I finished my story, I waited for the explosion. It didn't take long.

"You cursed a Pennywise doll and let it have a knife?" Mom screeched at Aunt Tillie.

"I don't appreciate your tone," Aunt Tillie replied. She'd found a bottle of her homemade wine and was busily sipping from it.

"I don't appreciate you always taking it a step too far," Mom argued. "Why can't you ever just do a little mischief? You always have to be the biggest and baddest witch on the block."

"I am the biggest and baddest witch on the block."

"I don't think you can reasonably say that with Bay, Scout, and Stormy running around," Graham interjected. He shrank back when Aunt Tillie attempted to peel his skin with her glare. "Or I will sit here and mind my own business."

I let loose a hollow laugh. "You're right, but that doesn't matter. Aunt Tillie managed to resurrect her clown dolls and send them into the woods. Something tells me we're not done with them."

"They won't be a problem," Aunt Tillie insisted.

"They're definitely going to be a problem," Marnie said, "but we can't go looking for them tonight."

"No, tonight we have a different problem."

Graham shifted on the couch. "I only know the basics of the situation. I know the warden was following you around, making demands. How much trouble does Landon think you're going to be in?"

That was a good question. "He didn't say, but he's worried."

"Landon always worries about things he shouldn't worry about," Mom pointed out. She almost looked as if she was seeking confirmation.

"He does tend to overreact," I agreed. "Chief Terry is worried too."

"If you ask me, this is a blessing for us," Aunt Tillie said. "We no longer have to worry about that guy spying on us."

"He's dead," I shot back. "Landon said it looked as if he had a broken neck. I guess it's possible he fell, but..."

"But we don't have a lot of accidents in this town," Mom finished. "He was likely killed."

"Which begs several questions," Graham said. "What was he doing at Margaret's house? Was he working with her on something? Was he on his way here to spy? Did he know that you were going there?"

"I just don't know." Briefly, I shut my eyes. "Landon said we have to be ready for the investigator to come here."

Mom looked at the clock. "Tonight? It's after eight o'clock."

My mother was a night owl. She loved watching horror movies once the sun set. However, in her world, decorum dictated nobody visit after eight o'clock.

"I don't think he'll care," I replied.

"Then I guess we'd better put a charcuterie board together." Mom was resigned. "We can't have an FBI agent present and not feed him."

We could, but that wasn't how it worked in the Winchester house. "I could use a cupcake," I said.

"We hid a whole container from Landon earlier," Marnie volunteered. "Go nuts."

I needed the sugar rush. "Thanks. It's going to be a long night."

"Definitely," Mom agreed. "A very long night."

3
THREE

The charcuterie board was ready when Landon and Chief Terry walked into the dining room with a thirty-something man in tailored pants and a powder blue polo shirt. His hair was dark blond, and his green eyes seemed friendly enough. He carried himself in a way that left no doubt that he was in a position of authority.

"Hey, everybody." Landon brightened when he saw the food. "I see you're expecting us."

"Guests first." Mom slapped Landon's hand as he reached for a slice of summer sausage.

"You're so mean," Landon complained.

"That's a mother-in-law's job." Despite her words, Mom smiled at him. "Winchester is sleeping in the living room."

"Thanks." Landon gestured to the table. "This is Special Agent Zach Hodgins. He's been with the Traverse City office a few months. Zach, this is … everybody."

"It's lovely to meet you." Hodgins bobbed his head. "How about some individual introductions?"

Landon looked surprised that Hodgins was getting to business so quickly. "Sure. This is Winnie Winchester. She's my mother-in-law."

Hodgins shook her hand in perfunctory fashion.

"She's also Terry's fiancée," Landon added. He seemed unsure if he should've added that part, but he kept going. "This is Marnie and Twila Winchester. They own The Overlook with Winnie. And this is Tillie." He sent a warning look to my great-aunt, who was still clutching her bottle of wine at the head of the table. "Then we have Graham Stratton. He's chief of police in Hawthorne Hollow. I'm not certain you've had a chance to meet him yet."

"Not yet." Hodgins shook his hand. "Am I missing something? Is there some tie to Hawthorne Hollow that I haven't been made aware of?"

"No, I'm here with Marnie," Graham explained.

"Ah." Hodgins smiled. He turned to me. "That would make you Bay. I recognize you from the photos Landon has on his desk. Not that he's ever in the office much."

"I'm glad I look like my photo," I said.

"And that leaves Thistle." Landon looked around. "Where did she go?"

"Home," I replied. "I didn't realize you needed her."

"You can talk to Thistle tomorrow," Landon said to Hodgins. "She lives in the barn by the petting zoo."

"She lives in a barn?" Hodgins's eyebrows hopped.

"There are two barns," Twila offered. "One is for the animals. The other was converted to a house. Thistle lives there with her boyfriend."

"Marcus," Landon supplied.

"Okay." Hodgins sat down at the table and glanced at the charcuterie board. "Is this for everybody?"

"Absolutely." Mom bobbed her head. "Bay suggested we would be having guests, so I whipped up a snack."

Hodgins looked over the heaping mound of food. "You just whipped this up?"

"That's normal around here." Chief Terry gave Mom a pat on the shoulder, and in a move I wasn't expecting, he sat next to her on the opposite side of the table from where he normally sat.

When Landon sat at Hodgins's left, I realized it was a strategic move. The three law enforcement representatives—including Graham—were scattered evenly around the table. They looked relaxed, but an air of unease filled the room.

"The medical examiner has a team collecting the body," Hodgins started. He added numerous pieces of meat, hunks of cheese, grapes, and crackers to his plate. "It looks like Brad Childs suffered a broken neck. We won't know for certain if that's what killed him until the autopsy. It's possible something else happened, and he broke his neck falling."

Nobody spoke.

Landon finally made a motion with his chin to get me to cross to him and sit.

"I need to know what you were doing at Margaret Little's house," Hodgins continued. "I guess we'll start with that question."

"We were just taking a walk," Aunt Tillie replied, speaking for the first time. "We happened to see the body in the ditch."

I wanted to kill her. That wasn't the story we'd agreed on.

"We were playing a prank on Mrs. Little," I clarified. There was no way Mrs. Little hadn't already told the FBI agent at least some version of the story. There was no sense painting ourselves as innocent victims. "I tripped over the body."

Aunt Tillie shot me a death glare. "We were walking," she gritted out.

"He knows we weren't just walking," I shot back.

"He's 'The Man,'" Aunt Tillie said in her darkest voice. "What did I teach you when you were a kid?"

"Never to trust 'The Man,'" I replied without hesitation. "Unfortunately, he's not an idiot. Plus, I'm married to 'The Man.' I don't have the same aversion to the police that you do."

"You'll have to excuse my aunt," Mom offered. "She's a bit—"

"Senile?" Hodgins assumed.

"What did he say?" Aunt Tillie barked.

"Tempestuous," Mom supplied. "I was going to say that she's tempestuous."

"Tillie and Margaret have a storied past," Chief Terry said. "They have been at each other's throats for a very long time."

"Since they were children," Marnie volunteered.

"That was all Margaret," Aunt Tillie countered. "I was an angel. She was the Devil."

"I see." Hodgins didn't smile, not a good sign. "What sort of prank were you playing?"

"Oh, just the normal stuff," I replied. "You know ... make Mrs. Little think her house was haunted. That sort of thing."

"You do that often?"

I scratched my cheek. "More often than I feel comfortable admitting to a stranger."

"It's an active rivalry," Chief Terry explained. "It's been going on for a really long time. When Bay and her cousins were children, I had to go out to Margaret's house more than once because Tillie had them out there throwing toilet paper around."

"Oh, please." Aunt Tillie was offended. "I would never stoop to throwing toilet paper around."

"Then what were those things hanging from Margaret's trees?" Chief Terry countered.

"Tampons."

"Is that better?"

"Yes."

Hodgins shoved a cracker in his mouth—I had to think he was buying himself time—and smiled when he swallowed. "So you would say your actions this evening were normal?"

"There's nothing normal about me," Aunt Tillie replied.

"I'm sure that's true."

"As for Margaret, she's a bit of an exaggerator. You can't believe anything that comes out of her mouth."

"But I should believe everything that comes out of yours?" Hodgins challenged.

"Yes." From all outward appearances, Aunt Tillie was the picture of serenity. She was gauging exactly how far she could push Hodgins. If she didn't like the answer she came up with, I had no doubt that she would start working against him ... and that was something we didn't need.

"Paint a picture for me," Hodgins said to me. "I need to know exactly what happened."

"We walked up the driveway when we got there," I explained, "after we parked on the road."

"Did you pass the ditch where the body was found?"

"Not heading up." I shook my head. "We were focused on each other."

"Doing what?"

"For the walk up, we were reminiscing about all the other times we'd tortured Mrs. Little."

"And you don't feel guilty about that?"

"Nope." I was careful not to act gleeful, but if he expected me to apologize for giving Mrs. Little exactly what she deserved, he was going to be sorely disappointed. "The thing with Mrs. Little is that she's been, well, not nice I guess would be the best description I can use, since we were kids.

"Now, I know that Aunt Tillie isn't innocent in all of this," I continued, "but Mrs. Little is terrible. She was mean to us as kids. She's been trying to buy up property in town so she can name herself queen. She's not a good person."

"Why do you care if she buys property in the town?" Hodgins looked baffled.

I wasn't going to like him. That much was obvious. I wanted to like him —if only to make things easier on Landon—but that wasn't going to happen. I could tell already that he didn't trust us. Sure, he probably shouldn't trust us, but he didn't know that yet. He could at least pretend not to be suspicious.

"No," I replied. "Mrs. Little doesn't get to secretly buy up half the town so she can ... do whatever weird things she wants to do. That's not how it works."

"How does it work?"

Chief Terry cleared his throat to draw Hodgins's attention. "This is a small town. There are a lot of deep relationships that we deal with. Not all of those relationships are good."

"I understand," Hodgins said. "But it sounds as if Mrs. Michaels was there torturing an older woman."

It took me a second to figure out who "Mrs. Michaels" was. "Oh, I go by the last name Winchester," I said.

"Okay, so it sounds as if Miss Winchester was out there torturing an older woman."

"Ms." I had no idea why I felt the need to correct him a second time. Everything about him rubbed me the wrong way.

"She uses her maiden name because of her job," Landon volunteered. "It's not that she doesn't want to be Mrs. Michaels."

I shot him an odd look. He was the one who argued that I should keep Winchester as a last name. It was feared in magical communities, and for good reason. We had decided to revisit the conversation when we added children to the mix because I didn't want to have a different name from my children. That was still a few years down the line.

"Sorry." Landon's smile was sheepish. There was an edge to his tone, and I made a mental note to ask him what was going on later.

"I'm not trying to cast aspersions on your character, Ms. Winchester," Hodgins said. He was going back for more food. Apparently, all FBI agents were gluttons. "I'm simply trying to understand why you were there."

"Because Aunt Tillie likes to torture Mrs. Little, and I like to help," I replied. "We've been doing it since we were kids. Yes, it's immature—and Aunt Tillie is even more immature—but it's what we do when we're bored."

"Mrs. Little mentioned clowns."

This was the sort of lying I excelled at. "She called me a clown?" I feigned outrage. "Did you hear that?" I shot Aunt Tillie a pointed look. "She called you a clown."

"I'm going to teach her a thing or two about clowns," Aunt Tillie intoned. "She'll wish she'd never used that word."

"She suggested that there were clowns running around in the yard," Hodgins pressed. "Were you dressed as clowns?"

"This is exactly how I was," I assured him. "Aunt Tillie had her combat helmet on and her whistle. No stick tonight, though."

Hodgins merely nodded. "Okay, I..." He trailed off when another noise became obvious:

snort, snort.

Peg the pig pushed her way through the swinging kitchen door, Winchester close on her heels, and the two of them took off running down the hallway.

"They'll be back," Mom promised when Hodgins focused his attention on the animals.

"Was that a pig?" he asked.

"No, that's a family member," Aunt Tillie replied. "She has feelings."

"Okay." Hodgins stared a moment longer, then turned to me. "My understanding is that you had a relationship with the deceased."

There was nothing technically wrong with what he'd said—I *did* have a relationship with Brad Childs—but it was the way he said it that bothered me. "I guess that depends on how you define 'relationship,'" I replied. "I knew him, but met him only recently."

"You helped bring in some of the escaped prisoners, correct?"

This was a slippery slope. "Yeah."

"Bay was with us when we got the call to go out to the prison," Chief Terry interjected. "We'd just finished eating and didn't have time to take her home. She was with us when we recaptured the first prisoner."

"That's a perfectly acceptable explanation," Hodgins said. "My issue is that Ms. Winchester was with you several other times."

"She and Landon are tragically codependent," Mom volunteered. "I've tried to get them to give it a rest, but you really can't talk to them."

"It's pathetic," Aunt Tillie said. "I raised those girls to stand on their own two feet, and this one spends all her time leaning on that one." She jabbed her thumb at Landon and me in turn. "It wouldn't be so bad if he wasn't such a whiner, but that's all he does. Well, that and eat bacon."

"Ignore her," Chief Terry said when Hodgins's eyebrows lifted. "She's..."

"Senile?" Hodgins volunteered yet again.

"Say it one more time," Aunt Tillie threatened, her eyes dark. "I dare you."

Hodgins must have seen something in her eyes—something to fear—because he straightened. "I only say that because of the level of commitment that Ms. Winchester—that would be the oldest Ms. Winchester—seems to be comfortable with boasting of torturing an old woman. It's either diabolical or crazy. Which do you prefer?" he asked Aunt Tillie.

"I'm fine being diabolical."

Landon rubbed his forehead. "Aunt Tillie and Mrs. Little hate each other. They do weird things to each other all the time. That's not going to change so there's no point getting worked up about it. You can't change it."

"It also has nothing to do with what we're dealing with now," Chief Terry noted. "Tillie didn't kill Brad Childs."

"That would not be my first assumption," Hodgins agreed. "My problem is that Ms. Winchester—the younger one—did have a problem with him."

"Call me Bay," I said. "It will cut down on all the 'Ms. Winchester' nonsense. Why would I kill Brad Childs?"

"He was stalking you, correct?"

That word—stalking—felt dangerous given the way he was looking at me. "He seemed sad," I replied, opting to give some of the acting lessons Aunt Tillie had bestowed upon us as children a workout. "He lost his job. When you're that close to retirement, it has to be hard."

"So, you weren't afraid of him?"

I couldn't look at Landon. "He made me nervous," I hedged, acting as if I was giving it a great deal of thought. "He would show up outside work. He made really strange demands. I tried telling him just because we pretend to be witches in this town to appease tourists doesn't mean we are witches."

"Yes, it's like Disney World," Aunt Tillie agreed. "We're just characters dressed in ridiculous costumes." Her tone was edgy enough that I was worried. "We even pose for photos."

Hodgins nodded at my great-aunt as if she were a small child. "I heard all about how the town rebranded. It was actually a brilliant move. Hemlock Cove seems to be thriving as every other town around it is dying. What about you, Tillie—"

"Call me Ms. Winchester," she corrected him, ignoring the look I shot her.

Hodgins didn't miss a beat. "What about you, Ms. Winchester? Did you have a reason to want Mr. Childs dead?"

"I wasn't a big fan," Aunt Tillie replied as I held my breath. "I'm not a big fan of crazy. Like, there was this one time Old Man Doherty decided that the Civil War was still going on. This was when I was a teenager, so you wouldn't have even been a blob in your daddy's scrotum."

Landon choked on the water he was drinking, and I had to thump him on the back.

"Old Man Doherty kept hiding in the bushes, trying to shoot anyone he thought was on the side of Northern aggression," Aunt Tillie continued. "Most of the time he was harmless. He had an old musket that he normally forgot to load. One time, though, Constanza Bishop told him he was being an idiot. She didn't run when he pointed the gun at her. She was dead before she even realized what had happened. Apparently, that time he'd remembered to load his musket."

Hodgins sat there and took it all in. Finally, he lifted one hand. "What does that have to do with this conversation?"

"You tell me. You started it."

Hodgins almost looked helpless when he turned to me.

"I didn't kill Brad Childs," I assured him. "I was as shocked as anyone when I realized it was him. I know you have a job to do—and we'll answer any questions you have—but I don't know anything that can help you."

"I guess that means we're done for today." Hodgins stood and glanced around. "Thank you so much for your hospitality. I'll be in touch." With that, he swept out of the room, leaving us to stare in his wake.

That was it? That was all he was going to ask?

He couldn't be anywhere near done.

4
FOUR

"Do you want to talk about it?" I asked Landon at the guesthouse on the inn property.

"Yeah, but give me a minute." Landon managed a quick smile. He tossed his keys on the coffee table and disappeared into our bedroom. I had no idea what he was doing, but when he reemerged, he was in boxer shorts and a T-shirt. Winchester had followed him into the room but not back out.

"Is he in bed?" I asked as Landon settled on the couch.

"If you mean our bed, yes."

I frowned. "I thought we were going to train him to sleep in his bed."

"He's just a baby."

I was fearful about what raising children with an indulgent man like him was going to look like, but that was tomorrow's problem. "Fine." I stripped off my shirt and pants and crawled onto the couch next to him in my underwear. I grabbed the blanket from the end of the couch and tossed it over us. "Let's hear it."

"Hear what?"

"I know you're angry."

"I'm not."

"You have your mad face on."

"I don't have a mad face."

"Seriously?" I was too tired to play this game.

"Fine, I'm a little mad, but not at you."

"Really? I would be mad at me. We were out there torturing Mrs. Little with clowns. If we'd stayed home this wouldn't have happened."

"Childs would still be dead."

"Yes, but you wouldn't have to explain to a co-worker why your wife— *Mrs. Michaels*—was out doing weird things with her cousin and aunt."

To my surprise, Landon now smiled. "You didn't like being called Mrs. Michaels."

"It felt like a power play."

"How so?"

"It was like he was putting me in my place. Like the only reason he was even pretending to be pleasant was because he was your co-worker."

"I can see that." Landon lifted his arm and shifted so I was pressed against his side.

"He was there out of deference to you, and he wanted me to know it."

"He wasn't showing me deference. Well, he was, but we're not exactly friendly."

"I didn't realize you had enemies in your office."

"He's not an enemy. He's just ... a real pain in my ass." A muscle worked in Landon's jaw. "He came in a few months ago, was friendly to everybody, but it was obvious from the start that he's competitive."

"With everybody or just you?"

"He thinks I get special treatment."

"Because you don't have to go to the office every day?"

"That and I don't have to live in Traverse City."

Landon's living arrangements had been difficult when we first started out. His job required him to live in Traverse City, so I only saw him a few nights a week. For a brief period, I toyed with the idea of moving there so we could be together. Ultimately, Landon's boss worked out a way for him to live in Hemlock Cove and keep his job.

I was always worried that deal would dissolve.

"I'm sorry," I offered.

He angled his head to look down at me. "What exactly are you sorry about?"

"You moved here for me."

"I moved here for us. I love this town, however wacky it is. I'm never going to be sorry about that. This is your town. Now it's ours. I want to raise our children here."

"But if this guy is giving you trouble..."

"Zach is full of himself," Landon replied. "He managed to make a name for himself in the Chicago office. He was riding high. Then he got in a bit of trouble. He had to pick a smaller venue to transfer to and ended up here."

"What sort of trouble?"

"I don't know. They're pretty tightlipped about it, which makes me think it was bad. Zach was part of the anti-crime initiative in Chicago, and he's made no bones about the fact that he thinks Traverse City is too small of a market. He wants a big city so he can be in on the big cases."

"Do you want that?"

"I used to think I did."

"But not now?"

"No." He rubbed his hand over my back. "Maybe at one time. I think when I first joined the Bureau I wanted big things. Now I want bigger things."

My eyebrows knit. "I'm not sure I understand."

"You're my big thing, Bay."

I made a face.

"I didn't mean it in a derogatory way." He poked my side. "It's just ... what you do here is more important. The magic you wield, the battles you win, the monsters you keep from the world, that's all bigger than anything I've ever done. I want to be part of that."

I went warm all over at his explanation. "That's kind of sweet."

"I'm a sweet guy," he agreed, giving me a tickle for good measure. Then he sobered. "Zach doesn't get that I'm happy where I am. He thinks I'm biding my time for some reason, and he's marked me as the guy he wants to beat. That puts us in competition with one another."

"You don't have to compete with him," I argued. "You could ignore him."

"What fun is that?" He laughed at my furrowed brow. "I occasionally like to compete. He doesn't realize I've already won. I don't want to leave this place. He can't understand that, so he tries to push my buttons."

"You could try not having buttons to push," I suggested.

"And Aunt Tillie could try not torturing Margaret Little. Some things are out of our control."

"I guess." I rubbed my cheek against his shoulder. "Why did Steve assign Hodgins to this case?" I asked, referring to Landon's boss Steve Newton.

"I can't ask, but I can guess."

"He wants to make sure nobody can say your wife got favors."

He nodded. "I don't know what to do here, Bay."

"We have to go with the flow." That was all there was to it. "We'll answer his questions and try to be on our best behavior."

"Aunt Tillie is going to be on her best behavior?" He was understandably dubious.

"Probably not. Maybe he'll just decide she's senile and leave her alone."

"If he keeps using that word, he'll end up with boils in bad places and wonder why he smells like a pile of manure."

That wasn't out of the realm of possibility. "If he gets too close, we can cast a memory spell." Even suggesting it made me queasy, but we didn't have much choice.

"You don't like memory spells," he reminded me.

"I'll cast one to save my family."

"Well, we're not there yet." He kissed the top of my head. "You need to be prepared, Bay. He's going to be all over this town asking questions about you."

"Do you know what Mrs. Little told him?"

"No. We were not allowed to be present for his session with her."

"I'm sure it wasn't good."

"I don't know. It might work out okay for us."

"Since when are you an optimist?"

"I've been looking on the bright side of life ever since I met you," he teased with a tickle. "Seriously, he kept saying that you guys were torturing an old lady. It's possible that whatever Mrs. Little told him he discarded right away."

"Because she sounded like a crazy old bat?"

"He won't be predisposed to believe that Aunt Tillie sent an army of clown dolls after her."

"Yeah, speaking of that." I leveled up enough to look him in the eye. "The dolls are on the loose. There's no way she put them in stasis. They're out there, and they're on the hunt."

"Zach might not believe his own eyes if he sees one. I mean ... up until you, I didn't know anything about magic. I wouldn't have believed it possible for a doll to come alive and sing."

"Burt is carrying a knife."

"We should probably find him."

"Or he'll find us."

"Did you have to put that idea in my head?" Landon sounded pained. "I'm going to have nightmares, Bay."

"I stole two cupcakes from Mom's secret stash at the inn. They're in my purse. Will that help?"

His expression turned serene. "You do know the way to my heart."

IT TOOK ME LONGER TO FALL ASLEEP THAN Landon. He was one of those people who could crash in the middle of a tornado.

Around two o'clock, something woke me. I remained in bed, quiet, and tried to figure out what had roused me. Landon's soft snoring told me he wouldn't get up unless I shook him awake. On his other side, Winchester was curled into his back. The puppy, much like his daddy, slept hard.

The guesthouse was quiet. The pedestal fan that we kept pointed at us continued its low hum. The familiar noises of a house, the ones you search for when comfort is needed, were all there. That left the outside to worry about.

I left Landon to sleep. I had no intention of going outside unless I saw something dangerous. Even then, I would wake Landon. I'd made a promise. He hated—absolutely loathed—when I left in the middle of the night without telling him. Often there was nothing he could do. He just wanted to know.

I moved to the bedroom window on my side and looked out. The wind was blowing, but I saw nothing moving.

When I moved to the other window I was almost robbed of breath. There was definitely movement, and it wasn't of the human variety.

Burt, half his chest missing and part of his face mangled, waved at me from the tree line. He still had the knife he'd been in possession of at Mrs. Little's house and the smile he graced me with was of pure mayhem.

"Crap," I muttered.

"Bay?" Landon stirred, his hand moving to my side of the bed. When he realized it was empty, he bolted to a sitting position. "What are you doing?"

"Burt's outside."

When I looked through the window again, the clown was gone.

"He was there," I insisted when Landon joined me. "He was waving."

"Are you sure it wasn't a dream?"

"Why would I dream about him?"

"Because he's traumatizing."

"I would love to know what the psychology is behind fear of clowns," I muttered.

"I actually know the answer to that." Landon steered me back toward the bed, suggesting that a clown hunt wasn't in the cards tonight. It was probably for the best. If Burt was trying to lure me out, there was probably a sinister reason. "Studies suggest that people who are afraid of clowns are actually bothered by uncertainty of harmful intent."

"You're making that up."

He chuckled as we rolled back under the covers. "It's a commentary on unpredictable behavior fueled by the media's influence."

"Did you read that in a book?"

"I took a lot of psychology classes at the academy."

"We need to go out there in the morning and look around. If Burt is going to be hanging around the property, we need to set a trap."

"That sounds doable."

"He's smart."

"He's still just a doll."

"Aunt Tillie thinks he's sentient."

"Or she's just saying that to get a rise out of you."

He was determined to sweep it under the rug—probably so he could get some sleep without nightmares—so I opted to let it go. "You're really smart, huh?"

"The smartest." He curled up behind me. "Get some sleep, Bay. Morning will come soon enough."

On that sentiment, I let myself drift off again.

THE NEXT TIME I WOKE, THE SUN WAS shining through the windows and Landon was making happy noises. I felt the warmth of his body pressed against mine. I shifted and saw his back was to me and he was cuddling his puppy.

"I think I've been replaced," I complained.

"Of course not," Landon said. "He's just a baby, and he needs his morning cuddles."

"He also needs his morning walk." Before we got the dog, Landon and I would've spent an hour in bed playing grown-up games. Since we were still house-training the dog, things had changed a bit. "Come on." I threw off the covers and rooted around on the floor for a pair of jogging pants and a hoodie.

"We have time to play," Landon complained. He enjoyed his morning rituals. His pout told me he wanted to play a few games with me too.

"Nope." I shook my head. "We had to pick up all the rugs because he keeps peeing on them. We're getting him house trained."

"Fine." Landon grumbled as he sat up. "You're kind of a taskmaster this morning."

"I want to look for footprints."

His forehead creased and then smoothed as reality hit him. "Right. The clown."

"Burt."

"Why did she name him Burt?"

"You'll have to ask her."

The snow was mostly gone but there were still small pockets in the shaded area of the woods that got no sun. Landon took his happy puppy to the left. I went to the right.

"Bay, if that clown is over there, I expect you to kill it before he traumatizes our son," Landon called out.

I waved to let him know I was on it. As I approached the woods, I looked in every direction to make sure Burt wasn't about to run in behind me and start stabbing. When I got to the place I was certain he'd been standing, I dropped to my knees and started searching.

I was so intent on what I was doing I didn't realize Landon and Winchester had followed until the puppy threw himself at me and started licking my face.

"Good morning," I said as I tried to lift my chin to evade his enthusiastic tongue.

"It would've been better if you'd let me wake you up with kisses," Landon said.

"I don't know. He seems to have learned your tongue technique."

Landon looked down at the ground. "Anything?"

"Footprints." I pointed to the rounded spots on the ground. "His shoes wouldn't leave regular prints, but this was him."

"That means he was outside our bedroom last night." Landon planted his hands on his hips. "Lovely."

"I have to talk to Aunt Tillie," I said as I straightened. "We can set a magical trap for him. He's the clown we need to worry about most."

"I would argue that Zach is the clown we need to worry about most."

"You really do have it out for him." I smiled despite the heavy nature of the discussion. "What are you going to do today?"

"Have breakfast with my wife."

"You mean you're going to make out with your bacon."

He pretended I hadn't spoken. "Then I'm going to talk to Terry. We need to work together on this. What about you?"

"I'm going to have breakfast with my husband," I teased.

"You mean you're going to make out with your hash browns."

"And my tomato juice. Then I'm going to make sure my mother can take care of Winchester. I don't think it's wise to take him with me ... just in case I need to be incognito."

Landon nodded knowingly. "That makes sense."

"After that, I don't know. I'll probably see what you're doing and check in with Aunt Tillie. Then I will decide what I'm doing."

"Can we make out before we head to the inn? You kind of stole my morning thunder."

"I'm sure that can be arranged."

He smiled, and it made him just a little bit too handsome. "My morning is already looking up."

5
FIVE

Winchester took off so fast his nails clacked on the hardwood when we got to the lobby of the inn. He knew exactly where he was going, and Peg's enthusiastic greetings could be heard long before we hit the dining room.

Snort. Snort.

The whole crew was at the table, including Clove, her husband Sam, and their baby Calvin, who was starting to develop a personality. When he'd first been born, he was like a lump that just sat there and occasionally cried. Now he smiled and clapped his hands when he saw us.

"Hey, buddy!" Landon waved at the baby, who was in his highchair. "How's it going?"

Calvin babbled something incoherent and then grabbed Cheerios from the highchair tray and stuffed them in his mouth.

"He's getting close to crawling," Clove said proudly. "It won't be long."

Aunt Tillie's expression was blank. "Are we supposed to applaud for that?" she asked.

Marnie shot her a dirty look. "He's a baby. We're supposed to applaud everything he does."

"Nobody applauds me when I crawl," Aunt Tillie argued.

"Get down on the floor now," Thistle suggested. "If you crawl, we'll applaud."

"Keep it up," Aunt Tillie warned. "I'll hex you so no matter what pair of pants you wear they'll be an inch from being able to be buttoned."

Thistle narrowed her eyes. "I guess I'll have to wear elastic band pants then."

Aunt Tillie scoffed. "That will be a good look."

"Works for you," Thistle shot back.

Mom slammed her fist on the table, jolting everybody. Poor Calvin froze with his Cheerio halfway to his mouth and stared at her with wide, glassy eyes.

"I'm sorry," Mom said to the baby. "I didn't mean to upset you. You're fine. Keep eating." She gave him an encouraging smile. "He's very cute," she said to Clove. "Bay, you'd better get on the stick. I want a grandchild—not just a dog—to spoil."

"Yeah, Bay," Thistle taunted. "Get on the *stick*."

Mom shifted her gaze to Thistle, who shrank in her chair. "I'm not so old I don't know you think you're being cute, Thistle. If you want to be cute, bring Marcus for more meals. We like him."

"He's getting ready for the petting zoo to open," Thistle replied. "I'll send your message along."

"See that you do."

"We like him way better than you," Aunt Tillie added.

"You stuff it," Mom said. She was a proponent of respecting elders, but apparently Aunt Tillie was already on her last nerve this morning. That was fairly impressive in my book. The day hadn't even started yet.

"Now, everybody fill your plates," Mom continued. "We have some things to discuss."

Landon didn't need to be told twice. He had eggs, hash browns, bacon, and toast on his plate before I could even finish filling my juice glass.

"Take a breath," I admonished when he started shoveling it in. "You're only getting those three slices of bacon this morning."

"You're not the boss of him," Aunt Tillie challenged.

Landon swallowed the eggs he'd just forked in and looked between us. He almost seemed nervous. "Three slices is fine," he said, making me realize he was sacrificing his own happiness because he didn't want to agree with Aunt Tillie.

"You can have five," I said indulgently.

Landon brightened and immediately snagged two extra slices.

"What's going on?" Clove asked as she put dabs of scrambled eggs and hash browns on a small plate for Calvin. She made sure to cut them up even further so there were no choking hazards and then put the plate in front of her son, who shot her a gummy smile. "Why did you insist we all come for breakfast?"

Up until she said it, I'd assumed it had been a happy coincidence. In hindsight, that didn't make a lot of sense given what we were up against. "You made them come here?" I asked my mother.

"I figured it was best we come up with a plan," Mom replied. "We're going to have FBI agents crawling up our backsides."

"Crabs would be preferable," Aunt Tillie drawled.

Mom jabbed a finger in Aunt Tillie's direction, but her gaze never moved from Clove. "We need to agree on how we're going to deal with these FBI agents."

"I don't see why we have to deal with them at all," Thistle argued. "Can't we just ignore them?"

"Not if you don't want them to become suspicious," Landon replied. "Listen, I know you all want me to swoop in and fix this—"

"We don't expect that," Mom countered. "You're not responsible for this, Landon."

"Bay is," Aunt Tillie said.

I glared at her. "Excuse me?"

"You're the one who brought the warden to town," Aunt Tillie argued. "You're the reason he was here."

I dropped my fork on my plate with a clatter. Part of me was irritated. Part knew she was right. "I'm sorry. Aunt Tillie is right. You're dealing with this because of me."

"That's a bunch of crap," Chief Terry exploded, taking everyone by surprise with his vehemence. "None of this is your fault, Bay."

"I beg to differ." Aunt Tillie was a snotty mess this morning, and I couldn't decide if she was angry at Mom, me, or herself. It could be a combination of all three.

"You're going to want to shut up now," Mom snapped at Aunt Tillie. "I'll take away that new four-wheeler you've got hidden in the woods if you're not careful."

Aunt Tillie's mouth fell open. "How...?" She trailed off and readjusted. "I have no idea what you're talking about."

Mom rolled her eyes. "Please. You might've arranged for the delivery when we were busy spring-cleaning the pantry, but we're not idiots. Marnie saw it being delivered and you spiriting it away to the woods."

"Thanks," Marnie said dryly.

Mom didn't look sorry. "You could've refused delivery."

"She already had it in gear and was speeding off."

"You can't take Big Bertha away from me," Aunt Tillie argued.

"Big Bertha?" Sam asked, his brow creasing.

"She names inanimate objects," Clove explained.

"That's how we got Burt," Thistle said.

"Speaking of Burt," I interjected. "He was outside our window last night."

Aunt Tillie whipped her eyes to me. "He didn't cut any fingers or toes off?"

"No. Wait ... is that a possibility?"

"It had better not be a possibility," Landon warned, his mouth full of bacon. "I'll arrest you."

"Yeah, you've got a bit of grease on your chin there, Skippy," Aunt Tillie replied.

"The four-wheeler is staying here until the clown mess is cleaned up," Mom ordered Aunt Tillie. "I'm not bending on that. You're getting the clowns taken care of today."

Aunt Tillie grumbled. It sounded like, "You don't say what I do. I say what I do," but I couldn't be certain.

"As for the FBI agents, we should defer to Terry and Landon on this one," Mom continued. "You're the experts. How should we do this?"

"Wow, I never thought I would get to be an expert on anything in this family," Landon teased in an effort to lighten the mood. It didn't work, so he sobered. "I already told Bay, but I should tell the rest of you as well. Zach Hodgins isn't what I would call a friend. He's trying to make a name for himself.

"At one time he was in Chicago working big cases, but something went sideways, and he was sent here as punishment," he continued. "I don't know what went wrong. That isn't public information. I do know that he's desperately trying to make a name for himself here so he can transfer out and start working his way up again."

"He has a rivalry with Landon," I added.

"I wouldn't call it a rivalry," he countered. "It's more of a workplace standoff."

"You mean a rivalry," Mom said. "The guy wants to take you down a peg because he thinks you're his competition."

Landon considered it for a second, then shrugged. "He doesn't understand me. He thinks this is all an act." He gestured around the table. "I was once interested in advancing to bigger cities too. That all changed when I met Bay. He likely believes I have a strategic reason for wanting to stay here."

"Can't it just be that you love Bay?" Mom asked.

"No." Landon was grim. "He's been trying to one-up me since he arrived in the office. I haven't shown a lot of interest in his efforts. To him, that's pretty much the worst thing I can do. He's angry that I don't engage with him."

"Has he tried engaging with you?" Chief Terry asked.

"Several times," Landon confirmed. "Normally, I go there on Wednesdays. I meet with Steve. I have lunch with a few of the other guys. I try to be as down to earth as possible."

"Do they give you grief about giving up your trajectory for a woman?" Chief Terry asked.

I didn't much like how he phrased it. "Excuse me?"

"Sorry, sweetheart." Chief Terry sent me an apologetic look. "You're well worth whatever he had to give up."

Did he think that was better? "Exactly how much trajectory have you lost?" I demanded of Landon.

He straightened. "Bay—"

I shook my head. "Tell me."

"It's not measurable, Bay." Landon dropped the piece of bacon he was holding.

"I don't want you giving anything up for me."

"I'm not giving up anything," he argued. "I decided on a different path. This place and you are what I want. Don't turn into a martyr for no reason. That's an added problem we don't need right now."

"You do tend to turn into a martyr," Thistle said.

"It's true," Aunt Tillie agreed. "It's very annoying."

"I'll ground you from that four-wheeler for even longer if you're not careful," Mom threatened.

Aunt Tillie puffed out her chest. "I'm not afraid of you."

Mom narrowed her eyes. Aunt Tillie mimicked her. It was a standoff.

Aunt Tillie finally averted her eyes. "I said I would take care of the clowns," she grumbled.

"Holy crap," Thistle said in a reverent tone. "Did Aunt Tillie just lose a battle of wills?"

"I'll make it so your legs constantly grow hair and you can never wear a skirt again," Aunt Tillie barked.

I had to hide my smile behind my hand. Then I remembered we had a serious situation to deal with. "What is this going to mean for you?" I asked Landon. "Is this guy going to report back on the situation here to your boss?"

Landon lifted one shoulder in a shrug. "I don't think Zach is coming after me personally. He's not trying to throw my wife in jail or anything. I think the next time I go there, I will be dealing with questions about my wife the delinquent who goes on missions to terrorize a helpless old lady with her great-aunt."

I had never really considered it from his point of view. I couldn't help feeling guilty. "Landon—"

"Don't." He shot me a warning look. "I am not sorry we're together. I'm not sorry I chose this life. If you act weird, I'm going to think you're sorry, that you're being a martyr, and that will upset me."

"I'm not being a martyr."

"You are, and I don't want to deal with it." Landon reached for another slice of bacon. His stare practically dared me to call him on the fact that he was surpassing his allotted five slices. "You're my wife, Bay. If this wasn't the life I wanted, I wouldn't be here. Let it go."

"Fine." I threw my hands in the air. "We're in trouble. This guy is going to call a team here. They're going to be crawling through our business."

"They're also going to go out of their way to catch you having the sort of conversation that you wouldn't want to have in front of them," Chief Terry warned. "Landon and I can't intervene. You have to be careful, because you tend to run your mouths when you shouldn't."

"I can't help but feel there's an insult coming my way," Mom said stiffly.

"Don't do that." Chief Terry mimicked Landon's earlier face. "You're not the problem. You're never the problem."

Mom's expression softened.

"Let me guess," Thistle drawled. "Bay is never the problem either, right? Not your little sweetheart."

Chief Terry murdered her with a look. "That won't work on me. And Bay is a problem."

"Hey," I protested, hurt despite my determination to let the martyr thing go.

"I'm sorry, but you are," Chief Terry insisted. "You, Thistle, and to a lesser extent Clove tend to run your mouths all over town. That's on top of Tillie's antics." He turned to my great-aunt. "By the way, you need to stop. Torturing Margaret Little is off the table until the Feds are out of our backyard."

Aunt Tillie's mouth fell open.

"No." Chief Terry tapped his finger on the table to show he meant business. "You cannot make the unicorns fart ... or dance ... or blow glitter out of crevices they shouldn't. We do not want these people looking at us too closely."

"Why not just kill me now?" Aunt Tillie countered.

"Don't tempt us," Thistle fired back.

"The only joy I get is torturing Margaret." Aunt Tillie adopted a piteous tone that I knew was for show. "I have so few years left—forty at the most —and you're taking my joy from me." She turned to Mom. "How can you allow this?"

"Oh, don't even," Mom said. "Nobody is falling for that."

"Fine!" Aunt Tillie turned from weak and sad to angry and roaring in the blink of an eye as she slapped her hands on the table. "How about this? You can't tell me what to do. I'm going to do what I want. That includes torturing Margaret."

"You can't," I protested. "You'll get us all in trouble if you're not careful."

"I'm not worried about 'The Man.' I've been beating 'The Man' since I was in diapers."

Thistle opened her mouth but shut it when Mom glared at her.

"This isn't about beating 'The Man,'" Mom said in the most controlled voice I'd ever heard her use. "This is about keeping our family safe."

"I always keep our family safe." Aunt Tillie flounced toward the swinging doors. "You can't tell me what to do. I'll handle this. You have nothing to worry about." With that, she disappeared into the kitchen.

"That was quite the exit," Chief Terry said after a few seconds. "She's going to make a mess for all of us."

"She is," Mom agreed. "I'll handle it."

"As for family conversations when the FBI agents are around, there's an easy fix for that," I volunteered. "We'll just start talking about the wedding whenever we think someone is around. It's a big event for us and makes us seem innocent."

I expected everybody to applaud my smart idea. Instead, Mom scowled. "What is it with you and this wedding?" she demanded. "Why do you have to make such a big deal out of it?"

"Because I want to. It's a good idea and you know it."

"Fine. I'm not going to argue." Mom's eyes darted to the window when the unmistakable sound of an engine firing to life in the backyard became evident. "Son of a witch," she hissed, hopping to her feet and scurrying to look through the glass.

Even though I knew exactly what was going to happen, I watched, holding my breath until the huge four-wheeler zoomed past the window. I caught a brief glimpse of Aunt Tillie. She had a new helmet with flames on it. She looked like she might be wearing leather chaps over her leggings. She was gone before I could commit all the finer details to memory.

"She's going to be a problem," Chief Terry muttered.

"She's always a problem," Landon said. "We can't control her. All we can hope is that Zach really does think she's senile."

Chief Terry wasn't convinced. "And if he figures out the truth?"

"Then we're in a world of trouble."

6

SIX

We left Winchester with Mom. I had plans to take him to the office when he was a little older. Given that the FBI would be crawling all over town today, I didn't want to have to worry about him if something that required me being sneaky popped up. Besides, he was happy playing with Peg all day. Mom said they ran around the inn, delighting the guests. Then they ran around the yard until they tired themselves out.

The newspaper building was quiet, so I went straight to my office and booted up my computer. After checking emails and firing off replies to the page designer and advertising clients, I went looking for Viola, The Whistler's resident ghost. I found her exactly where I expected, in the kitchenette watching television.

"What are you watching today?" I asked, cocking my head to figure out what was on the screen.

"It's a show about sex," Viola replied. "I'm not sure what sort of sex, but it involves a lot of feet licking."

I made a face. "You're watching porn?"

"It's on Netflix. It can't be porn."

I had my doubts. "I have a job for you." Despite my determination to be professional, I couldn't stop looking at the scene on the screen. The position was ... well, frankly I didn't see how it was possible. "This is on Netflix?"

Viola nodded. "I was going to cancel my membership, but now I'm holding off."

Since she was using my membership—and almost nobody could see or talk to her but me, Aunt Tillie, and weirdly, Landon—that seemed unlikely.

"I need you to go on a spying mission for me," I announced.

Slowly, Viola tracked her gaze from the television to me. "I'm listening."

"Mrs. Little." I'd given this a great deal of thought and knew exactly how I wanted to play things with the old bat. "There are some FBI agents in town."

"Yeah, you're married to one." Viola bobbed her head. "I can spy on him if you want."

"He can see you," I reminded her.

"Only when you want him to see me."

I hadn't yet worked that part out yet. I was a necromancer apparently. I could control ghosts, not just see them as I originally thought. When I was a teenager, the "gift" felt like a curse. I'd grown into my abilities, though, and was no longer perpetually worried about who might hear me talking to invisible friends. One of the side effects of getting stronger was that Landon could see ghosts when I wanted him to.

"Actually, he's seen ghosts when he hasn't been with me," I offered, remembering a child ghost who had gone to him when I was in trouble. "I think he's predisposed to it. His mother has a bit of witch in her."

"I can spy on him. Do you think he's cheating on you?"

Cheating was something I never worried about with Landon. Even if I caught him making out with his bacon it wasn't a terrifying prospect. "I don't want you to spy on Landon. At least right now. It might be fun to spy on him when we don't have something big going on. There are other FBI agents in town."

"Why?" Viola almost looked bored. "Are they here for Tillie? I bet they're here for Tillie. It was only a matter of time."

"They're not here for her, but if you see any possessed clown dolls running around, I want to know about that too."

Viola looked horrified. "Clowns?"

"It's a long story."

"She cursed clown dolls to go after Margaret, didn't she? That is diabolical."

Apparently, the story wasn't that long after all. "She did. Then she sent them scattering into the woods. I don't want the FBI agents to see any of them."

"I don't want to see any of them either."

"Mrs. Little is the one I'm worried about. When we were in her yard last night running—"

"Why would you run from Margaret?" Viola scoffed. "Did she have that mud mask on that she insists on using even though nobody has used masks like that since the '80s?"

"She had a shotgun."

"Oh." Viola nodded sagely.

"She was shooting at the clowns first. Then she saw us and changed targets."

"I'm on your side, but you can't say you didn't have it coming."

I agreed. "When we were running, I tripped over a body. You know that warden who has been hanging around?"

"The one stalking you?"

"Yes. He's dead."

"He was in front of Margaret's house?" Viola looked puzzled.

"Yeah, I haven't figured out what he was doing out there. I want you to eavesdrop on her. Find out what she's saying to her friends."

"I hate those harpies."

Viola used to be one of those harpies. "Say whatever mean things you want to say to them."

"They can't hear me."

"Well, maybe I'll try to figure out a way so they can as a reward."

Viola was intrigued. "Okay. What do you want me listening for?"

"I want to know if she says anything about Brad Childs—that's the warden—and I want to know what she said to the FBI agents who were called to the scene last night."

"Why would you need more FBI agents when you already sleep with one?"

"Because it's a conflict of interest for Landon and Chief Terry to investigate. They filed a complaint about Childs stalking me."

"Ah." Viola wasn't as dim as she often pretended because she understood straightaway. "They're going to think you did it."

"It doesn't look good that we were in Mrs. Little's yard when the body was found. I'm not sure how long he had been there, but we're going to be their focus for a little bit. Mrs. Little is going to try to make trouble for us."

"Oh, absolutely," Viola agreed. "She's going to try to use these other FBI agents as leverage against you guys."

I hadn't figured out exactly how Mrs. Little was going to do it, but that's exactly what worried me. If she could get me locked up, she would. "Just find out what she's saying and report back."

"No problem." Viola turned back to the television. "I just want to finish this movie before I head out."

I didn't get the point of watching porn when you couldn't benefit from it, but arguing with Viola had proven pointless more often than not. There was no reason to needlessly pick a fight I couldn't win. "Okay. I'm going to Hypnotic."

She gave me an absent wave.

I started for the door but paused long enough to look at the screen again. "Seriously, how are they even in that position?"

"She's double-jointed."

CALVIN WAS IN HIS PLAYPEN IN THE MIDDLE of Hypnotic, the magic shop Clove and Thistle owned across the road from the police department. He was all smiles when he saw me, his eyes going to the wind chimes over the door as they lightly clanged.

"Hey, handsome." I kissed the top of his dark head. He had brown eyes like Clove and boasted most of her facial features, including her ski-slope nose and dimple.

"Bah," he said. It wasn't language—he was still a few months from that —but there were times when he babbled where I got the feeling he was actually trying to communicate.

"Bah," I agreed.

Clove walked out from the storage room, a rag in hand. "Oh, it's just you." She looked disappointed.

"I love you too," I said.

"I thought it was a customer. We're getting close to that time of the year when the foot traffic is going to pick up."

I wasn't a fan of winter, but Hemlock Cove was a tourist town, so I appreciated the few months we got off to enjoy a little downtime. She was right, though. Festival season was right around the corner. Soon we would be inundated with tourists. They were our bread and butter, but sometimes they got annoying.

"Sorry to disappoint," I drawled as I flopped on the couch.

"It's just Bay," Clove said to Thistle when she appeared from the same storage room.

Thistle shook her head. "I thought it was a customer."

"You guys really know how to make a witch feel welcome." I offered up a sarcastic thumbs-up. "They're very mean," I said to Calvin.

"Sah," he said in agreement.

"We weren't expecting you," Clove said. "We're always happy to see you."

"I'm not," Thistle countered. "Whenever Bay comes calling in the afternoon, it means trouble."

As if on cue, the wind chimes sounded again to tell us someone else was entering. When I looked to the door, I saw a woman in her late twenties in a smart suit. Her shoulders were squared, and I pegged her for an FBI agent right away.

Here we go.

I smiled in greeting but didn't say anything. I was going to let her make the first move.

"Welcome to Hypnotic," Clove offered. "Can we help you find anything specific?" She also recognized the woman for what she was.

"I'm just looking around." The woman went to the nearest shelf and eyed the skull candles Thistle had made. "You have some interesting stuff." She wrinkled her top lip. "It's very ... eclectic."

She said "eclectic" like I might say the word "moist." With a whole lot of disdain.

"Thank you," Thistle said with a blinding smile. Only someone who didn't know her would fall for it. "That's just the word I like to hear when it comes to my work."

"Oh, you made these?" The woman feigned surprise. "You have a lot of talent."

If she thought that compliment was going to work on Thistle, she was going to be sorely disappointed.

"I know," Thistle replied. "Can we help you, agent?"

The woman's lips pressed into a thin line. "What makes you think I'm an agent?"

"That suit is a dead giveaway," Clove replied. "Nobody wears suits like that around here."

"I'll keep that in mind." The woman flashed a smile, then sighed when none of us reacted. "I'm Cam Riddle. I'm part of the team investigating the death of Brad Childs."

"We figured," Thistle said. "If you have questions, just ask. We don't go in for subterfuge here."

Cam took in Thistle's purple hair and made a face. "Weren't you part of the team that was terrorizing an old lady last night?"

"Her," Clove replied before anybody else could. "I was home with my baby like a good girl." She gestured to Calvin, who was busy sucking his pacifier and watching the conversation play out.

"Thank you, Clove," Thistle said. "I'm sure the knowledge that you were home acting like a good girl last night will help Agent Riddle sleep at night."

Clove made a wounded face. "I was just saying."

"It's been duly noted that you weren't at the scene last night," Cam assured Clove. "You two, though..." Her gaze bounced between Thistle and me as she waited for us to acknowledge our presence at a crime scene.

I didn't give her the satisfaction.

Disappointment flashed on Cam's face, then she covered. "I've seen photos of you," she said to me. "Landon has several on his desk. There's one from your wedding. My favorite is the one where you're making duck lips at one another."

I hadn't realized he had more than one photo on his desk. "I guess I'm famous in your office."

"Definitely." Cam looked like a bobble head she was nodding so fast. "Most of the women of a certain age in the office were crushed when Landon married. There was a pool, because nobody believed it would really happen."

What an odd thing to say. "Well, it happened."

"Obviously." Cam's smile was supposed to be friendly, but there was no light in her eyes. "He crushed a lot of hearts that day."

"How long have you worked with Landon?" I asked.

"I've been at the Traverse City office a few years. When Landon first joined the team, he was considered a ladies' man with potential."

"What sort of potential?" Thistle asked. She looked annoyed on my behalf.

"Landon is one of those guys who lived large, but you could always tell he would eventually settle down. Players play until they find the right person. There was some jockeying going on in the office to make sure they were the right person, but he fell for you."

"I feel as if you want me to apologize for falling in love with my husband," I said. "I won't."

"I wouldn't apologize in your position either," Cam readily agreed. "You won. That should be celebrated."

I didn't like her attitude. It was as if she was trying to pretend that she was interested in Landon. As if the interest wasn't really there, but she wanted me to believe that it was.

"Do you need something?" I asked.

"Oh, I'm just looking around." She was back to looking at the shelves. "Warden Childs's death is a big deal. We're going to be here for a bit to sort everything out. We can't do nothing when one of our own falls."

"He wasn't one of your own any longer," Thistle pointed out. "He lost his job because the security at his prison was lax and a bunch of dangerous prisoners escaped on his watch."

"He was still a law enforcement representative."

Thistle wasn't about to let it go. "Who was stalking my cousin."

"Yes, I have some questions about that." Cam flicked her eyes to me. "Why do you think he fixated on you? I get that his beliefs were fantastical. My guess is that he was emotionally overwrought about losing his job so close to retirement, and he fixated on you to fill the void because he didn't want to accept reality. I'm curious why he fixated on you."

The goal was to keep the story as close to the truth as possible. Landon and I had talked about what we would say to anyone if they questioned why I was in on so many prisoner recaptures.

"I think he fixated on me because I was with Landon and Chief Terry for that initial takedown," I replied calmly. "I happened to be with them when they got word there was a prison break and they didn't want to waste time dropping me off, so they took me with them. It was a fluke I was there at all."

"But why focus on you instead of Terry Davenport or Landon?" Cam adopted a quizzical expression that felt wholly out of place. It was an act, and I wasn't going to fall for it.

"Maybe because it felt like a small miracle that we lucked into finding them," I replied, holding out my hand. "I'm not sure why he focused on me. He kept letting himself into the newspaper office when I was in the back working. Then he would magically stumble across me on the street."

"And Landon just allowed that?"

"Landon asked him to stop."

"Landon is a very proprietary man. I'm surprised he would allow someone to get so close to the woman he loves and do nothing about it."

"Landon is not a Neanderthal," I replied. "He felt bad for Childs. He even said that not everything that happened was Childs's fault. Someone had to pay for what went down, though. Landon told Childs to stay away, but he didn't want to compound the man's problems."

"How magnanimous of Landon."

I wanted to punch her. Hard. Like, so, so hard. Me losing it wasn't going to make things better for any of us. "I don't know what to tell you."

"Oh, well." Cam lifted one shoulder in a shrug. Then she headed toward the door. "It's a nice story. Cute baby, too."

"That's all you want?" I called after her.

"For now." Cam didn't look at us again before disappearing.

"She's going to be trouble," Thistle said as the door shut.

I nodded. "Big trouble. She acts interested in Landon, but it's a diversion. She's interested in something else."

"What do you think that is?"

"I don't know. I'm almost afraid to find out."

7
SEVEN

We went to lunch at noon. Thistle and Clove shut down the store and we took Calvin's stroller so we would have a place to plant him for his nap. Once inside the diner, we found Landon and Chief Terry already sitting at one of the bigger tables.

"Were you expecting us?" I asked as I sat next to Landon.

"Hoping," he replied, offering me a kiss. "How has your day been going?" he asked when he was finished kissing me breathless.

"Um ... what?" He could still befuddle me at the oddest of times.

He grinned. "What have you been doing?"

I shook myself out of my reverie long enough to look up and find Chief Terry scowling at us. "It's been enlightening. Tell me about Cam Riddle."

Landon's smile disappeared. "Is she here?"

I nodded. "Yes, and she made a big point of telling me that you broke hearts in the office when you married me."

"Oh, I did not." He rolled his eyes. "She's making that up."

"She acted as if she almost wanted me to believe she was interested in you."

"Do you think it was a test of some sort?" Chief Terry asked.

"I don't know. It felt off. She mentioned the photos on your desk, even going so far as to talk about us making duck lips at each other."

"Like she wanted you to know that she was paying attention to Landon's desk," Chief Terry mused. "That is odd."

"The whole thing was weird," I agreed. "She came into the store, called Thistle's candles eclectic, commented on us terrorizing an old woman—she used that exact phrasing again—and then brought up Childs."

"What did she ask you about him?"

"Not much. I don't think she was actually looking for answers. It was more that she was feeling me out."

"Weird." Landon moved his hand to my back and idly rubbed. "I saw Zach. He stopped at the police station to make sure I knew he was here 'in the spirit of cooperation and good relations.'"

"That sounds practiced."

"Yup." Landon was grim. "I have no idea who else they've got here. Cam is kind of a surprise. She doesn't spend a lot of time out of the office."

"Meaning she's lazy?" Thistle asked as she plopped down next to Chief Terry. "You're not going to cry because I'm not your little sweetheart, are you?"

Chief Terry gave her a dirty look. "You are all sorts of annoying right now," he complained.

"That's because I'm not a sweetheart."

Chief Terry worked his jaw. "I don't favor Bay."

Snorts erupted at the table. I was the only one who refrained. That was probably why I was his little sweetheart.

"I don't." He looked pained. "I treated you all equally." He glanced at Clove, who was settling Calvin between her and Landon at the head of the table. "Tell her."

"I want to agree with you simply to annoy Thistle, but we all knew that Bay was your favorite growing up," Clove replied.

"I stood up for you multiple times," Chief Terry argued.

"Stood up for me? Yes. Favored me? No. It was enough to make me cry myself to sleep a couple of times."

Chief Terry made a morose face. "Don't say things like that."

"It's the truth. I cried and cried."

"She's making that up," I interjected. "She never cried. She said things like, 'I'm way cuter than Bay, it makes no sense that he would like her more.'"

"Well, it's true." Clove puffed herself out. "I was always the cutest."

"That's because you were a foot shorter than everybody else and people thought you were five years younger than us," Thistle countered. "Once they realized you were the same age, the cuteness factor disappeared because the whining was endless."

Clove blinked twice. "You're dead to me."

"Yeah, yeah, yeah." Thistle craned her neck and looked around the diner. "No Feds?"

"Not yet," Landon replied. "I don't expect them to leave town for lunch, so keep your eyes open."

"We don't want 'The Man' to eavesdrop," Thistle agreed. "I'm on it."

I smirked at the Aunt Tillie impersonation. "What's Cam's deal?"

Landon held his hands palms out. "She's always been a little odd. She's working at upward momentum too, but she prefers to work in the office. I think she's better suited for financial crimes—you know the ones where you have to spend six months digging through documents to find the dirt —but she's insistent on sticking where she is."

"Has she ever flirted with you?" I asked.

Landon's gaze was heavy when it landed on me. "You're not worried about something like that?"

"Of course not."

He waited.

"I'm not," I insisted. "I know you're loyal."

"He'd better be," Chief Terry said. "I don't care what he does for a living. I can hide a body if I need to."

"Aunt Tillie can help you," Thistle said. "That's one thing she's good at."

Landon turned his sharp gaze to her. "How do you know that?"

"We've had to dispose of more than one monster," I replied. "Relax. She's not arranging for humans to be buried." A memory pushed forth. "Except Floyd, and she didn't kill him. She just helped cover it up."

Landon made a face. "Don't remind me of the pesky poltergeist. As for Cam, she's odd. She kind of acts as if she's flirting sometimes, but it's not real flirting. There's no natural flow ... or charm."

"Maybe she's just awkward," Clove suggested. "Not everyone is a natural at flirting. Bay and Thistle are terrible at it. I tried to give them lessons, but they were never very good at learning."

"Like you were some master flirter," Thistle scoffed.

"I was. I'm the one who got married first."

"Because you got pregnant. Just imagine if you hadn't forgotten how birth control works. You and Sam would probably still be dancing around one another."

Clove's mouth fell open. "You take that back."

Thistle blew a raspberry.

"If Cam isn't interested in flirting with Landon, why would she push that particular button?" Chief Terry asked. He was used to tuning out our cousinly bickering.

"She was probably testing Bay," Landon replied. "The people at the office are curious about her. It's not just that I got special dispensation to live over here—although that seems to have rubbed a few people the wrong way because Traverse City is an expensive town to live in—but it's also because they don't get to see her.

"Like Philip Hargrove," he continued. "Everyone knows his fiancée, Lanie. Bay wasn't there so she wasn't included in the outings."

I never pictured Landon going on group outings with his co-workers when we lived separately. "Did you go out with them a lot?"

Landon shrugged. "I was bored on the nights I was stuck there without you. Before you came along, I went out with them three or four times a week. Sometimes it was just for dinner, but we had drinks fairly often. Once you and I got together, it was less than that. I was still there four nights a week, but I didn't spend all that time pining for you."

"That makes me kind of sad," I said. "I pictured you drinking a bottle of wine in a hot bath with a Lush bath bomb and crying because you missed me so much."

"I did that some nights too."

I grinned. "Good answer."

"I thought you'd like that." He sobered. "I'm something of an anomaly in the office. I get along with most everyone. The two I would single out as enemies are Zach and Cam."

"And they're here together," I said.

"Steve did it strategically," Chief Terry supplied. "He doesn't want there to be any questions about what happened to Childs."

"Cam suggested that they were being extra diligent because Childs was a former member of law enforcement," I said. "It was almost as if she was trying to gauge my reaction. Thistle even pushed her on Childs losing his job, but she seemed uninterested in that."

Landon tapped his fingers on the table, clearly lost in thought.

The server arrived to take our orders. Nobody needed to read the menu. We ate at the diner at least three times a week.

I went with a cheeseburger and fries and waited until our drinks were delivered to talk again. "I found her odd."

"She's someone to keep an eye on," Landon said. "I don't know how we do that without looking obvious."

"I put Viola on it." I didn't realize I was going to admit that until the words were already out of my mouth. "I asked her to listen for dirt on the agents and watch Mrs. Little. I didn't think it could hurt."

"Viola is a nut," Landon complained.

"She was watching porn. Really weird porn. They were doing this move —" I raised my arm to demonstrate but Chief Terry cut me off.

"Don't you dare," he warned.

I dropped my arm. "Sorry. Anyway, if there's something to find, Viola will find it. Spying is her forte."

"If you say so." Landon clucked his tongue. Then he froze when the bell over the door jangled.

I turned in that direction.

Mrs. Little, her hair unkempt and her eyes a bit wild, pulled up short when she saw us. "You," she growled.

"Us," Thistle agreed.

"You're the reason my life is falling apart," Mrs. Little barked.

I was distinctly uncomfortable as I felt eyes swinging in our direction. "Do you need something?" I asked.

"The Feds are on to you," she replied. "They know what you are. They know what you've been doing to me. You're going to be locked away."

"I have no idea what you're talking about," I lied.

Her eyes went even rounder, which shouldn't have been possible. "You set the clown alley on me."

My eyebrows moved toward one another. "The clown alley? I don't know what that is."

"It's what they call a group of clowns," Landon replied.

I shifted my gaze to him.

"How do you know that?" Clove asked.

"Seriously, how *do* you know that?" Chief Terry demanded.

Even baby Calvin looked baffled.

"I looked it up once," Landon replied. "Don't look at me that way," he barked at me. "It's not a big deal."

I was beyond confused. "What is it with you and the clowns?"

"They're creepy and weird. There's a reason clowns are so often used as killers in movies."

"What movies are clowns killers in?" Clove asked. "Other than *It*."

"*House of a 1,000 Corpses. The Devil's Rejects.*"

"Technically that's the same clown," I argued.

"*Terrifier. 31. Killer Klowns from Outer Space. Clownado.*" He ticked them off on his fingers.

I did a sharp double take at the last one.

"It's a real movie," Landon said. "I had a lot of time to burn when I was taking baths and missing you. The amount of bad movies I watched is staggering."

I patted his shoulder because I didn't know what else to do. "We'll see about getting you a therapist."

He rolled his eyes.

Mrs. Little's face had grown red during the time we'd been discussing the clown alley. "Do you need something?" My tone was cold. I had no more sympathy for the woman. Yes, we'd spent the better part of the last few months torturing her, but she'd earned everything we threw at her.

"Look at you all, sitting around as if you own the place." Mrs. Little had looked evil plenty of times in her life. The expression on her face now was straight out of my childhood nightmares. "You don't own this town. This is my town."

"Margaret, maybe you should take a seat," Chief Terry suggested. "You're getting worked up, and there's no need for that."

"Maybe you should take a seat," Mrs. Little shot back.

Chief Terry looked down at his chair. "I am sitting."

"So stay there. I don't need to take a seat. I'm perfectly fine. In fact, I'm better than fine. I know what I have to do now."

The way she said it threw me. "You know what you have to do about what?"

"Well, *Bay*, I realized last night that I've been going about this the wrong way. I've been trying to be reasonable."

"I'm not sure you know what that word means," Thistle challenged.

Mrs. Little glared at her. "I kept telling myself that it wasn't your fault.

That it was Tillie. She tried to corrupt you. You were children and didn't know any better. But now you know better. Do you know what I know?"

I wrinkled my nose when she swayed a bit closer and I got a whiff of her. "That perhaps you should've showered today?" I asked.

Chief Terry shot me a quelling look. "Bay."

Just the sound of my name escaping his lips had me holding up a hand. "Sorry."

"You're not sorry," Mrs. Little continued. "You're evil. You take good men and make them evil too. Look what they've done to you, Terry." She looked legitimately sad. "You were a good man, and they ruined you. They did the same to this one." She jerked a thumb at Landon.

"Sure, he's always shown signs of perversion, but he wasn't abject evil until he joined their coven," she continued. "He was a law enforcement representative, above reproach."

"I'm still a law enforcement representative," Landon argued.

Mrs. Little ignored him. "You were supposed to fight for the good people of this town. Instead, you joined with evil." Her eyes moved back to me. "The best thing I could've done for this town, for myself, was to drown these three when they were little."

"Hey!" Chief Terry got to his feet. Mrs. Little wasn't the only one with a red face, because he looked as if he was about to blow a gasket. "Don't say things like that about them."

"It's true," Mrs. Little spat. "That one spent all her time in cemeteries talking to evil things when she was little." She jabbed a finger at me. "That one spent time trying to perfect love spells to entice men." She pointed at Clove. "And that one didn't even try to hide the fact that she was whole-hog evil." Now she glared at Thistle.

"She's not entirely wrong," Thistle said blandly.

"Knock it off, Thistle," Chief Terry barked. "Margaret, I think you should sit down. You don't look well. Maybe go home and get some sleep."

"I know what you're doing." Mrs. Little practically sang out the words as she wagged her finger. "I won't fall for it again. I won't let you gaslight me. I won't fall victim to you again. No, I'm going to end this. All of this." Her eyes snagged with mine. "I won't let you destroy this town."

"You definitely need a nap." Chief Terry reached out to grab Mrs. Little's arm, but she slapped his hand away.

"Don't touch me, foul hell beast!" Mrs. Little roared, drawing every set of eyes in the restaurant. "I won't be fooled again. I know what has to be done." With that, she turned on her heel and marched to the door.

The FBI agents who had entered the diner during her diatribe without us noticing parted to give her a clear path to escape. Cam and Hodgins, standing shoulder to shoulder, raised twin eyebrows as they regarded us.

"I don't think she got much sleep last night," Landon explained.

Hodgins nodded, managing a smile. "That must be it." He led his team to the opposite side of the diner to sit.

"Well, that was freaky," Clove said in a low voice.

Thistle nodded. "She's always been a freaky woman, but that was freakier than anything else she's ever done. What do you think is wrong with her?"

"Maybe we finally pushed her too far," I suggested. "Maybe the clowns were her breaking point."

"The clowns were a terrible idea," Landon agreed.

"You didn't argue when we were marching them out last night," I reminded him.

"Only because I wanted them out of the inn. In hindsight, it was a bad, bad idea."

"Well, it's done now." Chief Terry returned to his chair, looking resigned. "She's going to be a problem if we don't get her under control."

I darted a look to the table where the FBI agents—four of them in total—were watching us. "She's already a problem. I'm not even sure she's a problem we can mitigate. We just need to make sure she doesn't make things worse."

"How do we do that?" Landon asked. "She seems pretty far gone."

It was a fair question. "I don't know, but we'd better figure it out ... and fast."

8
EIGHT

My plan was to return to the newspaper office to get actual work done after lunch. With that in mind, I waved Clove and Thistle off and started in that direction. Landon caught me before I could cross the road.

He took my hand and tugged me against his chest.

"If you're planning on getting freaky, we should probably go to the newspaper office," I teased. "If we do it in the street, your FBI friends will arrest us."

Momentary intrigue lit in Landon's eyes, but then he sighed. "If I can carve out some time in an hour, I'll find you." He kissed the tip of my nose, then turned serious as he stared down into my eyes. "Bay..."

"I know," I assured him. I couldn't stand that he was so worried. "I'll be good."

"I'm not worried about you being good. You're smart and strategic. You'll do what you need to do."

"Aw, that's kind of sweet."

He briefly rested his forehead against mine. "They'll be watching you closely, Bay. Make sure they don't see anything."

"You mean like Aunt Tillie riding her scooter with a cape while Mrs. Little's unicorns fart glitter?"

Landon opened his mouth, then shut it. "That would be bad," he said finally.

"So, so bad," I agreed.

"It wouldn't be the end of the world, though."

I didn't know how he could say that with a straight face. "How is that not the worst thing in the world?"

"We can chalk that up to theatrics," Landon replied. "We can say it was theater. Nobody dies in that scenario."

That's when reality hit me. "You're worried about a different sort of magic becoming obvious."

"I'm worried that you'll be exposed." He stroked his hand through his hair. "It won't be good for any of us if the truth comes out. I'm especially worried for you."

"Why me?"

"You're the most powerful witch in the family, Bay. You're always the one rushing in to save the day."

"I told you, if we have to, I'll cast a memory spell."

"That's all well and good, but what happens when Zach files daily reports and then forgets what he wrote to the boss?"

"You're saying we can't cast a memory spell," I realized.

"That wouldn't be my first choice," he agreed.

"Then what do we do?"

"Be really, really careful."

"And when that fails?" I wasn't being funny. The Winchesters weren't known for flying under the radar.

"I don't know."

I leaned in and hugged him, my gaze going to two people standing in front of the police station. Cam and Hodgins were watching us with overt interest. I forced myself to pull back before I was ready.

"We have an audience."

Landon kept his gaze on me. "I don't care. Be safe and try not to text anything weird. Call instead."

"You think they're monitoring our texts?" I couldn't believe things had gotten so bad this fast.

"I want to be proactive about protecting this family."

I nodded. "I'll be good."

"Keep in touch." He gave me a quick kiss.

. . .

I HUMMED TO MYSELF FOR THE walk back to the newspaper office. We had a lot to deal with, and I had no idea where to start. I was so lost in thought I almost missed the woman bending over the mulch bed that lined the walkway to the front door. She appeared to be tidying up.

I stopped, stared for a moment, and then looked around to see if a yard crew had arrived early for the spring cleanup. There was a vehicle in the parking lot, a nondescript SUV, but nothing else.

"Can I help you?" I asked.

The woman jerked at the sound of my voice and her cheeks were red when she turned. "I'm so sorry. I just ... was waiting. Then I saw the mulch was on the sidewalk and I ... um..." She straightened and met my gaze head on. "I'm Tricia Childs."

I'd never heard Childs's wife's name. "I'm so sorry for your loss," I blurted.

She smiled, but it was a sad sort of gesture. "Thank you. I understand someone at this building found his body. I'm looking for Bay Winchester."

Growing up, feeling awkward had been part of my reality. As I matured, I became more confident. I was right back to feeling awkward in the face of this woman's sad countenance. "I'm Bay." I stuck out my hand.

Tricia's grip was weak. "I was hoping for a few moments of your time."

"Absolutely." I pulled my keys out of my purse and opened the door. "Come in."

Tricia was silent as she followed me into the lobby. Her gaze bounced from wall to wall. As far as decorations went, the lobby was cute but not overflowing with personality. I had new decorations on my list of things to do, but it kept getting pushed aside as catastrophe after catastrophe popped up.

"Why don't you come this way?" I gestured for her to follow me to my office. Thankfully, for once, I didn't hear the television in the kitchen. Viola was likely out on the mission I'd tasked her with.

At least I had that going for me.

I got her settled in one of the chairs across from my desk and offered a bottle of water, which she politely declined.

"I'll cut right to the chase," she started. "I know you're a busy woman. I understand you found Brad in a ditch last night. I'm trying to understand how that happened."

This was the part of the conversation I was dreading. "I was out with my great-aunt and cousin—"

"Looking for Brad?" Tricia seemed confused.

"No, it was more of a family project."

She just blinked, which forced me to make a decision.

"My great-aunt and Margaret Little have been playing pranks on each other since they were children seventy years ago."

Tricia just stared.

"My great-aunt calls Mrs. Little her arch nemesis."

That elicited a small smile.

"Ever since we were little, Aunt Tillie has tapped my cousins and me to help her torture Mrs. Little."

"Like, physically torture her?"

"Oh, no. We're nowhere near that sophisticated." I leaned back in my chair, resigned. "In the winter Aunt Tillie mixes yellow food coloring so it looks like all the snow in Mrs. Little's front yard has been peed on. Once she used tape to place outlines of bodies in her front yard and closed her front door with police tape to confuse Mrs. Little."

Understanding dawned in Tricia's eyes. "The sort of pranks teenagers pull on people."

"Yes, and I'm not proud." I rolled my neck. "We have a long history with Mrs. Little. Recently, she angered me with news that she'd been buying up property in an effort to control the town. We were out there for mischief. It is what it is."

"I'm not judging you," Tricia assured me. "I was confused as to what you were doing there in the middle of the night."

"It wasn't that late. Aunt Tillie talks big, but she's a monster if she's not in bed by ten o'clock, so we carry out our hijinks under the cover of darkness, but it gets dark here at six o'clock this time of year."

"I understand."

"Mrs. Little got worked up last night and brought her shotgun to the front porch," I continued. "We ran, and that's when I found your husband. I accidentally tripped over him."

Tricia ran her tongue over her lips and shifted on her chair. "Do you know what he was doing there?" she asked.

"No. I'm sorry. I was kind of hoping you knew. Mrs. Little's house is set back from the road. There's nothing on either side of her for an extended stretch. She's not far from the inn but it's still a hike."

"I'm just as curious as you are." Tricia's eyes flicked to the window. "Brad hadn't been himself for months. He was ... spiraling. I knew he was in trouble, but I had no idea what to do for him."

"I knew your husband somewhat," I hedged. "I met him during the prison break."

"I know." Tricia looked tired now. "He mentioned your name nonstop after he lost his job."

I swallowed hard. "I see."

Tricia's gaze was heavy when she turned back to me. "You're worried that I believe the things he was saying. I don't. I could see he was losing his grip on reality. He didn't even resemble the man I married."

I felt mildly guilty. "He seemed to think I could somehow fix things for him." I chose my words carefully. "I tried explaining that I had no power to do what he was asking, but he wouldn't let it go."

"That job was his whole life," Tricia said. "He got his self-worth from being the warden. I'm not sure when the shift happened, but he could never disassociate himself from his job to be just a husband and father.

"When we went to the school for a parent-teacher conference, he would always talk about the things he was doing with the education program at the prison—as if that was the same thing—and he spent more time talking about himself than the kids," she continued. "If we went to a holiday party, he had to be the center of attention. I could see he was too attached to the job and no longer cared who he was as a person, but I didn't know how to fix that."

My response was measured. "I don't think it was your job to fix it."

"Maybe not," she agreed. "We said 'for better and for worse' in our vows, though. I feel as if I should've done something. It was too late by the time he lost his job."

"He didn't seem to take it well," I agreed.

"He melted down," Tricia confirmed. "He knew he was in trouble—he wasn't naive—but some part of him thought he could hold onto his job."

"You can't be the warden during a jailbreak and keep your job. Especially when you're dealing with that many prisoners," I said.

"And a guard was involved," Tricia added. "A guard he personally hired.

I knew he was going to lose his job. He could've retired early. Or taken a year to lick his wounds and then gotten a job in security. We would've been fine."

"He didn't want that," I surmised.

"No, he wanted his job back. He didn't want to be known as the warden who let prisoners escape. He wanted to be back on top. I think that's why he glommed on to Hemlock Cove's witch mystique."

So she knew about that, too. "He asked me for things I couldn't provide," I said. "I was going to see if I could find a company that needed security." That was a lie, but it made me look good, so I went with it. "He was uninterested in that."

"Oh, I know." Tricia's eyes crinkled with weariness. "When he first mentioned it, I thought he was joking. He was drinking a lot after losing his job. It wouldn't have surprised me if the alcohol had him thinking strange thoughts. It was more than that."

"Why do you think he latched on to me?" I already knew, but it couldn't hurt to see where her head was at.

"You were a handy target for his rage. When the prisoners were on the run, he marveled that you guys lucked into that first set of escapees. Then you got more ... and more. He started getting suspicious. I think reality was setting in. At the same time, you were getting accolades for finding prisoners, he was getting lambasted, and it became obvious he was going to lose his job."

"I'm guessing Hemlock Cove's unique way of making money didn't help."

"What the people here have done is nothing short of genius," Tricia said. "You turned everything around, to the point neighboring towns are starting to take advantage by emulating you. It was a great idea. Brad never said much about the witch stuff until you brought in those prisoners and everyone started whispering about how amazing you are."

"I wasn't alone," I argued. "I had the chief of police and my husband, an FBI agent, with me. They did the bulk of the work. I just helped them set a trap."

"I'm not blaming you for any of this, Bay. Can I call you Bay?"

I nodded. "Please do."

"My husband became obsessed with you very quickly. When I asked what he was doing, he said he was looking for a new job. I knew better. He was here, watching you."

Stalking was more accurate. "He approached me sometimes. He thought I could cast a spell to make his life better. I tried talking him down, making him realize that wasn't possible. He didn't seem to believe me."

"He was lost," Tricia said. "I can't help but wonder if there was more I could've done to bring him back. I let things float believing he would eventually snap out of it."

"You don't know what he was doing here last night?" I pressed.

"I assumed he was following you."

It bothered me that she was so blasé about him following me. It wasn't worth challenging her. Not now. Making Tricia Childs an enemy would work against us. "I hadn't seen him for a few days," I said. "If he was hanging around the inn, we might not necessarily see him. We spend more time on the grounds than at the front."

"You live at the inn?" Tricia's forehead creased in concentration.

"My husband and I live in the guesthouse on the inn grounds. It's tucked away in the woods."

"He wasn't hanging around your home, was he?" Tricia looked horrified at the thought.

"Not that I'm aware of." In truth, thanks to the wards we'd erected, Childs couldn't get close to the guesthouse. That didn't mean he wasn't planting himself in the woods to spy on us.

"Well, I guess that's something." Tricia looked momentarily lost. "I'm not sure what to tell the kids. They're old enough to understand but..."

"Nobody really understands this," I surmised. "I get it."

"Well, I've taken up enough of your time." She stood. "I'm sorry Brad made your life so difficult."

"I'm sorry he didn't find peace at the end."

I walked her to the door and watched her leave. She seemed lost as she made her way along the sidewalk. She didn't seem to be grieving her husband as much as the man who used to be her husband.

I was about to turn back inside when a blur of movement on the sidewalk across the lot caught my attention.

I registered two things right away. One was that Cam and Hodgins were sitting on the bench in front of the newspaper, their backs to the building, their heads bent together in conversation.

The second thing I noticed was Aunt Tillie. She was on her four-wheeler —not the scooter—dressed in full camouflage. There were two clown dolls in the four-wheeler with her, their hands raised as if they were on a roller-coaster.

It was obvious something bad was about to happen, but there was no stopping it. It was far too late.

As Aunt Tillie cruised past The Unicorn Emporium, she raised her hands in the air with the dolls. Mrs. Little's building exploded in a huge glitter bomb.

The glitter seemed to come out of every nook and cranny of the building. We're talking pink glitter, green glitter, purple glitter. It went everywhere, including all over the FBI agents on the bench.

My mouth fell open as I registered the mess Aunt Tillie had left behind. As for my great-aunt, she just kept going.

I was still standing there gaping when Cam and Hodgins stood, incredulous, and turned in tandem to look at me.

I straightened and waved like an idiot. I figured it was better to pretend this was normal and that they were overreacting.

"Nice day, huh?" I said blandly.

Cam's eyes were the size of saucers. "Are you serious?"

"The sun is great."

Hodgins, his mouth open, looked to the store and back at me. "Was that your aunt?" he demanded.

"Yup. Looks like it's going to be a colorful day." With that, I walked back into the building.

9
NINE

I was still a bit nervous when I got back to the inn. I was looking for a snack and a planning session on how to deal with Aunt Tillie. I found several vehicles in the lot, including what looked to be some sort of equipment van. It had "FBI" splashed on the side of it.

"Oh, crap," I muttered.

I went through the front door, where I found several people—including Hodgins—standing in front of Mom. He was all smiles when he turned to mark my arrival.

"Hello."

"Hello," I replied. I met Mom's gaze, but there was no hint as to what was going on to be found in her unreadable eyes. "Have you been interrogating my family?" I asked.

"Interrogating?" Hodgins's forehead creased. "No. We're checking in."

Checking in? Did that mean they were staying at the inn? What in the fresh hell? "You're staying here?" Wasn't that a conflict of interest? It had to be.

Hodgins must have read my mind because he bobbed his head. "This is the inn closest to the scene. You were there, so we felt it best to have easy access to whatever information you can provide." He leaned forward, as if to impart some great wisdom. "Plus, after that charcuterie board last night —and the great things people in town are saying—this is the best place for food."

He was right. Still, if I thought I was agitated before, the mere thought of the FBI sharing a roof with Aunt Tillie was enough to send me to Nervous Breakdown Land. "You won't be sorry," I replied because I had no idea what else to say.

"Here are your keycards," Mom said. From all outward appearances, she seemed relaxed. "You have four rooms. You can decide among yourselves who gets what room." She gave the keycards to Hodgins. "Dinner is in an hour, so go ahead and get settled. There's a drink cart in the library if you want a cocktail before the food is served. Just head into the dining room at seven o'clock."

"Awesome." Hodgins beamed at her. "I'm looking forward to whatever you have going for us this evening."

"It's Italian night," Mom said. "Lasagna, pasta, breadsticks, salad, and stuffed mushroom caps."

"Yum." Hodgins made a big show of rubbing his stomach.

The woman and man with him smiled at me, but there was nothing friendly about the gesture.

"Where's Aunt Tillie?" I asked Mom to stop myself from freaking out.

"Kitchen," Mom replied.

"Great." I flashed one more smile that I didn't feel and started in that direction. "I'll see you guys at dinner."

"Looking forward to it," Hodgins said.

I waited until I was around the corner to increase my pace. I was almost at a dead run when I burst into the kitchen. My entrance was so wild that Marnie and Twila jolted at my arrival.

"What are you doing?" Marnie demanded.

I looked at the empty recliner in the corner. "Where is she?"

"Aunt Tillie?"

"No, the Queen of Sheba. Of course, Aunt Tillie."

"She's not here." Marnie looked puzzled. "I haven't seen her in hours."

My gaze was accusatory when I turned to look at my mother, who was joining us in the kitchen. "You said Aunt Tillie was here."

"Technically I just said 'kitchen,'" Mom countered.

"You implied she was here."

"No, you assumed that. I wanted you in the kitchen so we could talk." Mom calmly placed her hands on the counter. "It seems the FBI will be staying here while they investigate what happened to Brad Childs." She said it as if I should be shocked by the news.

"I just saw them in the lobby," I exploded.

Mom's eyes moved to the ceiling and then back to me. "Watch your tone."

That was rich in this house. Nobody watched their tone. Ever. "They can't stay here," I argued.

"Well, they are. Their credit cards cleared."

"Send them someplace else."

Mom's hands moved to her hips. "And how is that going to look? They'll think we're hiding something."

"We *are* hiding something."

"We're not hiding what they think we're hiding."

"It doesn't matter." I forced myself to take a deep breath in an effort to calm myself. "Do you know what she did this afternoon?"

"It's hard to tell with Aunt Tillie."

"She exploded Mrs. Little's store."

Abject horror flooded Mom's eyes. "The Unicorn Emporium exploded?"

"Well, not exactly." I shifted from one foot to the other, uncomfortable with my own theatrics. "She made glitter explode from every freaking crevice in the building. It went everywhere ... including all over Hodgins and Cam Riddle."

"Who is Cam Riddle?" Twila asked.

"She's one of the FBI agents. I didn't see her in the lobby. Is she not staying here?"

"I have no idea." Mom held out her hands. "They said they needed four rooms."

"I don't want her here." I sounded petulant but didn't care. "She was saying weird stuff about Landon."

"What sort of stuff?" Marnie asked. "We say weird stuff about Landon all the time. Was it that sort of stuff?"

"She insinuated she has the hots for him."

"Well, I wouldn't worry about that." Mom patted my arm. "Landon is devoted to you. He would never stray."

I shot her a "don't even start" look. "I'm not worried about Landon cheating. I'm worried about her motivations."

"Even if she got naked and danced in front of Landon, he wouldn't look," Twila said. "Well, maybe if she dressed like bacon."

Since I'd dressed as bacon as a joke—it had really got Landon going—I opted not to comment on that suggestion. "I don't trust her. That's the point."

"We can't trust any of them," Mom agreed. "They could be perfectly nice people, paragons of virtue and dedicated to bettering the world, but they're still a danger to us. That's why it's best to have them stay here."

She wasn't seeing the bigger picture. "And what happens when Aunt Tillie's dolls—she had two of them in the four-wheeler cheering her on—start wreaking havoc during meals?"

Mom's expression darkened. "I told her to get rid of those dolls."

"Yes, because she always does whatever you tell her to do."

"She's going to do this." Mom was matter of fact. "I'll take that four-wheeler away from her."

It might've been a good threat, but we all knew if Aunt Tillie wanted that four-wheeler, she was going to get it. In fact, now that Aunt Tillie knew that Mom wanted to take her new toy, she would make sure Mom couldn't get near it.

Mom might've been a formidable force, but she was a dabbler when it came to magic.

"They can't stay here," I gritted out. "It's a bad idea."

"We have no choice," Mom replied. "Terry called and said they were on their way. They showed up five minutes later. What did you expect me to do?"

"Chief Terry sent them here?"

"He must have had a reason."

Clearly, he wanted me to have a nervous breakdown. "Does Landon know?"

"I can't answer that. I did what Terry wanted. They're here. We'll have to deal with them. That means you need to adjust."

Did she think ordering it would magically make it happen? "This blows."

Mom merely shrugged. "We've been in worse situations."

Off the top of my head, I couldn't think of any. Rather than respond, I stalked toward the family living quarters. "Where's my dog?"

"Sleeping in a sunbeam by the window," Mom replied. "I hope you don't think you're grabbing that dog and fleeing."

That was exactly the plan.

"You're expected for dinner," Mom insisted, reading the guilt on my face. "They are here because of you, Bay."

I didn't need her reminding me.

"Whatever." I was resigned to my fate. "I'm taking Winchester outside. I don't want to talk to them."

"Well, you'll have to talk to them eventually."

"We'll just see about that."

TURNS OUT MY MOTHER WAS RIGHT. I didn't really think I'd be able to avoid the FBI agents forever. I would've preferred more than twenty minutes of solitude, though. When the two agents who had been in the lobby with Hodgins appeared on the back porch, I knew it was going to be a long evening.

"We didn't get a chance to meet earlier." The man, in his twenties and ridiculously good looking, with a shock of dark hair that offset vividly green eyes, stepped forward and extended his hand. "I'm Spencer Briscoe."

"Hey." I shook his hand because manners dictated I not be a jerk. "I'm Bay Winchester."

"Landon's wife." Spencer bobbed his head. "I've seen photos of you on his desk."

"That's what everyone keeps telling me." I glanced at the woman with him. She was older, in her fifties, and immaculately dressed. Her suit looked expensive, her shoes even more so. "And you are?"

"Patrice Griffin," she replied. "I mostly handle the equipment. I'm something of a computer nerd, so you'll see me around more than the others."

"She likes to sit around and type on the computer while the rest of us work," Spencer teased.

Patrice shot him a dubious look. "When was the last time you actually worked instead of relying on your looks to get your way?"

They had an easy rapport. Under different circumstances, I would've probably liked them, but I wasn't about to let my guard down now.

"So, you work with Landon," I said.

"We do." Patrice moved to one of the chairs that had only recently made its way back to the porch after being stowed away for winter. "I've known Landon since he joined the team."

"I've only been with the team a year," Spencer volunteered. "Landon was one of the first people to welcome me."

"Are you close with him?" I realized I knew almost nothing about Landon's work environment. He went to Traverse City once a week to check in, but we never really talked about what he did there. I felt guilty that so much of our lives revolved around my stuff and made a mental note to question him further.

"Landon? He's my boy." Spencer said in charming fashion, and yet there was something about his smile I didn't like.

"I like Landon," Patrice volunteered. "I didn't like him at first—boy was full of himself—but he's calmed down a lot. I think that's probably your influence on him. You made him grow up."

Given how crazy my family was on any given day, that seemed impossible. I smiled all the same. "He's pretty great."

"Aw." Patrice grinned. "I can see you're as gone for him as he is for you. He broke a lot of hearts in the office when he took himself off the market."

I wasn't nearly as irritated when she said it as when Cam did. "Did you have a crush on him?" I teased.

"Oh, no." Patrice wrinkled her nose. "Splashing around with him would feel like I was trapped in the kiddie pool. Now that tall drink of water Terry, he's..." She let loose a lascivious chef's kiss that had my eyes popping.

"He's engaged," I blurted without thinking.

"Engaged is not married."

"To my mother," I added.

Patrice didn't look bothered in the least. "Well, I have time to work on him."

I wasn't worried about Chief Terry stepping out on my mother—I'd never met a more loyal man—but for some reason the idea of Patrice flirting with him in front of my mother filled me with grim satisfaction. If Mom didn't want to acknowledge my reservations regarding Cam's interest in Landon, then I would sit back and watch the sparks fly when the pointed boot was on another foot over dinner.

The conversation was stagnating, so I decided to redirect it toward something productive. "Do you have a cause of death on Brad Childs?"

"We can't share information like that," Spencer replied. "Wait, does Landon share privileged information with you?"

"Of course not," I replied automatically. Landon didn't keep anything from me, but I wasn't stupid enough to volunteer that information. "I was just curious. Finding him that way ... well ... it gave me a few bad moments last night. I was hoping he didn't suffer."

"It's a strange situation," Patrice said. "Zach said you were there toilet-papering that crazy old woman's house."

They kept referring to Mrs. Little as an old woman. Aunt Tillie would have them begging for forgiveness if they referred to her that way. "There was no toilet paper."

Before Patrice could say anything more, the sound of an engine filled the air. I wasn't surprised when Aunt Tillie appeared on the hill on her four-wheeler, her combat helmet skewed on her head. She didn't slow as she zipped past. In fact, she didn't even look in our direction.

"Who is that?" Spencer asked. He looked confused ... and maybe a little intrigued.

"Aunt Tillie," I replied grimly.

"She's supposed to be fun." Patrice perked up. "Was she wearing a combat helmet?"

I nodded.

"I think she had a stick too," Spencer noted. "Why would she need a stick?"

I'd often wondered that. "She's just ... eccentric."

"I heard she was batshit crazy."

I gave him a dirty look. It was one thing for me to call her crazy. "She looks at life through interesting glasses."

"I can't wait to meet her." Spencer sounded far too happy. "I heard she threatened to hex people and pretends to slay zombies."

"Pretty much," I confirmed.

"Awesome." Spencer grinned when Winchester came bounding up the hill. "Hey, boy." He hurried down to the ground to roll around with the puppy. That made me like him more.

"Is this Landon's dog?" Patrice asked.

I was surprised. "How did you know?"

"He has a photo of the dog on his desk now. It's bigger than your photos."

"Does he have a framed photo of bacon, too?" I was joking, but the look Patrice shot me suggested that maybe I'd hit the nail on the head. "Seriously?"

"Actually, he has a photo of you dressed as bacon."

Of course he did. "Well, more power to him. I..." Aunt Tillie appeared from behind the greenhouse. Her four-wheeler was gone, but I had no doubt she'd warded it to make sure my mother couldn't steal it. "Well, well, well," I said when I was certain she was within hearing distance. "If it isn't my favorite aunt."

Aunt Tillie recognized my tone but didn't acknowledge the game we were playing. "Guests?" Her smile was a little too smug for my liking as she beamed it at Patrice and Spencer.

"FBI agents," I replied. "It seems they're going to use The Overlook as their home base."

"Ugh." Aunt Tillie didn't hide her disgust. "I hate when 'The Man' comes to visit."

Spencer looked delighted at her attitude. Patrice was more thoughtful. She smiled at Aunt Tillie, but there was a wariness about her.

"You and I should go for a walk," I suggested to Aunt Tillie. "I bet your legs could use a good stretch, what with you taking your new toy downtown today to pay Mrs. Little a visit."

Aunt Tillie didn't care in the least. "I'm fine." She started up the steps. "What's for dinner?"

"Don't you want to walk before dinner?" I asked.

"No, I don't want to walk. Geez, Bay, stop being needy."

I glared at her as she skirted around me and headed for the back door. "What did you say was for dinner tonight?"

"I didn't," I replied grimly. "It's Italian night."

"Ooh. Garlic bread." Aunt Tillie nodded. "That sounds like the perfect reward after a hard day." With that, she opened the door. "I hope you find who you're looking for," she said to Spencer and Patrice. "It's a shame when someone dies under any circumstances. To be left in a ditch like that." She made a clucking sound with her tongue. "It's a downright tragedy."

She walked into the inn, leaving me with two FBI agents who seemed gobsmacked by her entrance.

"She's awesome," Spencer said when the door closed. "She reminds me of my Nana. Although my Nana smokes a pipe."

"Aunt Tillie likes to smoke," I assured him.

"A pipe?"

"Pot." Marijuana was now legal in Michigan, so I wasn't worried about the admission. Aunt Tillie used to claim that her pot was medicinal. Now she didn't even bother. It had been at least a year since she'd claimed she had glaucoma.

Spencer raised an eyebrow. "I think I'm going to like her."

"Yeah, talk to me again in an hour."

10

TEN

I planted myself in the lobby to work on my phone until Landon and Chief Terry arrived. They talked in low voices as they entered, both of them registering surprise when they saw me.

"Which of you should I yell at first?" I asked as I lowered my phone.

"Not me." Landon sauntered over for a kiss. "I'm an angel."

"I guess that means I'm going to yell at you." I focused on Chief Terry. "You are the reason we have FBI agents crawling up our butts."

Chief Terry darted a look down the hallway, as if expecting Hodgins to appear. Then he fixed me with a dark look. "Be careful, young lady."

"They're in the library drinking," I replied. "It's fine."

"How can you be sure?"

"Aunt Tillie is spying on them." I pointed to the corner of the hallway that stretched beyond the curve that led to the west side of the inn, to the figure on the floor using a mirror to spy. "If they leave the library, we'll know."

"Ah." Chief Terry scratched his chin. "I didn't see her there. What is she doing?"

"Who knows. After what she did this afternoon downtown, she's feeling full of herself. She won't come near me. When I try to give her grief, she takes off."

"We need to talk to her about that," Landon said. "Hodgins had a few questions."

"I'll bet. What did you tell him?"

"That she likely dressed as a ninja and put small exploding packets all around the building and then set them off with a remote."

My mouth fell open. Then I reconsidered. As far as lies went, it was about as good as we could manage under the circumstances. "Well, that is just ... better than what I was coming up with."

"What was that?"

"Trained mice."

Landon smirked. "Mine is better." He pushed my hair back from my forehead. "What's up? You seem more tense than usual."

"They're staying here." I darted a dark look to Chief Terry. "Apparently, you told them to stay here."

"If I hadn't recommended the inn where I live, you don't think they would've found that suspicious?" Chief Terry demanded.

"We can't have them underfoot. There are rogue clown dolls running around. Did you tell him about the clowns?" I demanded of Landon.

"I did," Landon confirmed. "I thought your mother was going to force Aunt Tillie to deal with the clowns."

"When has Aunt Tillie ever done what my mother tells her to do?"

"A few times," Landon hedged. "I can think of at least one."

"Aunt Tillie is full of herself right now."

"I'm not deaf," Aunt Tillie bellowed from the hallway.

"Are you sure?" I fired back. "Listening isn't one of your strong suits."

She rolled to her elbow and glared at me. "You're on my list."

"Whatever."

"Yes." Landon pumped his fist. He seemed to catch himself when I glared at him. "I like when you're on her list," he said apologetically. "It always benefits me."

"Yes, because if she makes me smell like bacon now—what with the FBI agents on the prowl—that won't be suspicious at all."

"It could be perfume," Landon offered.

"That makes it weirder."

"Take a breath, Bay," Landon instructed. "You're tying yourself into knots over things we can't control."

"Brad Childs's wife stopped in for a visit today," I blurted.

"At the paper?" Chief Terry straightened. "What did she want?"

"She heard I found her husband. She had questions."

"What did you tell her?"

"Mostly the truth. I left out the clowns for obvious reasons, but otherwise I stuck to the real story."

"Where are those clowns?" Chief Terry asked Aunt Tillie.

She was back to using her mirror to spy. "I have no idea what you're talking about," she replied.

"I hate when you do that," I complained. "I'm not going to let you gaslight us. Not this time."

"I seriously don't know what you're talking about, Bay." Aunt Tillie was the picture of innocence. "Have you considered a therapist? You seem to be wrapped a little tight."

Landon laughed until he caught me glaring at him.

"Maybe you're not doing your job and relaxing her at night like you're supposed to," Aunt Tillie suggested to Landon. "How hard is it to make her giddy before you fall asleep like a slug on top of her?"

Landon might've thought it was funny when Aunt Tillie gave other people a hard time. When she directed her acid tongue toward him, though, he turned sullen. "You mind your own business," he said. "As for you, Bay, take a breath." He looked concerned when he turned back to me. "You'll give yourself a panic attack or something if you don't get it together."

"This is going to come back to bite us," I insisted. "We can't have them under this roof when Aunt Tillie is petulant. It's going to get ugly."

"We'll deal with it," Landon promised. "It's going to be okay."

Nothing felt like it was going to be okay. "Let's see if you still feel the same way after dinner."

"It will be fine."

He was going to regret saying that. Mostly because I was never going to let him live it down.

THE DINING ROOM WAS FULL OF LAUGHING PEOPLE. Landon and Chief Terry had excused themselves to have cocktails with the agents—claiming it was the polite thing to do—and left me stewing in the lobby. I waited out front for an extra ten minutes after the others had made their way into the dining room out of spite.

This was going to be bad. I could feel it to my bones.

All eyes turned to me when I took my normal spot between Landon and Chief Terry.

"There you are." Hodgins beamed at me. "I was starting to think you were avoiding us."

"Sorry." I returned his smile, but it was as fake as the one he graced me with. "I was talking to my layout person."

"Your what?"

"Bay owns the newspaper in town," Landon explained. "She has to handle everything—from stories, to advertising, to coming out with the layout each week—so some days are busier than others."

Hodgins bobbed his head. He had a glass of wine clutched in his hand, and one look at the bottle on the table told me they'd uncorked Aunt Tillie's special blend.

Wasn't that interesting? Or frightening. Yeah, it was definitely frightening.

"It must have been great to grow up here," Cam said. Her cheeks practically glowed, making me think she'd already imbibed a few glasses. She was going to hate herself in the morning. "Having all this space to run around in. Did you have a fort?"

I nodded. "Chief Terry helped us build a treehouse when we were kids."

"What a man," Patrice intoned, winking for good measure.

Across the table, Mom readjusted on her chair and darted a dirty look in Patrice's direction.

Next to me, Chief Terry shifted on his chair, clearly uncomfortable.

"It was quite the project," I agreed. "He wanted to put in a staircase for us, but we were worried that would mean more visits from Mom and the aunts, so he put a rope ladder up instead."

Chief Terry chuckled at the memory. "The first time Clove went up she fell backward and snagged her leg. She was hanging there a good twenty minutes before anybody helped her down."

"Did you spend a lot of time with Bay when she was a girl?" Hodgins asked. "Where is your father?"

The question wasn't entirely unexpected. Thankfully, my mother took matters into her own hands.

"Bay's father—as well as Clove and Thistle's fathers—left when they were younger," Mom explained. "They moved down south and lived there for a number of years. They saw the girls frequently, though."

"Frequently" was a bit of a stretch, but I let it go.

"Recently, they moved back to the area and opened their own inn," Mom continued. "The Dragonfly."

"Sounds nice." Hodgins nodded approvingly. "It must be great to have your father back so you don't have to lean on Terry so much."

I narrowed my eyes. "I happen to like leaning on Chief Terry."

"And I like when she leans," Chief Terry agreed. "I'm still close with all the girls. No matter what Thistle says," he added darkly. I could tell Thistle's assertion that he favored me was still weighing on him. There would have to be a reckoning on that front. "Soon I will be Bay's stepfather. Not much has changed."

"Except now Bay walks in on her mother and Terry having sex," Aunt Tillie volunteered. "That never used to happen, so that much is different."

Those who had been in the middle of sipping their wine choked on it. Others let their eyes go wide. Me? I calmly reached for the pasta bowl. If Mom, Landon, and Chief Terry wanted to pretend everything was going to be okay, who was I to argue?

"You walked in on your mother and Terry having sex?" Cam, horrified, asked.

"What type of sex?" Patrice demanded. "Did it look acrobatic?"

I cast a sidelong look to Chief Terry, whose cheeks were the color of the tomatoes that would be ripening in Aunt Tillie's garden in a few months. "Fairly acrobatic," I replied.

"Bay." Chief Terry's voice was full of warning. He could read my mood and knew I was going to be difficult for the duration now.

"I mean ... Chief Terry complains about his knees all the time, but it looked fun." I shot Patrice a happy thumbs-up.

"Nice." Patrice nodded knowingly and took another sip of wine. "Very nice."

I felt Chief Terry's glare on the side of my face. "Stop it," he hissed.

I ignored him. "So, how goes the investigation on Brad Childs?" I asked.

"I'm not sure how much we can tell you," Hodgins replied. "It's an active investigation, which means I can't share much. I'm sure you're used to that." He gave Landon a pointed look.

"We're not used to it," Aunt Tillie countered. "Landon is a regular blabbermouth. We know all the details when he has a case."

Landon continued glaring as he reached over and took the glass of wine from in front of Aunt Tillie and moved it out of her reach. "I think you've had enough," he said. "Don't think you're going out driving that four-wheeler when we're done here."

"You're not the boss of me," Aunt Tillie snapped. She used her magic to move the glass of wine back in front of her. "Mind your own business."

I glanced around the table to see if the agents had noticed, but none of them were reacting. Did they not realize what she'd done?

"How does this work?" Cam asked. She seemed to be gauging the tension at the table, and unlike the others wasn't content to watch things play out.

"How does all what work?" Landon, still glaring at Aunt Tillie, asked.

"Your living arrangements," Cam replied. "Terry lives here at the inn, but you and Bay don't, correct?"

Landon dragged his eyes from Aunt Tillie by sheer force of will. "Bay and I live in the guesthouse on the property. It's a five-minute walk, and about that long for a drive. In the summer we tend to walk here for dinner."

"So your mother-in-law cooks for you? That must be nice," she said to me. "I'm a menace in the kitchen. What a relief it would be to pawn that task off on somebody else."

She was poking me. Others at the table might not see it, but I did. Before I could respond, movement outside the window behind Hodgins caught my attention. I almost fell out of my chair when I saw Burt peering through the window. He caught me staring, waved, and then went back to staring, all the while his maniacal smile front and center.

"Bay, Agent Riddle is talking to you," Mom prodded.

"Sorry." It took everything I had to tear my gaze from the window. The clown had unnerved me. I darted a look to Aunt Tillie and found her looking in the same direction. "I'm not great in the kitchen," I admitted. "My mom and aunt are whizzes when it comes to anything culinary. Unfortunately for Landon, that gene skipped me."

"She has other gifts," Landon assured Cam.

"Yes, she's a pervert," Aunt Tillie offered. "She keeps him happy in the bedroom, so he forgets the other stuff."

Of all the things I expected her to say, that wasn't one. "Don't tell them I'm a pervert," I snapped.

"Definitely not," Mom agreed. "You're giving them the wrong idea."

"What wrong idea?" Aunt Tillie sniffed. I knew better. Everybody at the table who hadn't just checked in today knew better. That wasn't going to stop Aunt Tillie from showing everybody who was boss. "You haven't forgotten that your daughter dresses like bacon and Landon makes her sizzle to turn him on?"

Mom sputtered. "We have company," she reminded Aunt Tillie.

I managed a glance at Chief Terry and found he'd focused his attention on his plate. He didn't like when Landon got handsy in front of him, however innocent and playful. This conversation was completely out of his wheelhouse.

"We don't have company," Aunt Tillie countered. "'The Man' is not company."

"Do you not like law enforcement?" Hodgins asked.

"I hate being arrested," Aunt Tillie replied. "It's a real bummer."

Cam asked the obvious question. "Are you arrested often?"

"Oh, here and there." Aunt Tillie acted nonchalant. "This one time, my lesbian lover convinced me to be a drug mule. I was almost past the deadline for the statute of limitations, but then she turned me in to get a lighter sentence for herself, and I had to go to prison. There was a guard who liked to abuse people. His name was Pornstache."

"That's the plot for *Orange is the New Black*," I complained. "If you're going to lie, come up with a better one than that."

"Fine." Aunt Tillie's eyes flashed, telling me I was going to smell like something foul in the morning. I didn't even care at this point. "Once, when I was arrested, I had to trade smokes and sex for protection from one of the gangs. I obviously couldn't be with the white prisoners because I have too much flavor, so now I'm an honorary member of the Crips."

"Huh." Hodgins looked genuinely baffled.

Across the table, Mom hid her face and sucked down an entire glass of wine.

"You'll have to excuse them," Landon said. "This is part of the dinner theater they put on. They can't seem to turn it off."

Aunt Tillie placed her fingers into a complicated symbol that sort of looked like the shocker symbol. "That's my gang hello," she told Hodgins. "Look it up."

"I'll do that later tonight," Hodgins promised.

"She's never been in prison," Chief Terry said testily. "She has been arrested for general mischief, but she's never been in prison."

"Yeah, I figured," Hodgins said with a laugh. "She obviously says things to get a rise out of people. I find it interesting ... from a purely psychological standpoint, of course."

"You think I'm lying?" Aunt Tillie narrowed her eyes. "We'll just see if you feel the same way when I call in my gang."

One member of her gang was back in the window, his ruffled clown pants pulled down and his fabric butt on display as he mooned the diners.

"I can tell I'm going to like it here," Hodgins said. "Now I know why you moved here, Michaels. The place is a laugh a minute."

"I moved here because I love the town and I didn't want to be away from Bay," Landon replied. "I still do my job."

"Yes, they created a position so you could be here," Hodgins agreed. "It's all very enlightening."

I reached for the meat sauce and doused my spaghetti. Then I grabbed a breadstick and started dipping as conversation turned to how Hemlock Cove had managed to defy the odds in a dying industrial area and thrive.

Occasionally, I looked up to see what Burt was doing. I wasn't the only one who had caught sight of him. Chief Terry actually made the sign of the cross at one point and Mom continuously kicked Aunt Tillie under the table whenever there was a flash of his red hair.

If this was how all the meals were going to go now that we had federal agents under The Overlook's roof, I couldn't wait until breakfast rolled around.

11

ELEVEN

L andon had after-dinner drinks with the other FBI agents in the library. He didn't tell me why—he didn't have to—but his efforts to keep things friendly were starting to grate. I helped clear the table. I could feel Mom's eyes on me as I worked but she didn't say anything until I joined her and the aunts in the kitchen.

"Bay, you can't get angry at Landon for trying to make nice with them," Mom started as I looked for something to do to take my mind off things.

"I'm not mad at him," I assured her. "I'm just not sure it's a good idea to have them here." I darted a pointed look to Chief Terry, who was scrubbing a pan in the sink. I'd never seen him help with dishes before, but he looked intent on his project.

"If you think I want them here, Bay, then you're mistaken." Chief Terry's expression was grave as he turned to face me. "But it will look suspicious if we don't want them here."

"Something I'm sure they're counting on."

"We have to act as if we have nothing to hide. That's simply the way it is."

I muttered a profanity.

Chief Terry tried again. "I know you're nervous—"

"Of course I'm nervous," I exploded. "They're staying under this roof and there are clown dolls with knives running around."

Mom shook her head. "I told Aunt Tillie to get rid of them."

"Oh, right." I threw my hands in the air, frustrated. She was never this naive. "That must be why I saw Burt through the dining room window no less than six times during dinner."

"Is that what you were looking at?" Mom's eyebrows hiked. "I thought you were just being rude."

"That clown was screwing around at the windows."

"Are you sure?" Chief Terry, appalled, asked.

"Positive."

"Then let's see if we can find him." He abandoned the pot in the sink. "Let that soak," he instructed Mom. "I'll finish it when I get back."

"You're going clown hunting?" Mom's forehead creased. "Are you sure that's a good idea?"

"Compared to the alternative, I don't see that we have an option. We don't need the clown getting inside the inn and terrorizing the agents."

That was something I hadn't even considered, but it was a real concern. "I'm going to strangle her," I said without realizing.

"Get in line," Mom replied grimly. "You guys find the clown. I'll find Aunt Tillie."

The witch in question had disappeared before dinner was even finished. She excused herself to go to the bathroom, but we didn't see her again. In hindsight, the fact that she'd taken her own bottle of wine with her to the bathroom should've been a dead giveaway that she wasn't returning.

"Come on," I said, resigned. "Let's get this over with."

Chief Terry took a flashlight as we left through the back door of the family living quarters. He pointed the beam at the yard in an effort to catch signs of movement. A telltale giggle erupted from near the greenhouse, but I stopped him with a hand on his arm and a shake of my head before he started in that direction.

"That's one of the little ones," I whispered. "They're a problem, but Burt is the big problem."

Chief Terry nodded and turned the beam to the west side of the yard. "Why did she name him Burt?"

"I have no idea. She claims he's sentient, though."

Chief Terry took a moment to ponder it. "Is that possible?" he asked.

"It wouldn't be the first time she enchanted an inanimate object that developed a nasty personality. The lawn gnomes never acted as if they were great thinkers, but Burt is another story."

"Of course it happens to the most frightening one."

"Yeah. It's even worse now that he's been shot by Mrs. Little. Twice." I moved to get in front of Chief Terry. "You stay behind me."

He was incredulous. "I'm the chief of police. You stay behind me."

"I'm the one with magic."

"I have a gun."

"Which has proven ineffective against Burt."

Chief Terry scowled.

"You were timid when you were a little kid. More so than Thistle and Clove. Clove pretended she was timid, but she wasn't."

"Is that why you favored me?" We were shoulder to shoulder as we approached the trees on the west side of the property.

"I didn't favor you," Chief Terry insisted.

"It's not something to feel guilty about," I assured him. "Clove and Thistle are fine with it. They've always joked about it."

"I wanted to be there for them as much as you. It's just..."

"I needed you more," I finished.

He nodded, his eyes briefly moving to me before returning to the woods. "You were always searching for something. Thistle and Clove always knew who they were.

"You couldn't seem to decide what you wanted to do with your life. Things were rough for you with bullies at times, and you left town because you thought it would be easier. I thought my heart would break that day."

"I hated it down there, but I had to go to know. I wouldn't have believed it otherwise."

"That's exactly what your mother said."

I smirked. "She's pretty smart when she wants to be."

"She snagged me, didn't she?" Chief Terry swept the flashlight beam left and right as we searched the trees.

"If only she'd snagged you when I was a kid," I lamented. "That was the thing I wanted most."

"I'm not sure it would've worked then, Bay."

I didn't get annoyed when he stretched out his arm in an unnecessary protective measure to keep me from walking into the trees. "What do you mean?"

"Your mom and aunts had a dream. They wanted this inn. That took a lot of their focus. They worked hard to get here. They also had the three of you ... and Tillie, who was like three other children wrapped in one small package. No relationship would've thrived under those circumstances."

It made sense, but I didn't agree. "I think if you want something bad enough that you can make it work."

"What I wanted back then was to make sure you and your cousins were going to be okay," Chief Terry argued. "I didn't think running around with Tillie was in your best interests. I told your mother that more than once. She told me that you were perfectly fine with Tillie."

"We *were* perfectly fine with her," I assured him. "She got us into trouble, but we were never really in danger. She would've died to prevent that."

"She's so much work."

"And now you get to share a roof with her," I teased.

"She's threatening to move into the greenhouse. She says she needs her own space."

"We could probably get a space set up for her out there this summer. If that's what she really wants."

"You can't put an old woman in a greenhouse."

I grabbed his wrist to steady the beam when something caught my attention in the trees. Sure enough, about thirty feet back, Burt was hiding behind a big maple, the knife still clutched in his hand.

"There he is."

Chief Terry cringed when he saw the clown. "What was she thinking?"

"That he was terrifying."

"He has a knife."

I nodded. "Yeah."

"We can't go into the woods, Bay." Chief Terry was deadly serious. "We have to come up with a plan."

"I'm open to suggestions."

"Well, off the top of my head, I suggest you call Stormy tomorrow and get her out here to set him on fire. If that doesn't work, I'm thinking Evan."

Evan, a day-walking vampire, had become Aunt Tillie's primary sidekick. He was best friends with Scout Randall, a pixie witch who lived one town over in Hawthorne Hollow, and he'd been dividing his time between his job over there and his duties as Aunt Tillie's partner in crime for months. Things had been hopping in Hawthorne Hollow of late—there was even a loa hanging around not long ago—which meant he hadn't had as much time for Aunt Tillie.

"I did not consider that." I let out the breath I didn't even realize I was holding. "That's probably the smartest idea you've ever had."

"Definitely smarter than locking Tillie in the greenhouse, where she'll freeze to death during winter."

The previous conversation came roaring back. "She won't freeze to death."

"Do you know something about winter that I don't?" he challenged.

"Witches can make their own heat. Have you forgotten she has an inclement weather dome out there that we had picnics in all winter?"

Chief Terry faltered. "I didn't consider that."

"Well, consider this." I was serious when I focused on him. "Aunt Tillie is going to chafe with 'The Man' in the house. She's going to become paranoid and believe you're spying on her. We should work together to enlarge the greenhouse and give her enough space to be comfortable."

"But your mother will be upset."

Burt hissed to draw our attention, and when I looked up, he flipped me off.

"Right back at you," I snapped.

Burt let loose a maniacal laugh.

I tried to throw magic at him, but he ducked out of sight.

"Back to the house," Chief Terry ordered, the hand not holding the flashlight gripping my arm. "I don't want that thing creeping up behind us."

We were in total agreement there. To distract myself from the fact that Burt was here—I occasionally heard him laughing—I focused on Chief Terry's worry about Mom. "Mom will be fine because Aunt Tillie is still going to have her chair in the kitchen. She'll be at the inn for every meal. Heck, she'll be in the living room watching television every morning and night. She'll just have her own place to sleep ... and plot mischief."

"And you'd be okay with that?" Chief Terry looked baffled. "What about icy walkways during the winter? Do you want her to fall and break a hip?"

"We can use magic to keep the sidewalks clear. She wanders around in the snow all the time anyway."

"I know." He rubbed his hand over his cheek. "I don't want to be the reason she's removed from her own home."

"Aunt Tillie is going to do what Aunt Tillie is going to do," I said. "You can't stop her. If this wasn't something she really wanted, she wouldn't have suggested it."

Chief Terry worked his jaw. "I guess. I just—"

We almost came out of our skins when the back door swung open. Landon appeared with Winchester at his heels. He didn't look happy.

"What are you two doing?"

"Hunting clowns," I replied.

Landon's eyes jerked to the yard. "Find any?"

"Yes, but we've decided to be smart about things and send Evan after them," Chief Terry replied. "He'll have an easier time dropping in from above and killing that fool."

"How do we know he can kill it?" Landon asked.

"He can dismember it without breaking a sweat," I replied. I forced myself to be sunny when asking my next question. "Did you have fun with your friends?"

"Not really." Landon lightly brushed his thumb over my cheek. "Sometimes you have to do things you don't want to do."

"That's what I told her," Chief Terry said.

"Right now, I really want to go home and romance my wife." Landon held his hand out to me. "We have to walk. I had too much to drink."

"You want to walk with Burt on the loose?"

Landon froze. "Or you could drive."

I chuckled. "I knew you would suggest that."

"Let's go." He herded me toward the door, his eyes drifting to the trees. "I'm going to kill Aunt Tillie for this."

Chief Terry was just as disgruntled as Landon. "Join the club."

LANDON WOKE WITHOUT A HANGOVER, and we enjoyed our morning snuggle before resigning ourselves to the problems of the day. We took Winchester out for his morning bathroom break. While Landon was busy praising his dog, I looked for fresh tracks in the snow.

Landon almost looked afraid when he asked the obvious question. "Anything?"

"I don't see any fresh Burt tracks."

He exhaled heavily, relieved. "That's good."

"There are little ones around. I think three of the smaller dolls were here yesterday ... or last night."

Landon's smile disappeared. "Are you trying to give me indigestion before I even have breakfast?"

"No, but I do want to talk to you about something."

Lines appeared at the corners of Landon's eyes. "I'm going to hate this, aren't I?"

"How do you want me to approach these agents?"

"What do you mean?"

"Do you want me to try to befriend them?" The mere notion turned my stomach, but I pushed forward. "Do you want me to try to bond with Cam even though she's trying to get under my skin with all the flirting?"

"Cam is trying to get a reaction out of you," Landon agreed. "She wants to see what you'd do if you believe she has a thing for me."

"Why would I do anything? I'm secure in our relationship."

"Maybe she's testing that."

"Or maybe Hodgins instructed her to keep me off balance," I suggested.

A muscle worked in Landon's jaw. "That's also a possibility."

"He's the one who makes me nervous," I said.

"He's the one to fear," Landon agreed. "He wants to get one over on me. There's no better way than going after my wife."

"It's going to be okay," I assured him. "We didn't kill Brad Childs."

"We need to figure out who did so we can get ahead of this."

"Could it be Mrs. Little?"

"Why would she kill him?"

"Maybe she thought it was us." That possibility didn't sit right with me, but it wasn't something we could overlook.

"Mrs. Little seemed even more off than usual yesterday," Landon acknowledged. "Maybe she's losing it."

"When we were kids, Chief Terry used to warn Aunt Tillie about pushing Mrs. Little too far. He said she would take us all by surprise one day, that she would win, and we would be sorry for everything we'd done. What if that day has finally come?"

"She seemed to be struggling yesterday," Landon said. "I think it's best we check in on her again. Just because you found Childs's body in front of her house doesn't mean she's responsible. It's possible someone followed Aunt Tillie there when she was coming up with her plan and killed him."

"That doesn't feel right, though, does it?"

"No." Landon shook his head. "This feels pointed. We need to figure out why."

"After breakfast, right? Because I'm starving."

"Of course after breakfast. It's almost bacon time. Like we're going to skip breakfast. Don't be ridiculous."

I smirked. "The FBI agents will be there."

His mouth flattened. "I know it's hard for you to have them there, but you need to try. It's best for all of us."

"I'll do my best."

"You don't have to be best friends with them. Just don't be rude."

That felt like a tall order.

12

TWELVE

Evan was in the lobby when Landon and I entered. Winchester immediately ran to him, tail wagging, and yipping.

"Hello." Evan dropped to his knees and stroked his hand over Winchester's soft fur. "How are you?"

Winchester yipped in response.

"Sounds good." Evan grinned at the dog before turning his smile to me. It faded quickly. "You seem tense."

Tense was a good word for what I was feeling. "Did Chief Terry call you?"

He looked surprised by the question. "No. Am I under arrest?"

I shook my head and edged forward to look down the hallway that led to the dining room.

"If you're looking for the FBI agents, they're already in there," Evan volunteered.

"All four of them?"

He nodded.

I exhaled and bobbed my head. "That's good. We need your help."

"I'm almost afraid to ask."

"You should be," Landon said. "Aunt Tillie has really done it this time."

Rather than appear worried, Evan smirked. "She's been quiet for days. I was becoming concerned. Seems that was a wasted effort."

"I'll say," I agreed. I told him about the dolls. When I got to the part about Burt, he cocked his head. He obviously hadn't heard about Childs's body, because he straightened at that news.

"What was Brad Childs doing in front of Margaret Little's house?" he asked.

"That is the question," Landon said.

"How did he die?"

"We don't know that either." Landon was grim. "He had a broken neck. That much was obvious. It's possible he died from something else and broke his neck when he fell. They are not sharing information with me on that front."

"Because they think Bay is a suspect," Evan surmised.

"Pretty much," Landon confirmed. "It doesn't help that Bay had to explain what she was doing at Mrs. Little's house when she tripped over the body."

"I'm assuming you left the clowns out of the retelling."

"Yes, but Mrs. Little likely filled them in," I said.

"She's another problem," Landon supplied. "She seemed unstable when we ran into her at lunch yesterday. There's no telling what she's saying to the other team."

"Why is there another team?" Evan looked perplexed. "Why aren't you and Terry handling this as you normally would?"

"Because two weeks ago, I filed a report with my boss about Childs stalking Bay."

"Ah." Evan bobbed his head. "In case we had to kill him, you wanted a paper trail that he was acting odd."

"Yes, but we didn't kill him, and we have a very big problem."

Evan clucked his tongue. "This isn't good."

"No, it's very bad," I agreed. "Burt has shown up several times now. Chief Terry and I went looking for him last night. We found him in the trees on the west side of the property. We decided that we could use your help getting rid of him."

"I'm not afraid of a clown doll," Evan agreed. "Even if he is sentient."

"He has a big knife," Landon complained.

"I can heal."

"We need him gone," I explained. "Also, because I can't be seen openly working with Landon, I thought you might want to work with me after breakfast."

"You want me to be your sidekick today," Evan teased.

"I just want backup in case," I replied. "If you're too busy..."

"I'm not too busy," he assured me. "I came because Tillie sent me a text last night ranting about all of you. When I got here, I found her passed out from too much wine. I thought I would check in with her this morning."

"That must have been after we left," I assumed.

Evan agreed. "Are we conducting a clown hunt today? I mean, is that all we're doing?"

"To start," I replied. "I thought we could steal Aunt Tillie's four-wheeler—she doesn't need to know about it—and head into the woods. I might be able to cast a spell once we're far enough away from the inn to draw them to us."

"Are we destroying them?"

"Yes," Landon answered before I could.

"I think that's the best option," I replied. "Aunt Tillie won't like it, but..."

"It's pretty much where we're at," Evan said. "You head into breakfast. I'll make sure the four-wheeler is gassed up and steal the keys."

"Aunt Tillie probably has them on her," I said grumpily.

"There are two sets. I know where she hid the second set." Evan was all smiles.

"That's because you helped her hide them," I realized.

He shrugged. "I find her entertaining. Times like these, however, remind me she can do a lot of harm if she's not reined in."

"She seems to have her nose out of joint about the FBI agents and the clowns," I confirmed. "Mom ordered her to destroy the clowns."

"Instead, she set them free." Evan smirked. "It's going to be a fun day. I'll search the property while you're eating. Appearances must be kept up. They'll question why you're leaving with me if you skip breakfast. I'll meet you in the greenhouse in an hour."

"Thanks for doing this." I meant it.

"It's my pleasure."

"I appreciate it too," Landon said. "We have to be careful that she's not seen working with me. At least I know she's safe with you."

"She's safe with herself," Evan replied. "With this many dolls running around, though, it's good to have several sets of eyes."

Landon's lips curved down. "Why did it have to be clowns?"

Evan shrugged. "She's Tillie."

"Yes, she's Tillie."

We left Evan and headed into the dining room. I pasted a smile I didn't feel on my face as we entered.

Chief Terry was already seated in his usual spot. He didn't smile in greeting when he saw us. Instead, he pinned Aunt Tillie with the sort of look I remembered from my childhood, when he caught us tormenting Mrs. Little.

At the other end of the table, Cam, Hodgins, Spencer, and Patrice were seated and drinking coffee. They had notebooks in front of them and seemed to be making plans for the day. There was no sign of Mom, Marnie, or Twila.

"What's going on?" Landon asked as he sat next to Aunt Tillie. She, of course, was busy glaring at Chief Terry.

"Nothing," Chief Terry replied. He flashed a smile for my benefit. "How are you?"

"Good," I assured him. I forced myself to smile at the FBI agents. "Big day?"

"We have a lot of legwork to do," Hodgins replied. "We're trying to track Childs's movements the day he died. We've figured out—through talks with his wife—that he was likely in town almost forty-eight hours before his body was discovered."

"How long had he been dead?" I asked.

"We're still trying to pin that down. At least a few hours."

"Which means he died when it was still light out."

"We can't confirm anything yet," Hodgins said. "I'm sure you under-stand. While we're on the subject, where were you that day?"

I should've been expecting the question—they'd asked me some ques-tions already, but we really hadn't gotten into the nitty-gritty—but I was surprised all the same. "That was the day before yesterday." I racked my brain. "We had breakfast here."

"We have breakfast here every morning," Landon explained to Hodgins. "Bay isn't much of a cook."

I gave him a dirty look. "You could cook."

"Sorry, that came out wrong. I didn't mean I want you to cook. It's easy for us to come here because we live on the grounds. We know the meal schedule and that allows us to save time."

"Plus, Landon is a glutton who eats his weight in pork products at every meal," Aunt Tillie volunteered, speaking for the first time since we'd entered the room.

"I *do* like my bacon," Landon agreed. He looked uncomfortable but tried to play it off as a joke. "I'm pretty easy when it comes to food, though."

That was the most ridiculous thing I'd ever heard. "You're easy with food?"

He shot me a pointed look. "Don't I eat anything?"

"Anything and everything," Aunt Tillie added.

I was rankled by the show Landon put on for the other agents' benefit. He was never one to kiss official bottoms, and yet here he was smooching.

Chief Terry, perhaps sensing that I was about to snap something out, shot me a warning look. "Breakfasts here are a family affair. We like to eat together before separating for the day. It's a bonding exercise."

"Yes, we're all bonded to each other like glue," I said.

"Or like flies to manure," Aunt Tillie offered.

"As for what I was doing the day before yesterday, after breakfast I went to the newspaper office. I was there until lunch. Then I went to the diner with Clove and Thistle. After lunch, I had to work on some advertising back at the office. Then I came here for dinner."

"And then you went with your great-aunt and cousin to torture an old lady," Hodgins said. "Sounds like a busy day."

I didn't like his attitude. "You keep referring to Mrs. Little as an old lady. She's more than that."

"I didn't mean to disparage her," Hodgins said. "Although, to be honest, I'm confused about why you would care given the things you've done to her."

Chief Terry cleared his throat before I could respond.

"As I told you before, Margaret and Tillie have a very long history. It's not all one-sided."

"What has Mrs. Little done to you?" Patrice asked Aunt Tillie.

"She dressed in a mask and tried to make me answer horror movie questions to save my life while threatening to hang me from a tree," Aunt Tillie replied.

"Isn't that the opening scene of *Scream*?" Spencer asked.

"Where do you think they got the idea?"

I rubbed my forehead and focused on the food that had appeared on my plate. Apparently, Landon had been busy without me noticing. "Mrs. Little has always been terrible. For as long as I can remember, she has gone out of her way to be mean to people."

"She was mean to you?" Hodgins asked. "What did she do?"

"When we were little, she used to tell us that our mothers chased our fathers away and made us unlovable." I didn't realize I was going to tell the story until it was already out of my mouth. "She said that our mothers cast spells on our fathers, and when they wore off, our fathers ran ... and they were glad to be away from us as much as our mothers."

Mom's eyes turned icy. "I didn't know that."

"Aunt Tillie paid her back by putting fish inside her hubcaps. Three days later, she was stinking up the town."

"Ah, yes." Mom nodded. "That was when Aunt Tillie used her paint gun to put brown splotches on the seat of Margaret's pants so everybody in town thought she'd crapped them and the smell was coming from her."

Spencer choked on a laugh. Patrice looked mildly amused. Cam and Hodgins didn't even smile.

"While I don't think it's okay to terrorize children, obviously you knew what she was telling you wasn't true," Cam insisted. "Your fathers run an inn in town. You clearly got over the things she said."

"At the time we believed her because we weren't seeing our fathers much," I replied. "That's neither here nor there. The stuff Mrs. Little did to us when we were kids was easy enough to get over. Kids say horrible things to each other and then get over it. The things Mrs. Little has done in recent years are worse."

"Yes, you mentioned her buying up land in town," Hodgins said. "Why is that a concern?"

"She's going to try to take over."

"She says she already runs everything in the town," Cam argued. "What would be different?"

"She says a lot of things," Mom replied. "That doesn't mean they are true."

"I need to talk to the people you saw the day before yesterday to nail down your timeline, Bay," Hodgins said. "We need to do this by the book. I don't want any accusations that we gave you special treatment because you're married to an FBI agent."

"I don't think we have to worry about that," Landon said. "Bay didn't kill Brad Childs, so there's no special treatment to give."

"I'm sure the evidence will support that." Hodgins's smile was brief. "Now, let's talk about who can corroborate your alibi."

I ticked off the list of names, relieved when I was finished and hoping the conversation would turn to something else. Hodgins focused on Aunt Tillie.

"I need to be able to corroborate your alibi too," Hodgins prodded.

Aunt Tillie barely blinked at the request. "My alibi?"

"Given your history with Margaret Little, we have no choice but to do our due diligence. You might be elderly—"

"I'm middle aged," Aunt Tillie fired back.

Hodgins pursed his lips, then smiled. "Okay, I still need your alibi."

"For how long?" Aunt Tillie demanded.

"Tell me where you were the day before yesterday and we'll go from there."

The way Aunt Tillie worked her jaw told me that breakfast was about to go sideways.

I shoveled eggs into my mouth and watched.

"I woke up around four in the morning," Aunt Tillie started. "That's normal for me."

"I can't imagine getting up that early," Spencer lamented. "That's an old person thing, right?"

"I'm going to give you an inverted penis thing if you're not careful," Aunt Tillie fired back.

Spencer laughed ... until he realized none of us were laughing. Then he shifted uncomfortably on his chair.

"I went to my greenhouse and worked there for a bit," Tillie continued. "I have some plants I'm getting ready to transplant outside as soon as the weather breaks."

"What sort of plants?" Patrice asked.

"Mostly herbs," Aunt Tillie replied. "Vervain. Henbane. Lady's Mantle. Marijuana."

Mom slapped her hand to her forehead.

"Okay," Hodgins said without missing a beat. "Then what did you do?"

"Then I went inside and had breakfast with the family. It didn't go well because Landon asked Winnie if she could figure out a way to stuff bacon in the pancakes and she told him that they would cook funny. He whined. Winnie made faces. Bay tried to replace some of Landon's real bacon with fake bacon."

I wasn't aware that she'd seen me do that.

Landon slid his eyes to me. "How could you?"

I shrugged. "You have got to start watching what you eat. I won't apologize for wanting to make you healthier."

"You haven't actually traded out my bacon, have you?"

"If you haven't noticed, why do you care?"

"The betrayal," Landon hissed.

Hodgins kept his gaze on Aunt Tillie. "And after breakfast?"

"I went to town with my sidekick. His name is Evan. He lives near Weldon Creek. I have two sidekicks but he's my number one."

"What does Evan do for a living?" Hodgins asked.

I became alert, ignoring Landon's exaggerated pouting. This was dangerous territory. I needn't have worried, though. Aunt Tillie's ability to lie on the spot kicked in.

"He fixes motorcycles," Aunt Tillie replied. "He works out of the Rusty Cauldron in Hawthorne Hollow. He lives in his uncle's house here. He mostly keeps to himself. I'm trying to make him more of an extrovert."

"He's your sidekick?" Hodgins prodded.

"Yup." Aunt Tillie's smile was serene. "I would make him my boyfriend but he's gay and, try as I might, he's not interested in female parts. I tried making him watch porn so he could be absolutely certain, but he didn't react at all. And I got really good porn and everything. I didn't steal it from illegal places on the internet or anything. I actually paid."

"So that's where that cable charge came from," Mom said. "I thought that was Terry."

"Hey!" Chief Terry looked offended. "Why would you assume that was me?"

"What were my other options?" Mom asked.

Chief Terry waved a hand at my smug-looking great aunt. "Isn't she always the answer to the question, 'Who did it?'"

Mom opened her mouth and then shut it. "You have a point."

"How about after you spent time with your sidekick?" Hodgins prodded.

To my surprise, Aunt Tillie offered up a happy smile. "You know what? You should probably come with me today. I can't remember everything, but I have a routine. If you come with me, you can go see the routine."

I sensed trouble. Big, big trouble.

Hodgins immediately accepted the invitation. "That sounds like a fabulous idea."

"Great." Aunt Tillie grabbed a piece of bacon. "The day is looking up."

13
THIRTEEN

I took the time to say goodbye to Landon in the backyard.

"It will be fine," I assured him. "We're just hunting clowns."

Landon wasn't appeased. "Can't you just leave them out there to rot?"

"That's not what you suggested last night," I reminded him. "You wanted Evan to take out Burt when I told you what Chief Terry and I discussed."

"I *do* want that," Landon agreed. "But I don't want you hunting clowns. Evan is more than capable of doing it alone."

"Thanks, man," Evan said as he slid to a stop in front of us on the four-wheeler. He wasn't wearing a helmet—he didn't really need one because he was a vampire—but he had one for me. "Ready?"

I eyed the helmet, bright pink with lightning bolts. "I'm ready."

"Wait." Landon held up his hand. "I didn't think you were serious when you mentioned this thing." He studied the four-wheeler. "Why do you have to take this?"

"Because the clowns are in the woods," I replied. "This will make searching easier ... and escape faster."

"It's cute you threw in that last part for my benefit." Landon sent me a tight smile. "There's just one problem."

"What's that?"

"I'm not an idiot. I know Aunt Tillie has this thing souped up. What happens if you get in an accident out there?"

"Have you forgotten the part where I have super strength and can run really fast?" Evan asked.

Landon shook his head. "Why can't you do that from the start instead of driving this thing around?"

"I didn't realize you were so cool."

Landon was instantly suspicious. "What do you mean?"

"I didn't realize you were game to have me carrying around your wife all day. I mean ... that's what's going to have to happen. She can't keep up with me, so I'll need to carry her. I didn't think you'd care for that. Now that I know you're game..."

Landon scowled. "I don't want that."

Evan's grin was easy. "I didn't think so. Stop being weird. You know she'll be safe with me."

"You haven't seen Burt," Landon countered. "He's all kinds of creepy."

"I can handle a doll." Evan sounded sure of himself. "Besides, don't you prefer the idea of Bay being with me instead of downtown, where she might run into Mrs. Little and make things worse?"

"Your mood this morning wasn't great," Landon hedged as he darted a glance at me. "If you want them not to like you, you're doing a bang-up job."

"I don't care if they like me," I snapped. "I don't particularly like them."

It was impossible to miss the look Evan and Landon exchanged.

"I'll talk to her about her bad attitude too," Evan offered.

Landon sighed. He liked Evan. He'd told me that more than once. Evan offered a sort of backup that differed from the normal magic and mayhem. That didn't mean Landon was happy with the idea of me taking off for an entire day with another man. "Just be careful," he said.

He leaned in to give me a kiss and cupped the back of my head. He looked as if he wanted to say more but was struggling. "I get this is hard for you," he started.

"I don't like them." I saw no reason to deny it. "They feel as if they are trying to get one over. If you peel back the layers, I'm not their target, Landon. You are."

"I know." He looked pained. "That doesn't mean they won't hurt you to get to me."

"I'm more worried about you. I can survive an 'eccentric' label. Just look at Aunt Tillie. You, however, have already given up so much."

Landon vehemently shook his head. "Stop that."

"Being with me is a sacrifice for you," I insisted.

"No, it is not." Landon's eyes flashed with annoyance. "You're the best thing that ever happened to me. This family is the best thing that ever happened to me. I didn't sacrifice anything. I got more than I ever dreamed of. Stop saying things like that."

His words warmed me. Still, I was worried how this was going to play out. "I think it's best that Evan and I spend the morning in the woods hunting clowns. It keeps me away from the agents and keeps the clowns on their toes. They'll be more worried about us than terrorizing people in town."

Landon pulled me in for a hug and kissed my cheek. "Be careful anyway. Burt is a menace."

"It will be fine. I have backup." With that, I took the helmet from Evan and pulled it on.

Landon grinned as he used his fingers to tuck my hair inside the helmet. "Be careful." He gave me a kiss and then focused on Evan. "Just because you're indestructible doesn't mean she is."

"I've got it," Evan assured him. "You have nothing to worry about. I could do this professionally."

Landon's smile disappeared. "You get more and more like Aunt Tillie with every passing day."

"I know," Evan agreed. "I even freak myself out sometimes."

"That's exactly how it should be."

Before Evan could take off with me holding tight behind him, a figure appeared on the sidewalk that stretched between the inn and the walkway that led to the guesthouse. Cam, dressed in black cargo pants and a green shirt, seemed surprised to find us together.

"What's this?" she asked.

I put my Aunt Tillie lying lessons to good use without thinking twice. "Evan lost his dog behind his farm. I'm going to help him find it."

"Who's Evan?" Cam's smile was a bit too flirty for my taste.

"Aunt Tillie's first sidekick," I replied. "She mentioned him at breakfast. He's a friend of the family."

"Have fun. I guess." Cam continued smiling. "I hope you find your dog."

"Something tells me we'll find exactly what we're looking for," Evan replied. "It was nice meeting you." With that, Evan took off like a shot and we headed toward the bluffs. I didn't look over my shoulder at Landon. I couldn't.

Today—just for today—we were on different paths. I couldn't risk him getting in trouble. That meant I was on my own. Well, other than Evan.

Perhaps that was for the best.

EVAN WAS A BIT OF A DAREDEVIL ON THE four-wheeler. He reminded me of Aunt Tillie. Only he couldn't get hurt while she was of an age that breaking a hip was a real concern. Despite how sharp he took the turns, I knew I wasn't in any danger. His reflexes were beyond anything I could imagine.

I relaxed and let him do the navigating. He didn't stop until we were at the creek three miles back in the hills.

"Wow," I said as I got off the four-wheeler and stretched. "I think you've been spending too much time with Aunt Tillie."

Evan grinned, and it lit up his entire face. He was handsome to the point of being striking. When he'd first entered our lives, he'd been a ragged mess. Having his soul repaired after being a blood-sucking fiend for several years had done a real number on his mental and physical health.

Scout had healed him. Then she'd fretted. She didn't know what to do with him. Weirdly, it had been Aunt Tillie who had brought him back to the land of the living. Nobody understood why she was constantly tapping him for revenge jobs—outings he seemed to hate—but now he'd grown to enjoy them—and his time with her.

Remembering that, the leading edge of irritation I felt thinking about Aunt Tillie and the clowns faded. She was a good person. She just had a nasty streak. Nobody was going to tell her what to do.

"What's with that face?" Evan asked as I began looking for prints.

I dragged my eyes to him. "I was just thinking."

"About the FBI agents?" Evan moved to the creek bed and searched the soft earth there for signs of the clowns.

"Not really. The FBI agents make me nervous. I wasn't thinking about them just now, though. I was thinking about Aunt Tillie."

"You're mad at her." It wasn't a question.

"Yup." I bobbed my head. "Uber mad."

"Because of the clowns?"

"There's a four-foot-tall Pennywise with two bullet holes in the chest running around town. He has a big knife ... and he's playing games with us. Am I supposed to like that?"

"No, but if the FBI agents weren't in town, you wouldn't be nearly as upset."

"I am ... conflicted ... about the FBI agents."

Evan looked up. "Why?"

He was a good sounding board, so I didn't feel bad about dumping all my feelings on him. "Well, for starters, it appears Landon has been less than forthcoming about his career prospects."

Evan cocked his head. "I don't know what that means."

"It seems everyone is in competition with him."

"In the office?"

I nodded.

"Why is that a problem? It means he's the one to beat."

"Yes, but beating him means that they move on to bigger markets. That's the end goal for all of them."

"And you're worried because Landon doesn't want to move on to a bigger market?"

"What if he does?"

"He doesn't."

"That's what he says, but I'm not sure it's true."

"Does he lie a lot?"

"Of course not. Not about anything big. He'll lie about how many slices of bacon he's had at any given breakfast, but that's not a real lie."

Evan smirked. "Why would he lie about being happy with his job?"

"I don't know." The conversation was making me uncomfortable. "It's just ... he wanted a big market before we got together. He says his goals changed when he met me. What if that's not the best thing for him?"

"Are you willing to move to a bigger market with him?"

I frowned. "I guess." I loved Landon enough to do what was necessary to make him happy, but the thought of moving filled me with dread.

"You wouldn't be happy in a big city. If you're happy here, why can't he be happy here?"

"I don't want him to sell himself short. If he has dreams, he deserves to make a go of them."

"Bay, you're his dream. This place is his dream. Do you want the same things you wanted when you were younger?"

"Kind of. I want to be happy. I thought one thing was going to make me happy, but it turned out to be another."

"Why can't it be that way for him?"

I took a moment to really think about it. "I guess I don't want him to ever look at me and regret his choice."

"He won't."

"How can you be so certain?"

"I've seen the way he looks at you. You're like the last slice of bacon on the plate. He'll always be happy with you. Trust in what he says, because this is not something he would lie about. Your marriage is too important to him."

I knew what he was saying was true. "I guess these other agents have thrown me," I admitted. "I never thought about there being competition in his office. Everything here seems to happen in a vacuum. He has other things going on."

"That's true for everyone."

"Yeah, but I liked it all being about me."

Evan barked out a laugh. "That sounds like something Tillie would say."

I fixed him with a wounded look. "That's the meanest thing you've ever said to me."

"I didn't mean it as a bad thing. Tillie is funny. She's smart ... and manipulative ... but has a soft heart. There are worse people you could emulate."

"Yes, well..." I moved to hunker down next to him to see what he was looking at, but his hand shot out to stop me. "What is it?" I hissed.

He shook his head and nudged me back. "The tracks are here," he said in a clear voice. "Rover was definitely here."

Rover? "I..." Before I could say anything else the sound of a twig cracking behind me had me straightening. I expected to find Burt advancing with his knife. Instead, I found Cam studying us.

"Oh, hello," she said. "I didn't realize you guys would be so far out."

"I didn't realize you were coming out so far either," I replied. Had she been listening? Did she hear what I'd said about Landon? Probably not. Evan tracked her as soon as she was within hearing distance.

"I'm trying to track the distance between the inn and the motel on the highway," Cam explained. "It's about five miles if you cut across the land and ignore the road, right?"

I glanced in the direction she was looking. "Are you talking about Independence Motor Lodge?"

"Yes. I believe that's the name."

"Why would you..." I trailed off, realization dawning. "Is that where Brad Childs was staying?"

"I'm not supposed to tell you that." Cam shot me a sheepish smile. "Nothing personal. We're trying to keep you separate from the investigation."

"Right." I smiled even though I didn't feel particularly happy. "I guess it's a fluke we ran into each other out here."

"I thought you were tracking a dog." Cam looked around. "I don't see a dog."

"His tracks are here." Evan pointed to the mud and, sure enough, there were what looked like paw prints. How had he managed that? "We're getting closer."

"I don't understand your part in all of this." Cam smiled at Evan. "Do you date one of the cousins?"

"I'm gay," Evan replied without hesitation. "There's no dating going on. I'm a family friend."

"Of Tillie's?"

"Of all of us," I replied. "Aunt Tillie adopted him not long after he moved to town. We're all quite attached to him now."

Cam kept smiling. "Well, I guess I should keep on my trek to the hotel."

"Yes, and we have to keep looking for Rover," Evan said. He motioned to the four-wheeler. "Let's head out to the bluff. I bet he's out there. He likes chasing the birds."

We left Cam, who determinedly walked toward the highway even though I knew darned well she wasn't going the entire way on foot. Evan raced off at a high speed again—causing me to hold on for dear life—and didn't stop until we'd gone at least two miles. Then he killed the engine.

"Do you think she followed us the entire way?" I asked.

He shrugged and surprised me when he dropped to his knees and started looking over the four-wheeler. After a few seconds, he came back with what looked to be a small mechanical square.

"What is that?" I asked.

"A tracker." He was grim. "I knew she couldn't have followed us on foot. Someone dropped her on the road to the east of where we were. From there, it would've been a ten-minute walk."

"So, she waited for us to leave and hiked back to where she parked."

"Yup." Evan crushed the tracker in his hand.

"Should you have done that? What if it makes them suspicious?"

"They're going to have to admit they put that tracker on the four-wheeler to say something, but they won't. For all they know, it fell off." He threw the tracker into the trees. "Good luck finding it."

"We should check all of our vehicles," I said.

"I'll handle it," he promised. "What do you think about what she said about the hotel?"

"That place is a hole in the wall. It's ... gross."

"And yet you wouldn't have seen Childs there. I'm betting that's why he was staying there."

"His wife didn't mention it."

"Maybe we should take a look."

"Let's do it. We're not really looking for a dog. But what about the clowns?"

"I'll start hunting them," he promised. "Gunner and Scout aren't doing anything today. They can help. Let's hit the hotel first."

14
FOURTEEN

The Independence Motor Lodge was the sort of place that people check into at the start of a horror movie and never check out of. The front office had a sign in the window touting Magic Fingers, which I was certain had gone extinct decades ago.

"You should bring Landon here," Evan said as we parked in the woods. His lips curved. "Something tells me he would like Magic Fingers."

"Yes, but I'm sure he wouldn't like the chlamydia he'd catch from the bedspread."

"Probably not." Evan climbed off the four-wheeler and cast me a serious look. "You stay here until I make certain there are no FBI agents present."

I wanted to argue—being left behind was no fun—but I nodded. This was a big deal, and we had to treat it like a big deal. "We need to find out what room he's in."

"I'll handle that. Give me ten minutes." He disappeared into the trees.

"I wish I could move that fast," I lamented.

"I can move that fast."

I jolted at the voice. It almost sounded as if it belonged to a child. When I turned, I saw a blue-haired clown doll—only about a foot in height—eyeing me from beneath a pine tree.

"Oh, geez." I glared at it. "Why?"

The clown shrugged. "Why not?" With that, it bolted into the trees, moving pretty fast for a doll.

I stared in its wake a moment and then followed. My legs were longer, so I caught up with the clown near the four-wheeler. I grabbed it by the back of its neck and whipped it around.

"Get off, wide load!" It screeched. "I'll rip your throat out and drink your blood!"

I rolled my eyes before jolting it with magic. The clown fell still in an instant. I kept hold of it and searched the area for more. I found three, which I took out in the same manner, and then carried them back to the four-wheeler. Evan returned as I dumped them onto the vehicle's seat.

"Where did they come from?" he asked, eyeing the dolls with a great deal of distaste.

"One of them came to visit right after you left. I found the others when looking around."

Evan shook his head. "I take it none of them are Burt."

"Burt is four times as big."

"That's terrifying." He shook his head, then grinned. "You have to love her style."

"I'm not all that fond of her style right now. Her style means Landon's co-workers think I'm a nut who tortures old ladies. That's what they keep calling Mrs. Little, an old lady."

"She is kind of old."

"She's also losing her mind. She was babbling like a crazy person in the diner yesterday."

"Think about it from her perspective." Evan turned philosophical. "Tillie unleashing a yard full of clown dolls on her might not seem like a big thing, but when you consider that Tillie does it at least once a week ... for fifty years or so ... it might be enough to drive someone crazy."

"She deserves it. It takes so little effort not to be a jerk."

"You do realize that you're the villain of her story?"

I frowned. "Me?"

"Well, Tillie would be her Lex Luthor. You're whoever Lex Luthor's henchman is."

I rolled my eyes. "She deserves it. She's the actual villain."

"In your story. Everyone has their own story, Bay. It's possible she wouldn't have turned anywhere near as evil if Tillie hadn't pushed her so often. That said, it's also possible Tillie kept her in check. She could've turned into a Kryptonian villain, destroying small towns with a single credit card charge, if Tillie hadn't constantly been on her."

It was something I hadn't considered. "I still hate her."

"Don't make me trot out Yoda logic." His grin was lightning quick. "You can't worry about Margaret Little right now. The FBI agents are here. We need to worry about them. Margaret will still be there when we're done."

He had a very good point. It was time to turn to business. "What did you find at the hotel?"

"You cannot call this establishment a hotel." Evan's upper lip curved into a sneer. "This is a motel. Motels should be outlawed."

"You're kind of fussy sometimes," I noted.

He shrugged. "I don't do motels. The Feds have already been here. It wasn't hard to get inside the clerk's mind. It's mostly full of porn. They did close off Childs's room. They told the clerk they'd be back after lunch to clean everything out."

"Which means if we want to see it, we have to go now," I surmised.

Evan nodded. "I checked to make sure the FBI doesn't have the property under surveillance."

"Then I guess we should go."

Evan led the way. He skirted the trees until we got to the rear of the building. Then we hugged the exterior wall until we found room four. He somehow had secured a keycard.

"We cannot dillydally," he said. "Don't move anything. Just look around and see what you find of interest."

I didn't have to look hard to find the biggest point of interest. I pointed to the wall next to the bed.

Evan followed my finger, his eyes narrowing as he took in the huge collage Childs had assembled. There was a map in the center of things. Locations of interest had been marked. All around it were photos of my family.

"He was spying on us," I said.

Evan nodded. "Snap photos of this. All of it. Get quite a few. Up close. Far away."

I pulled out my phone and did as instructed.

When I was certain I had captured it from every angle I moved closer to see what we were dealing with.

"He marked locations on the map," Evan said. He had his hands on his hips and didn't look happy. "Do these locations mean anything to you?"

"Well, he has The Overlook and Dragonfly noted."

"Do you think he went to the Dragonfly?"

The Dragonfly was the inn my father and uncles owned together. Even though they lived in town, I only saw them once a week or so. My father and I were getting along, and things were better between us than they'd been since he returned. I still didn't spend huge gobs of time with him, though. "I can ask."

"Do it." Evan nodded. "Hollow Creek is on here."

"Makes me wonder if Childs went out there," I said. Hollow Creek had been the location of more than a few magical fights. Months ago, it had been crawling with magical shards because we'd expended so much magic there the remnants built up and took on a life of their own. Luckily we'd managed to clean up that mess. There was, however, another problem out there.

"The vampire apex," Evan said when I sighed. "She's on the other side of the creek. It wouldn't be difficult to find her."

"I'm guessing she knows how to protect herself from this sort of thing," I countered.

"Probably," he agreed. "I'll stop and see her just in case." He pointed at the map. "There's the Dandridge."

The Dandridge was the lighthouse Clove shared with Sam and Calvin. It had also proven to be a magical stronghold. However, it wasn't the magic drawing Childs. At least I didn't believe it was. "He's got the barn where Thistle lives on here too," I argued. "I think he was tracking us, not our magic."

"What about the school?" Evan pointed to the marking for Stonecrest Academy, which was where one of our more recent magical battles had occurred.

"He could've known we were spending time out there."

"Yeah." Evan rolled his neck. "He doesn't have maps of Hawthorne Hollow or Shadow Hills, which means he was not paying attention to Stormy and Scout."

I hesitated, then nodded. "It's possible he was intrigued by them but didn't get time to dig. Obviously, we're the ones he was focused on."

"Obviously," Evan agreed. He touched his tongue to his top lip before turning to the photos. "When were these taken?"

"How should I know?" My response came out shriller than I expected. Evan leveled a serious look at me, and I adjusted my tone. "Let me think."

"Take your time." Evan moved to the window to check we were still in the clear, and I focused on the photos.

"This one was taken at the Valentine's Day Festival." I pointed but made sure not to touch the photo. "It was right before Landon loaded up on maple bacon cupcakes and spiked hot chocolate. Then he paid to take over the kissing booth for an hour."

Evan smirked. "He does like to play his part as the glutton."

"It's not a part."

"Yes, it is. The man likes his bacon, but he plays it up for you."

"Why would he do that?"

"Because you fight the big fights and sometimes it drags you down. Even in the thick of things, when you're frustrated and want to cry, if only for a split second, you laugh when he's a glutton. He keeps that schtick in his back pocket to make you happy."

Was that really true?

"He also loves bacon," Evan added.

I laughed. "So very, very much." I turned back to the photos. "This was just a few days ago." I pointed to a photo of Thistle and me in the window of Hypnotic. "That shirt is new. Thistle was talking about the new window mural she plans for spring."

"Anything else stand out?" Evan prodded.

"I don't..." I trailed off as one picture caught my attention. "That's Scout helping Aunt Tillie mess with Mrs. Little. I was there but I wasn't the star of that incident."

"Was that when Scout helped Tillie enchant the unicorns to sing 'Twelve Little Unicorns Jumping on the Bed' for twenty-four hours?"

"Yup. I thought Mrs. Little was going to pop an aneurism."

Evan nodded again before moving to the closet. "He has enough clothes in here for about a week. I think we need to talk to the clerk again."

"Why?"

"I don't think Childs did this in a few days. I think he was here for weeks."

"His wife said he was home."

"Maybe he was just touching base at home." Evan's expression was grave when his eyes met mine. "Or maybe she was protecting him."

We did a quick trip around the room and then let ourselves out. The clerk was exactly what I expected: skinny and wearing a stained T-shirt. The television above his desk was playing porn.

"Netflix?" I asked as a joke when the clerk looked up at me.

"Pornhub."

"Ah."

"Do you two need a room?" the clerk asked.

"This is Barry," Evan volunteered as he rested his elbow on the counter. "Barry and I go way back."

Barry narrowed his murky gray eyes. "Aren't you the guy who was in here a few minutes ago?"

"Astute as always, Barry," Evan drawled. "We have questions."

"This isn't the sort of establishment where we answer questions," Barry countered. "It's a no-tell motel." He was talking to us as if we were stupid.

"We've heard of that, but you're going to tell." Evan slapped his hand down on the top of Barry's head and froze him in place. "How you feeling, Barry?" he asked after a few seconds.

"Awesome," Barry replied. He looked like a very happy, very dazed, individual. "It's a beautiful day."

"Yes, it's lovely," Evan agreed. "This is my friend Hannah."

I made a face at the name but didn't say anything.

"I want you to answer her questions," Evan ordered.

"Hannah." Barry nodded. "That's a pretty name."

"Her black hair is pretty, isn't it?" Evan continued.

"So pretty."

"That hairy mole on her lip is a turn on."

"I love moles," Barry agreed.

Evan looked smug when he turned to me. "He's all yours."

I smiled at Barry, but his eyes were unfocused. I dropped all pretense. "Tell me about Brad Childs."

"That's the guy this guy was asking about a few minutes ago," Barry replied, gesturing to Evan.

"Yes," I said. "I need to know about Brad. How long did he stay here?"

"He rented a room by the month. We don't get a lot of business, so we gave him a deal. He didn't want housekeeping to go in his room. He brought his own towels. He spent two or three nights a week here."

"Did he tell you why he was staying here?"

Barry shrugged one shoulder. "I didn't ask. I assumed he was having trouble with his old lady. You know how bitches be."

I frowned. "I'm not sure I do."

Evan sent me a warning look. "We don't have time for you to give this idiot a lesson in manners."

I sighed. "Fine. Did anyone ever visit him here?"

"His mom."

"His mom?"

"Yeah. I mean ... I assumed she was his mom. She was an old lady. Much older than him. Even if his wife kicked him out, he wouldn't go for the old ones that way. He could still snag middle-aged. He didn't have to settle for old yet."

"You really are a great guy," I muttered, shaking my head. "Did he call this woman 'Mom?'"

"I don't know. I never got near them. She parked in front of his room."

"Can you describe her?"

"Gray hair. Short. She wore a lot of pink. I think she might've been slow, because she had a unicorn painted on her car."

I froze in place.

"What color was the car?" Evan asked, taking over.

"Gray," Barry replied. "Not like a cool gun-metal gray, more a powder gray."

"What color was the unicorn?"

"Oh, it was so cool." Barry rubbed his hands together, relishing the retelling. "It was pink with fairy dust all around. It even said unicorn on it. Unicorn ... something."

"Unicorn Emporium?" I supplied.

"I don't know what an emporium is."

"It doesn't matter." I turned to Evan. "We both know who that vehicle belongs to."

"Margaret," Evan confirmed. "Didn't she tell you she didn't know him?"

"She said she'd seen him around town," I replied. "She acted as if she'd never met him."

"Obviously that was a lie."

"A big lie," I agreed.

I tapped my fingers on the counter. "We can't get any more information here. We need to leave before the Feds return."

Evan turned back to Barry. "When the Feds come, you won't remember any of this. You won't remember me, or Hannah."

"I've already forgotten you," Barry assured him.

Evan put his hand to my back and prodded me outside. We made our way back to the four-wheeler. Evan made sure to move us even farther back in the woods so we could watch for a few minutes and talk.

"What do you want to do?" he asked.

"I'm going to talk to my father. He had photos of the Dragonfly. It's possible Childs was pumping them for information."

"Wouldn't he have told you about that?"

"Not necessarily."

"I'll drop you back at the inn so you can get your car. I'm going to check on Margaret."

"Be careful."

"I can handle Margaret."

Apparently, no one could handle Mrs. Little. She was even worse than we thought. "Be careful anyway."

15
FIFTEEN

My father was in the kitchen with Clove's father, Warren, at the Dragonfly. They had two cars in the lot, suggesting a few guests, but I didn't see anyone loitering about, and Thistle's father, Teddy, was nowhere in sight.

"Hello." Dad beamed when he saw me. "This is a surprise."

"I stop in." I didn't mean to be petulant, but I couldn't help myself. Occasionally, guilt got the better of me when I visited my father. We were in the same town, but I rarely saw him more than once a week.

"I wasn't giving you a hard time." Dad stopped chopping celery and looked me up and down. "Is something wrong?"

"Are you jumping to that conclusion because we always have trouble?" I tried to laugh. "I'm sorry," I offered when he raised an eyebrow. "It's been a rough two days."

"Does this have something to do with the body found at Margaret Little's house?" Warren asked. "We heard that Tillie was there when it was found."

"Thistle and I were there too."

"Doing what?" Dad asked.

"Oh, you know, hexing clown dolls to sing and torture Mrs. Little." This time I smiled.

Dad's mouth fell open. "You did what?"

"She's a horrible woman."

"Bay." Dad almost looked disappointed. "You're an adult."

"I'm not sorry." I folded my arms over my chest and jutted out my chin. "She's trying to buy up the town. She keeps partnering with evil people. She's not innocent in all of this."

"Maybe not, but do you really think the clowns were necessary?"

"In hindsight, it might have been overkill. Especially since the Penny-wise clown Aunt Tillie hexed—it's four feet tall—has a butcher knife and might be sentient."

Warren's hand hit his face. Dad just stared.

"It's not as bad as it sounds," I said hurriedly. "We'll find him. He seems more interested in stalking us anyway."

"Unbelievable," Dad said. "Bay—"

"I don't want to hear it," I shouted. "We have other problems. The clowns are low on the list of our worries right now."

"How frightening is that?" Warren drawled.

I shrugged. "We live interesting lives. What can I say?"

That nudged a smile out of Dad. "Who did the body belong to?" he asked after a few seconds. "They're saying it wasn't a local."

"Brad Childs."

"Brad?" Dad looked appalled. "Really?"

Well, that answered that question. "You knew him?"

"I did." Dad abandoned his culinary masterpiece and shifted closer to me. "What was he doing at Margaret Little's house?"

"We don't know, but I have to ask you a few questions."

"This is going to be bad, isn't it?"

"Well, it's not going to be good." This conversation wouldn't go well, and it was entirely my fault. I had no choice but to dive in. "What did you know about Brad?"

"What do you mean?" Puzzlement replaced worry on Dad's face. "He was looking in the area for a home for his family."

"Is that what he told you?"

"Is that not true?" Warren asked.

I shook my head. "Brad Childs was the warden at Antrim Correctional."

"Was he in charge when all those prisoners escaped?" Dad asked.

"He was. He lost his job over that." I took a deep breath. "In the weeks after, he became a bit obsessed with me."

Dad's forehead creased. "Sexually?"

"Magically."

"How would he even know?"

"I helped Landon and Chief Terry recapture a number of prisoners. Childs knew. He became curious." I held out my hands. "It wasn't the best situation."

"Why was he coming out here?"

"Did he ever ask questions about me?"

Dad opened his mouth—I was certain to say no—and then seemed to think better of it. "He did ask about my daughter. After I mentioned you lived in town. We never talked about your magic, Bay. I would never talk about that."

I believed him. "I'm not accusing you of anything," I assured him. "I feel bad because I didn't mention the problems I was having with Childs."

"That might've been helpful," Dad agreed.

"I'm sorry. I just didn't think about it."

"But you're thinking about it now for a reason," Dad pressed.

"Childs was making noise. A lot of it. He came in the office and tried to pressure me for a spell to help him get his job back. I didn't own up to having real magic. I told him he was seeing things that weren't there because the town's tourist draw was coloring his vision."

"I'm guessing he didn't believe that."

"Not even a little," I confirmed. "He was ... unpleasant. I magically banned him from the newspaper office, so I'd find him sitting on the bench near the sidewalk."

"Why not tell Terry?" Warren challenged. "Wouldn't he have been able to dissuade Brad?"

"Chief Terry knew what was going on. He was hoping Childs would lose interest."

"Perhaps Terry was too focused on his new marriage," Dad said with a resentment that surprised me.

"I'm the one fixating on the wedding," I countered. "Besides, what did you want him to do?"

There was no hesitation when Dad answered. "Arrest him. He was harassing you."

"And when we have to testify in court that he was asking me for magical spells?" I challenged.

"I don't care about that." Dad was furious. "You were in danger."

"He never overtly threatened me," I replied. "If he hurt me, he definitely wasn't going to get what he wanted."

"I don't like that Terry gave him the option."

Thorny situation, I thought. Dad had issues with Chief Terry because he'd been the one who had spent time with me as a kid. Dad was down state. I saw him, but not often. As I grew older, the visits stopped entirely until Dad moved back to town. Now Dad was determined to forge a bond with me. He saw Chief Terry as something of an obstacle.

"We all decided to sit back and see what Childs would do," I explained. "We were hoping he would lose interest. If that didn't happen, we were talking about a memory spell."

"And now Childs is dead," Dad said. "That makes you a suspect."

"What makes it worse is that Landon and Chief Terry have to be hands off with the investigation."

"Otherwise, the higher-ups will think you were getting special treatment," Warren assumed.

"Pretty much," I confirmed. "We have to be very careful. There's no other way around it. The FBI agents are even staying at The Overlook."

"That's deliberate," Dad said.

"We're in a bind. Aunt Tillie's clowns are running all over town. I took out a handful this morning when Evan was scouting the Independence Motor Lodge."

Horror washed over Dad's features. "Why were you there?"

"That's where Childs was staying. He was renting a room by the month. Evan and I got inside and looked around. We found a few disturbing things." I pulled out my phone.

"Who is Evan again?" Warren asked.

"He's the weird guy always running around town with Tillie," Dad replied. "I think they might be having an affair."

The mere thought of that had me giggling. It felt good to laugh after a rough morning. "Evan is gay."

"Then what is he doing with Tillie?" Dad demanded.

"He's ... different. He was going through a rough period and bonded with Aunt Tillie while recovering." I couldn't delve into the vampire with a soul thing too deeply. My father wouldn't understand. "He's a good guy. He's also great backup for things like I did today."

"Because he's a witch?" Dad assumed.

"He's not a witch, though he does have some witch in his lineage. I really can't get into all of that. Evan's secrets are his own. He helped me get into Childs's room. It turns out that was a good decision, because the FBI will confiscate his belongings later."

I showed Dad and Warren the photos of the collage, eliciting a low whistle from Warren and an extended scowl from Dad.

"He was stalking you," Dad said. His rage was palpable.

"I already knew he was stalking me, but he couldn't get close to the inn. We handled that."

"So he came to us to get information." Dad dragged a hand through his hair. "And we didn't recognize him for what he was."

"You couldn't have," I said. "Don't blame yourselves. If I had told you what was going on, you would've known. Blame me."

"Why didn't you tell me?"

That wasn't as easy to answer as he wanted. "I ... don't know. I get wrapped up in stuff. It's not your fault. I didn't think. I'm sorry."

"Is one of the things you're wrapped up in your mother's wedding?"

There was that hint of bitterness again. "Are you angry about Mom getting married?"

"Of course not!" Dad's eyes flooded with anger. "I wish your mother the very best."

"But that's the second time you brought up the wedding."

"You're imagining things."

I risked a look at Warren and found him studiously adding vegetables to a roasting pan.

"I don't want to argue," I said. "I really did think we could handle it ourselves. I just ... well ... it got away from us."

"Like the clown dolls?" Warren asked. He seemed eager to change the subject.

"The clown dolls are an issue. No matter what, if you see one that looks like it belongs in the movie *It,* run away. His name is Burt, and he's mean."

"I don't even know what to say to that," Dad lamented.

"Mrs. Little shot him twice, and he got right back up."

Dad shook his head. "Bay, that is just...not good."

"I know. We're dealing with it. The FBI agents are the priority, though."

"And what happens if the FBI agents come across the clowns?"

I would've been lying if I said I hadn't considered it. "Then we'll have to think of a good lie."

"What does Tillie say?" Warren asked.

"Aunt Tillie is a whole other problem. Her nose is out of joint about the FBI agents. They were bugging her at breakfast this morning and she claimed she couldn't remember her daily routine, so she insisted they follow her to see the routine themselves."

"That's going to get ugly," Dad said.

"Or it's going to be hilarious. If anyone can torture the FBI into submission, Aunt Tillie can."

"Isn't that the truth?" Warren offered up a smile, but it didn't last. "Do you think you're in danger of being exposed?"

"I don't know." I held out my hands. "If we are, hopefully we'll be able to mitigate it."

"With the memory spells you can cast?"

"That wouldn't be my first choice, but I have to do what I have to do."

"You'll figure it out." Dad squeezed my shoulder and went back to his cooking prep. "We were about to have some tomato soup and grilled cheeses once we get our roast in the oven. Are you up for it?"

I had to give him something, so I nodded. "Soup and a grilled cheese sound amazing."

Dad's smile was warm. "It should only take about twenty minutes. I want to talk more about that collage you found."

LUNCH WAS GOOD. THE CONVERSATION WAS a bit heavy. I preferred keeping my father out of the witchy stuff. He had never come right out and said it, but I got the feeling the magic was one of the reasons he ultimately couldn't deal and divorced my mother. Aunt Tillie was likely another reason. Mom, Marnie, and Twila weren't about to abandon their aunt. She'd essentially become their mother—an obnoxious flaky mother they often had to treat like a child, but a mother all the same—and when my grandmother died, Aunt Tillie was all they had left. She wasn't going anywhere.

I didn't blame my father for leaving. As a child I'd been sad. As an adult, however, I understood why it went down the way it did. I loved my mother and aunts, but they were a lot. Much like me, Dad thought that maybe there was more out there for him than Walkerville had to offer at the time. He learned the hard way—also like me—that he loved this place. It was too late when he returned.

Still, I was bothered by his reaction to the wedding. When lunch was finished, I cornered Warren in the library.

"What's the deal with Dad and the wedding?"

Warren looked pained. "Bay, I'm not having this conversation with you."

That meant there was a conversation to be had. "Why not?" I used my most reasonable voice. "If there's a problem, I can't help fix it if I don't know what's going on."

"You could ask your father what the problem is."

That sounded like zero fun. "Or you could just tell me."

"No." He was firm. "I'm not going to get into this. If you want to talk to your father about what's going on, be an adult and do it. You're here because you keep things from him. Is the irony lost on you?"

I wasn't sure it was irony as much as guilt. Despite that, I wasn't about to start taking blame I didn't feel was mine. "Listen—"

"No, you listen," Warren insisted. "We don't want to insert ourselves into your interactions with your mothers. It's not fair given how things went down."

"You mean when you all ran because you were afraid of Aunt Tillie?" I regretted it almost immediately.

Warren gave me a stern look. "I'm not going to pretend we weren't wrong—or that sitting around and lamenting our bad luck together was wise—but we're trying to make amends."

"I know. I shouldn't take it out on you. But Dad was weird. I'm just trying to understand why." I had to take a breath before saying the next part. "He's not going to do something to ruin Mom's wedding, is he?"

There was no hesitation before Warren answered. "Of course not. Jack isn't like that. You should know that."

"He was acting out of sorts."

"He has feelings, Bay. Just because he and your mother are divorced doesn't mean this is easy for him. You're his daughter, too."

It was the second part that threw me. "I don't understand."

He held up his hands. "I'm not getting involved. If you have questions, you need to ask your father."

I was about to press further, maybe sniffle to make him feel bad, when the front door opened and Evan strolled in. I could see him through the glass in the library door.

"What's wrong?" I asked, stepping out to join him.

"We need to head downtown." Evan was grim. "Tillie is ... well, Tillie-ing."

I closed my eyes and sighed. "Of course she is. Are the Feds downtown?"

"Some of them."

"She's trying to kill me," I muttered.

Warren smiled. "She does have a certain flair."

"This is Evan." I gestured to the vampire. "He's Aunt Tillie's number one sidekick."

"I'm not sure that's anything to brag about," Warren said.

"He's a good guy."

"This good guy says we need to get moving." Evan was forceful. "Some-body has to get her under control."

"Fine. Although ... what were you doing out here?"

"Hunting clowns."

"Catch any?"

"Five. They're slippery little buggers."

"What did you do with them?"

"I beheaded them."

That seemed brutal but effective. "As long as they're gone. No Burt?"

"No, but he's on my list."

16

SIXTEEN

The post-Valentine's Day festival—the Ready to Fling into Spring Festival—was essentially just like the previous festival. Hemlock Cove rarely had a week without a festival because the tourists absolutely loved them. Rather than take everything down and put it back up, the decorations were merely changed. Some booths came in and out because they weren't practical for a Michigan winter. The dunk tank and flower booths were examples of this. This week's festival had green decorations instead of pink and red. That was the only difference.

"Where is she?" I asked after parking in front of Hypnotic and scanning the downtown street.

"I'm not sure."

"Who called to tell you Aunt Tillie was up to something?" I hadn't asked the obvious question when he'd showed up the way he had, and now it was hitting me.

"Your mother. Apparently, she got a call from someone in town."

"Ah." I pressed my lips together and looked around. The telltale sound of small wheels spinning over pavement drew my attention. It was a wonderfully warm day for so early in the year—what locals referred to as fool's spring—and we were supposed to have a few more days of this before we crashed back to reality. Aunt Tillie was steering her electric kick scooter along the sidewalk.

The kick scooter had been around for almost two years now. My mother had freaked out when she saw it—convinced Aunt Tillie would break a hip —but after testing the contraption, it was determined that it only went twenty miles an hour and Aunt Tillie would simply retaliate by getting a much more dangerous toy if Mom tried to confiscate this one.

Aunt Tillie had her combat helmet in place, and for the first time this season she'd dug out her cape. It fluttered behind her, making her look like an octogenarian superhero as she blasted Beyoncé's country album from a speaker on the scooter and flipped Mrs. Little's unicorn store the bird as she passed.

I recognized the instant Aunt Tillie realized we were watching, because her eyes narrowed. She increased her pace and threw a bit of magic, causing us both to start sneezing as a noxious smell washed over us.

She was a blur as she wheeled past.

"Geez." Evan pinched his nose. "Was that sulfur?"

I nodded.

"Is that a gas leak?" a female voice asked from behind us. Cam stood with Hodgins, Spencer, and Patrice in front of the diner.

"That's just Aunt Tillie making people believe she's doing magic," I replied. The lie slipped off my tongue easily, and I faked a smile that promised sunshine and rainbows even as my inner witch wanted to curse them all.

"Well, it's lovely." Cam's smile was bright. "How's the dog?"

"Winchester?" I was momentarily confused. "He's out with my mom. He's fine."

"She means my dog," Evan interjected. "Rover."

"Oh, right." I faltered slightly. "We're still looking."

"That's why I asked to meet you," Evan said. "Scout called. She found him. You can stop looking." He was brutally pleasant when addressing Cam. "Bay and I separated because there was so much ground to cover."

"Yes, and I had lunch with my father," I added, just in case they'd been monitoring my activities. "We set up the date a week ago and I couldn't miss it."

"That's right." Hodgins nodded. "Your father owns a competing inn. That must make things difficult, what with him trying to sabotage your mother that way."

"My mother and father aren't in competition." I felt rather than saw

Landon exit the police station across the road. "There's more than enough business to go around."

"I still find it odd that your father returned so recently after such a long break from the area."

"You try living with Aunt Tillie." I held out my hands. "She was too much for the marriage to survive, but if she stays away from the Dragonfly, he's content sharing a town with her."

"Does she stay away from the Dragonfly?" Cam asked.

"She visits sporadically."

"I see." Cam smiled, then turned to look at the opposite side of the street, where Aunt Tillie buzzed back on the sidewalk, heading straight for Landon and Chief Terry.

"Oh, crap," I muttered.

Under normal circumstances, Evan would've used his super speed to cross the road and thwart Aunt Tillie. Or at least move Landon and Chief Terry to safety. That wasn't an option with federal witnesses, so we were forced to watch.

Aunt Tillie threw what looked like a glitter bomb at them as she sped past. It exploded outward—it was real magic, but not the sort that would get us in big trouble.

Landon and Chief Terry froze, pink glitter settling over them, and I could read every thought and curse going through their heads just by their body language.

"That looked fun," Hodgins said with a laugh.

"It won't be fun when Landon and I are still cleaning glitter out of our bed in a month," I grumbled. A sidelong look at Evan told me he was enjoying the show. "It's not funny," I growled.

"Oh, it's funny." Evan leaned close. "You know that wasn't just glitter?"

A sick sensation settled over me. "Crap on toast."

"Yup." Evan's smile grew wider. "I wonder what they smell like."

That answer became obvious as Landon and Chief Terry crossed the road. The closer they drew, the more obvious the smell became.

"What is that?" Hodgins waved his hand in front of his face. "Is that the sewer?"

"No," Landon replied grimly. "I'm going to arrest her," he said to me.

It was an empty threat, and we both knew it. Arresting Aunt Tillie would signal her victory. Plus, well, if she didn't want to go to jail she wouldn't. She seemed to have a bigger mission than she let on.

"Better than the smell of bacon, eh?" I was going for levity. The look Landon leveled at me suggested he didn't find anything about the situation funny.

"No, Bay, it's not better than bacon," he replied in a borderline shrill voice. "At least if I smelled like bacon, I would want to lick myself all day."

My stomach constricted when I got another whiff. "Well, um, at least she's still feeling strong and powerful at her age."

"That's exactly what I was thinking," Landon deadpanned. "It's strange how well you know me."

"Wow." Spencer waved his hand in front of his face. "That is foul, my man." He didn't look as if he was commiserating as much as trying to hide a smile. "Does this happen often?"

"She's an interesting woman," Evan replied. "Of course it happens often."

"You almost sound reverent," Hodgins noted, his full attention on Evan.

"I find her amusing," Evan replied. "I'll try to stop her before she does another loop." He started in the direction Aunt Tillie had disappeared in. "Text and I'll tell you where to find me when you're done," he said to me. "As for you guys..." He tipped an invisible hat. "I hope you find what you're looking for soon."

I watched him go, lamenting the fact that I couldn't go with him. It wasn't really an option. The Feds would be suspicious if I left my husband to take off with another man.

"You smell like tomato soup," Landon said. It was only then that I realized he had moved closer. I'd grown accustomed to the smell—as much as I could—so I didn't even gag. "Did you lunch cheat on me?"

"I had that lunch scheduled with my dad," I lied. "I told you."

"Oh, right. I would've gone with you if I knew there was tomato soup."

"Live and learn."

Hodgins, losing interest in the conversation, moved past us. "We'll leave you to that ... lovely smell. We're going to look around the festival."

What interest could they have in the festival? "Have fun," I said. I forced a smile and stood between Landon and Chief Terry until they were out of earshot. "Ugh. You stink." I pushed Landon away. "I love you, and if this never goes away, I'll figure a way around it, but that is foul."

Landon looked wounded. "I'm going to kill Aunt Tillie."

"Join the club." I moved into the road to look after Aunt Tillie and Evan. "What do you think they're doing?"

"Nothing good," Chief Terry replied. He looked as if he'd never heard the word "fun" in his life and it was a foreign concept.

"Well, while I have you here, there are some things we should discuss. Fast."

I cringed when they swung their eyes to me.

"What did you do?" Chief Terry demanded.

"It hurts my feelings when you say things like that," I complained.

"You'll live." Chief Terry shook his head. "Spill."

"Evan and I were by the little creek in the woods looking for clowns when Cam just 'happened' upon us." I used the air quotes.

"That's quite a ways out." Chief Terry was thoughtful when focusing on Landon. "Why do you think she was that far out?"

Landon shook his head, sending another burst of foul stench in my direction.

"Ugh, baby, no." I had to move farther away from him.

"This is hurtful, Bay," he complained. "Just downright hurtful."

I felt bad for him. Sort of.

"She said she was walking from the inn to the Independence Motor Lodge," I said.

"Why would she be going there?" Landon looked horrified. "That's where you go when you want to die in a horror movie."

I laughed. "That's basically what I said. She let slip that Childs was staying there."

"Interesting." Chief Terry tapped his bottom lip. "If she was going to the Independence, how did she end up in the exact place you were hunting clowns?"

"Evan found a tracker on Aunt Tillie's four-wheeler."

Chief Terry was grim. "What did you do with the tracker?"

"He crushed it and threw it in the woods. He said they might believe it was lost while we were out there."

"What if they don't believe that?" Landon challenged.

I held out my hands. "They would have to acknowledge its existence, and I don't see them doing that. Evan is going to check all our vehicles."

"I guess that's the smart play. I doubt they've put anything on my vehicle. I'm guessing it's just you and Tillie they're interested in."

"And their interest in Aunt Tillie is going to cause issues." It was the next part I was most worried about. "We went to the hotel."

Landon waited.

"Evan glamoured the clerk, a lovely guy named Barry who sits around watching porn all day."

"I've met Barry," Landon said. "He's a loser."

"He won't remember our visit. We got a keycard from him and let ourselves into Childs's room."

"You did what?" Chief Terry's face was so red I worried he might have a heart attack.

"We had to get in there," I insisted. "Once the Feds empty that room, the contents are out of our reach."

"Unbelievable." Chief Terry dragged a hand through his hair and looked to Landon. "Get her," he said when Landon remained silent.

"Why am I the one who has to get her?" Landon complained.

"You're her husband. She broke the law."

"You just want me to be the bad guy so you can be her favorite." Landon folded his arms over his chest. "She got in and out. I'm fine with it."

It was not the response I expected. "Seriously? No yelling?"

"I'm angrier about missing out on the tomato soup."

"Well, that couldn't be helped. What we found in Childs's room made it necessary to go there."

"I'm afraid to know what that is," Chief Terry said.

I pulled out my phone and showed him the collage. Chief Terry and Landon both swore.

"I knew he was watching you, but I had no idea he was so invasive," Chief Terry said. "He couldn't get close enough to the inn to spy, so he was doing it downtown."

"He was doing more than that," I countered. "The map contained a couple of interesting locations, including Hollow Creek. Evan is going to stop in and ask the vampire apex if she's seen anyone hanging around. I'm not particularly worried that Childs came across her because she can make him forget anything he saw. The Dragonfly was on there too."

Understanding dawned on Landon's face. "That's why you went out there. Had they seen him?"

"He befriended them," I replied. "He acted as if he was scouting Hemlock Cove to move his family here. He tried to engage Dad about me. Dad didn't mention my magic, but he did talk about me some."

"Why would he do that?" Chief Terry frowned. "He should have told him to mind his own business."

"He didn't know," I argued. "He thought he was just a guy talking about his family and asking about Dad's family in return. We can't blame him."

"Why not?" Chief Terry jutted out his chin.

"Because none of this would've happened if we'd filled them in on Childs in the first place. This one is on me."

"It's not on anyone, Bay," Landon argued. "It was a mistake."

"But now the Feds know exactly how much Childs was stalking me," I said. "They'll dig even harder now."

"Yup." Landon rolled his neck. "Unbelievable."

"Do you know how their morning with Aunt Tillie went?" I asked.

"Hodgins just said she's a nut," Chief Terry replied. "I guess she took them to random places ... the bakery, the alley behind Hypnotic to go through the dumpster, and the livery to talk to horses."

I frowned. "She doesn't do that. Well, we all go to the bakery."

"I'm well aware. She dragged them around town to mess with them."

"And now she's zipping up and down the sidewalks throwing around magic in plain sight," I groused.

"At least she's doing it under the guise of throwing fake magic," Landon argued. "It could be worse."

"I don't think you can smell yourself."

"You're mean today, Bay."

Before I could respond, the hair on the back of my neck stood up and saluted. I took another step into the middle of the street.

Magic was building. I felt it all around me.

One of the little clowns poked its head out from behind a bush in front of the police department. Then another appeared near the festival. This one was almost two feet tall, with a porcelain face.

"Oh, no," I said as more clowns became apparent. They were everywhere.

"What do we do?" Chief Terry demanded.

I had no idea. "We could run."

"We can't let them do whatever it is they're about to do."

I was right there with him but had no remedy. "This is going to be bad."

17
SEVENTEEN

Had Aunt Tillie called them? That was the first thought that entered my mind as I watched the clowns flood the downtown area. I didn't consider it long, because while obnoxious, there was no way she would have purposely unleashed them this way.

The clowns were here of their own volition.

I left Landon and Chief Terry and headed to the festival. It wasn't packed, but there were enough people milling about to be a problem, and that didn't include the Feds.

"Help!" a toddler screamed from between two booths. She was dressed in a pink hoodie and matching shoes, her blond hair in pigtails. I scooped her up before a clown grabbed her and transferred her to Landon, who I felt behind me.

"Hey." Landon smiled at the wailing toddler. "It's okay."

I lifted my boot and stomped the clown, who had the audacity to scream as if he was being killed. Sure, he *was* being killed, but he was just a doll.

"Bad," the little girl yelled. "Bad! Scary!"

Landon nodded. "Yes, it's very scary." He stroked her hair and then smiled at me.

"This is not funny," I barked.

"Of course it's not." Landon rocked back and forth with the weeping girl. "This is how I picture our life in a few years. Bad things come and I get to protect a little angel while you kill the clowns."

"Why do I have to kill the clowns?"

"They're your mess." Landon jumped when one of the clowns dove headfirst at his shoe.

I looked around for something to use as a weapon and came back with a mallet used to pound in stakes for the tarps that covered some booths. I smacked the clown in the head, and he crumpled. Unlike Burt, he did not get back up.

"See, we have it all under control," Landon told the girl.

She wasn't falling for it. "I want my mommy," she wailed, her lower lip trembling like a dog at the vet.

"You're Shawna O'Neill, right?" I asked.

The little girl nodded.

"Her mother should be at the kissing booth," I said to Landon. "Get her over there." I was grimly prepared to handle what was about to come. "I'll handle the clowns."

Landon hesitated. "I don't think I should leave you alone."

The words were barely out of his mouth before Evan landed on the pie table with a flourish. He'd once told me that in life he wasn't all that coordinated. Apparently, as a vampire he didn't have that problem.

"She's not alone," Evan announced.

Landon looked relieved to see the vampire. "Don't let her get hurt." He started down the aisle, then hissed when a two-foot-tall clown blocked his way. "Why did it have to be clowns?"

"They're effective." Evan grabbed a spatula from the counter and whipped it at the clown. He threw it hard enough that it embedded in the doll's head and sent him flying backward.

I waited to see if it would get up. When it didn't, I allowed myself to breathe. "Is that what we have to do with the cloth ones?"

"You can rip their heads off," Evan replied. "I took down a Raggedy Ann and Andy over there. They're sewed together surprisingly well, so you might not have the upper body strength."

"You'd better be saying that to her," Landon complained. "I'm all muscle, dude."

Evan smirked. "With a crispy pig fat center," he added. "Take the girl to her mother and hole up there. We'll handle the clowns."

Something occurred to me. "Where is Aunt Tillie?"

"I found her at the little park. She claims she's making things stink because Burt doesn't like pungent odors. I'm not sure I believe her."

"You definitely shouldn't believe her," I agreed. "It's a doll. It can't smell."

"Didn't that one scream when you stomped his head?" Evan pointed to the smashed clown head I'd stepped over a few moments earlier.

"I just cannot deal with that."

"Uh-huh." Evan's grin was lightning quick. "Are you ready?"

I nodded. "Let's do it."

Landon grabbed me. "Bay, the other agents are in here somewhere," he said.

"I will stomp and smash and keep all magic under the radar," I promised.

He nodded and let me go. Still, there was something about the way he tilted his head.

"What?" I prodded.

"Don't put yourself at risk," he said. "If the only option is using magic or getting hurt, use your magic, and we'll deal with the fallout."

"It will be fine," I assured him. "They're just dolls."

"I know you've seen the *Child's Play* movies. Don't ever say 'they're just dolls' again." He gave me a hard kiss and then started down the aisle.

Shawna had calmed some. "You smell bad," she told Landon.

"I'm aware."

"Really bad." Shawna gagged as he carried her away.

I forced myself to forget about Landon. There were clowns everywhere. While there was no way we could get them all, we had to take out as many as possible. That way the others might realize they were caught up in a losing effort and flee, which would at least buy us some time.

"Are you ready?" Evan asked.

I nodded.

"Together," he instructed. "We always need to keep each other at our backs so they can't sneak up on us."

"Do you think Aunt Tillie is here?" I asked.

My question was answered almost immediately when one of the clowns showed up with a familiar whistle. He stopped when he saw us, his eyes going wide. Then he blew the whistle as hard as he could.

"Witch alert!" he screeched. "Witch alert!"

I made a grab for him—I was desperate to shut him up—but missed. Evan, much faster, snagged the back of the wriggling clown and ripped the whistle out of his mouth.

"Where did you get this?" Evan demanded.

"Wouldn't you like to know," the clown shot back.

"I believe that's why I asked."

The clown lifted one shoulder. "Got it from a witch." His eyes narrowed when they landed on me. "She was tougher than you."

Evan ripped the clown's head off, throwing the parts in two separate directions. "Little rodent," he muttered.

I could think of a few other names for him. "I'm sure Aunt Tillie is fine." Aunt Tillie was always fine. She wasn't about to get taken out by a few clowns.

"I'm sure she is too." Evan gave me a reassuring smile. "Let's continue."

I took the lead, Evan at my back. When I saw a clown that could break, I hit it with the mallet. Whenever a fabric clown appeared, Evan ripped it to shreds. We made slow, methodical progress through the festival.

Then our luck changed.

Behind the cake booth—and, man, did that smell good—I caught sight of the one clown I didn't want to see.

"Oh, geez." Evan wheezed at the sight of Burt. "He's not terrifying or anything."

Burt, clutching his knife, offered me a wide grin. Then he picked his doll teeth—for the love of all that's holy, why did he have teeth?—with the tip of the knife.

"There once was a witch from the cove," Burt sang out, causing my shoulders to jerk. "She thought she was free to rove. Turns out she was wrong, now she's listening to this song, and she won't make it out of the stove."

I planted my hands on my hips. His voice was creepy, but the limerick was terrible. "Aunt Tillie should've put a bit more effort into teaching you to rhyme because that was weak."

Burt threw his head back and laughed. "I have another one for you. There once was a man from Nantucket..." That was all he got out before Evan leaped around me, planted one foot on the pottery booth and swung around. He was airborne and heading for Burt, but the doll wasn't like the others. He was fast, and armed with a knife.

I screamed when he slammed the knife into Evan's shoulder, catching the vampire on the way down. I heard the blade rip through Evan's flesh. Blood poured from his shoulder as he rolled away from the doll.

"Evan!" I dropped down next to him to check his wound. The look he shot me stopped me.

"Behind you!" he yelled.

My goal had been to take out as many clowns as possible without using magic. Knowing Burt was barreling down on me, butcher knife in hand, was too much. I lashed out with the first magic that came to mind. Unfortunately, it was accompanied by a purple flame.

Burt, knocked back by the burst, shook it off quickly. Then he resumed singing, which only made me more furious.

"There once was a witch from a small town," he bellowed. "She liked to keep others down. She had a mouth like a trucker and an attitude like a mother—"

I cut him off before he further horrified the kids, using magic to send the mallet at his face. The mallet hit hard enough to wipe away some of the paint, but he hit the ground, took a moment to shake his head, then snarled as he perched on all fours like a dog about to strike.

"Isn't he lovely?" Evan drawled. He'd abandoned favoring his shoulder and was now focused on the clown.

"He's the sweetest of the sweet," I agreed. "What do we do with him?"

"What do we do with him?" Burt mocked in an eerie approximation of my voice.

Heavy footsteps on the ground had me looking over my shoulder. Evan extended a hand to keep Burt at bay as I checked to see who was joining us.

Chief Terry looked ragged. He had a rapidly blackening bruise on his face and his hair was askew. "Is that the evil one?" he complained when he saw it.

"Is that the evil one?" the clown mocked, still using my voice.

Chief Terry's shoulders jerked.

"Let's just say it's not going to win any personality contests," Evan said. "What are you doing here?"

"What do you think?" Chief Terry fired back.

I checked Evan's wound. It had already nearly healed. "That's amazing."

"That's why I needed to handle that little beast," Evan replied. "You won't have the same luck if you misjudge a jump and land on a butcher knife."

Chief Terry's eyebrows made a run for the border of his hairline. "What's that?"

"I'm fine," Evan assured him. He turned to Burt, who showed no signs of moving. "He's all kinds of terrible."

"I'm going to kill Aunt Tillie," I said. "I'm going to..." I mimed crushing her invisible skull.

"I'll help you," Chief Terry growled. "Do you have any idea how much trouble this is going to cause us?"

"Evil clown dolls attacking the downtown? I have a slight idea."

"The Feds are that way." Chief Terry pointed vaguely in the direction Landon had taken Shawna.

"Did Landon make it there?" I asked.

Chief Terry nodded. "He had the O'Neill girl with him. She's with her mother now. He's safe. Hodgins, Cam, and Patrice are there."

"Is Cam hitting on him?" Why that was the first question that popped into my head I couldn't say.

"Landon isn't worried about Cam," Chief Terry replied. "He's worried about you. Bay. What are we going to do?"

It was a good question. Burt wasn't going down without a fight ... or a cauldron-load of magic. There were still other clowns running around. We couldn't enact a mass spell to kill them without exposing ourselves. Even after this ended, we were going to have to come up with a story.

"Where is Aunt Tillie?" I hissed when Burt started picking his teeth with the knife again. I saw Evan's blood on the blade. I reached out to grip Evan's forearm. "Your blood isn't going to make him even stronger?"

Evan appeared to consider it for several seconds. "He doesn't have a digestive system," he said. "I'm sure it's fine."

He didn't sound all that certain. "Maybe..." Before I could finish, music started blasting from Main Street. I straightened to look through the booth we were hunkered down in front of and focused on the area in front of the Unicorn Emporium.

Aunt Tillie, cape fluttering behind her, was on her scooter. She was blasting what sounded like Nickelback from her speaker as she slowly drove out of town.

To my amazement, the clowns—all except Burt as far as I could tell—lost interest in wreaking mayhem. They fell into a trance and started following Aunt Tillie.

"She's like the Pied Piper of Hemlock Cove," Evan mused. "Why Nickelback, though?"

"Isn't that always a good question?" I challenged. Remembering Burt, I swiveled quickly and found the spot he'd been standing in empty. "Son of a witch!"

Evan followed my gaze. "I could try to go after him," he offered. "Tillie seems to have the others under control."

The strains of "Hi-Ho" could be heard as the dolls followed my great-aunt out of town.

"I don't know." I started to turn around, then did a double take when I realized there was a person huddled inside the booth we'd been using as protection. "Spencer?"

Chief Terry was on his feet in an instant despite his bad knee. He was a protective force at my left as he stared down at the smiling FBI agent. "Your friends are looking for you."

"Is it safe to come out?" Spencer looked jittery as he rose. He made a big show of brushing off his jeans. "I was just about to make my move."

I waited for Chief Terry to say something.

"I'm sure you were," Chief Terry replied. "You should check in with your people. They're worried sick."

"You haven't said if it's safe," Spencer prodded.

"It's safe," Evan assured him. "That was just Tillie playing one of her little games."

"With clowns?" Spencer didn't look convinced.

"She has a sick sense of humor." Evan smiled until Spencer was out of the booth, then directed him to the kissing booth.

The three of us stood in uncomfortable silence, watching him go.

"How much do you think he heard?" I asked.

"Enough to make life difficult for us," Evan replied.

"It's possible he was too frightened to know what he heard," Chief Terry offered.

I waved my hand in front of my face. "You stink like Landon."

"Way to kick me when I'm down, Bay," Chief Terry complained.

"I still love you."

His expression softened. "Right back at you. That doesn't change the fact that we could be in real trouble."

18
EIGHTEEN

Cleanup was surprisingly minimal. The FBI agents watched from afar. When I informed Landon that Spencer heard something—and may have seen me use magic against Burt—he tried to put on a brave face.

We went home long enough to put him in a tub filled with tomato juice and then get him in the shower. He still smelled. Try as I might, I couldn't break Aunt Tillie's spell. I experimented, mixing odors until I managed to make him smell like cologne.

"Not too bad, huh?" He lifted his arm and smelled. "It's kind of nice."

I would've laughed any other day. His smile fled in an instant.

"It's okay," he said, pulling me in for a hug. The cologne was a bit much, but it was better. At least I could be near him without gagging. His lips brushed the top of my head. "If he saw something, we'll fix it."

"How can you be sure?"

"Because I will accept nothing less than happily ever after with you."

"Today was pretty far from happily ever after."

"It wasn't the worst thing in the world, Bay. Us not being together would be way worse. We're going to be okay."

"I haven't seen Aunt Tillie since she led the clowns out of town."

"I'm sure she'll be an absolute delight at dinner." He smiled.

"What about Burt?"

"Burt is terrifying. I don't want to think about him."

"He's not done."

"He's a problem for after dinner."

"You just want to eat. That's all you care about."

"Not all, but it is a top priority right now."

"Fine." I let him hug me a moment longer and then pulled back. "Let's go. Something tells me this is going to be the worst dinner ever."

"Those are bold words for this family. I've been to hundreds of dinners, a lot of them were bad. This dinner likely won't climb to the top of the list."

"I'm not sure that's something to brag about."

"I'm just looking on the bright side."

"Well, stop it. You're freaking me out."

THE FIRST THING I DID upon reaching the inn was track down Aunt Tillie. She was sitting in the dining room sipping wine. At the opposite end of the table, the FBI agents were already in their chairs, staring at her.

"What's going on?" Landon asked, his tone easygoing as he headed for the bar cart. "Wine, Bay?"

Wine often gave me a headache. The last thing I needed this evening was a headache. "I think I'll go to the library and make myself a cocktail," I replied.

One of Landon's eyebrows winged up, but he nodded. "Okay, that sounds good."

"Why don't you come with me?" I suggested to Aunt Tillie.

For her part, Aunt Tillie didn't look worried in the least that I was about to go off on her. "I'm good," she replied, taking another exaggerated sip. "In fact, I'm great."

"I think you'll feel even better with a cocktail," I stressed.

She shook her head. "Nah."

"Aunt Tillie—"

"I think your niece wants to talk to you alone," Patrice said. "She's just too tactful to say it."

"Oh, I know what she wants," Aunt Tillie replied. "I'm just not going to play that game."

"What game are we playing tonight?" Hodgins asked as he swirled what looked like cognac in a glass and eyed my great-aunt with so much suspicion I was surprised she wasn't already in cuffs.

"One can never tell," Aunt Tillie replied softly. "Let's see where the night takes us."

A tight thread of distrust had been stretched between Hodgins and Aunt Tillie. It was invisible to the naked eye, and yet it was clearly there.

"I definitely need a cocktail," I muttered before turning on my heel and stalking out of the room. I stayed in the library an extra five minutes—I needed to collect myself—and then made my way back to the dining room. Mom and my aunts were delivering platters of food to the table, and Chief Terry was seated in his usual spot.

"There you are," Mom scolded. "I was beginning to think you'd ditched us."

"Oh, if only," I drawled.

Mom shot me a "don't you make things worse" look before sitting. "We opted to barbecue tonight. I hope that's okay with everyone. You didn't mention anything about having any vegetarians."

"Even if we did, I wouldn't have mentioned it," Hodgins said. "I don't trust vegetarians."

"Why is that?" I asked, my irritation already clamoring to make an appearance.

"Because he likes to pretend he's an alpha," Aunt Tillie said before he could reply. "He has a teeny-weenie and he makes up for it by trying to dictate who can eat what ... or who can wear what ... or who can say what."

"I'm not an alpha," Hodgins insisted.

"Of course you are," Aunt Tillie replied. "You're trying to get one over on Landon. You don't care that it makes you look like a Kardashian at a sophisticated party and everyone is in the corner whispering about the fact that you need to display your butt in public. You just want to think you're beating Landon."

"Aunt Tillie!" That's all I said. I didn't disagree with what she'd said, but this was not the time.

"You'll have to excuse Aunt Tillie," Mom said to Hodgins. "She's had a long and trying day."

"I think we all have," Cam supplied, her smile was at the ready. It didn't escape my notice that she directed it at all the men first. The women were an afterthought. "There was a clown attack. Clowns. They weren't even human sized." She seemed baffled.

Before I could decide what to say, Aunt Tillie took control of the conversation.

"What clowns?" she asked.

"All the doll clowns that were running all over downtown Hemlock Cove this afternoon," Patrice replied.

Aunt Tillie was the picture of innocence. "I think you're mistaken. I would've heard if there were clowns running all over Hemlock Cove. You're the only clowns I know of in town."

I sucked down half my cocktail. I was both riveted and horrified by the tack Aunt Tillie had decided to take.

"We saw you leading the clowns out of town," Hodgins said.

"No, you didn't."

"Yes, we did."

"No, you didn't."

"You were wearing a combat helmet and a cape!" Hodgins exploded.

"I don't even own a combat helmet," Aunt Tillie argued. "I think you have me mistaken for someone else."

"No, it was definitely you."

"It was probably Millie."

I jolted at the name I hadn't heard in a really long time. Not since Chief Terry had caught Aunt Tillie teaching us to set magical fires outside Mrs. Little's house when we were kids. She'd told him that someone named Millie was responsible. Chief Terry hadn't believed her, of course, but Aunt Tillie had committed so fully to the lie that he'd eventually given up pushing her on the topic. He said it wasn't worth the headache because she would never break.

"Who is Millie?" Hodgins asked.

"Um..." Mom shifted on her chair. It was obvious she knew what Aunt Tillie was about to do and was also at a loss. "See, um..."

"Millie is my evil twin," Aunt Tillie replied before Mom could add to the mess with a ridiculous lie. "We were joined at birth, but after the separation surgery she decided I got everything good and she got everything bad. Ever since, she's embarked on a mission to make my life hell. That's probably who you saw."

Hodgins pursed his lips. "I don't think ... I mean ... there's no record of a Millie Winchester.'

"That's because she's married," Aunt Tillie replied. "Millie Rogers."

Hodgins pulled out his phone.

I split the seam of my lips with my tongue, debated, and then started adding huge portions of food to my plate.

"Aren't you going to say something?" Landon whispered as he took the tongs from me.

"I think I'm going to watch it play out," I replied.

"But..." Landon looked bewildered.

"We'll watch it play out," Chief Terry said decisively. "What can it hurt?"

"It's Aunt Tillie," Landon muttered. "It could hurt a lot."

"Or it might be funny." I dug into my ribs as I watched Hodgins stare at his phone. He made a series of faces that were right out of the David Hasselhoff School of Acting and then lifted his chin. "Did you know about the sister?" he demanded of Landon.

I almost choked on the bite of pork in my mouth. Had he found an actual Millie Rogers?

"I knew Tillie had a couple sisters," Landon, looking uncomfortable, hedged. "She doesn't talk about them much. Except for Ginger."

"And Ginger is your mother, correct?" Hodgins directed the question at Mom, as if Twila and Marnie weren't also sitting at the table.

"Yes," Mom replied.

"Do you have an Aunt Millie?"

"Not that we've met." Mom looked as distressed as I felt. "I have heard of her, though."

That was technically true. When I was a kid, after the initial incident, Aunt Tillie used Millie as a scapegoat whenever she didn't feel like dealing with the trouble she'd caused. That went on for a year before she dropped the Millie routine and moved on to something else.

"I see." Hodgins looked baffled. "You never mentioned a conjoined twin sister," he said to Landon.

"That's because I've never met her. I've only heard stories about Tillie's sisters in conjunction with her childhood. I never thought that much about it because ... well ... she doesn't speak to her sister Willa. I was told not to ask about that. I don't question the family makeup."

"That can definitely be a problem in this family," Twila agreed. "We have a tall tree and some of the branches fall off occasionally."

That might've been the wittiest thing she'd said all week, and she likely didn't realize it.

I remained silent as Landon pulled out his phone and started typing. Eating gave me something to do with my hands, so I took full advantage. After a few seconds, Landon held up his phone so I could see his screen.

It took everything I had not to burst out laughing. There was indeed an entry for Millie Rogers. The woman in the photo looked a lot like Aunt Tillie. Instead of hair that was more white than dark, though, the photo showed a woman clearly wearing a dark black wig ... and a mustache.

"There she is," I said. Slowly, I tracked my gaze back to Aunt Tillie. "It's like looking in a mirror, isn't it?"

Aunt Tillie calmly held out her plate to Landon. "Fill 'er up, Buttercup."

Landon grabbed a slab of ribs and tossed it on her plate, added some French fries, and then some corn. "Adequate?" he asked as he held up the plate for her review.

"That will do for now," Aunt Tillie confirmed.

I had a million questions. How had Aunt Tillie managed to get an actual record through the system. I couldn't ask her in front of the Feds. Apparently, she was finally going to get to use her evil twin alibi ... and she was going all in.

"So you're saying that was Millie we saw downtown today?" Hodgins pressed.

"It had to be," Aunt Tillie replied. "Once I came home for lunch, I was here all day."

"But we saw you on your scooter," Patrice insisted. "You had on a helmet and a cape and were throwing glitter on people. You saw her!" She excitedly pointed at Landon, Chief Terry, and me. "You know it was her."

"That was Millie," Aunt Tillie insisted. "I wasn't there."

"And it was Millie who led the clowns out of town?" Hodgins prodded.

"It sounds like something she would do," Aunt Tillie replied. "Animatronic clown dolls? That's just sick. It would take a diseased mind to come up with something like that."

Spencer, who had been silent since I sat down, flicked his eyes to me and then focused on Aunt Tillie. "They didn't seem like robots," he said.

"What do you know?" Aunt Tillie challenged.

"I was there when Bay and her friend Evan fought one that looked like it came from the movie *It*."

I continued eating. As lame as her lie was—and it was lame—somehow Aunt Tillie had managed the impossible. She had the Feds second-guessing themselves. Whoever had put that record together for her had done her a favor of epic proportions. It looked legit. Well, other than the mustache.

"You contend that your formerly conjoined sister who turned evil after you were surgically separated led the clowns out of town?" Hodgins asked. "Do you really think I'm going to fall for that?"

Aunt Tillie's primary response was a shrug. "I'm not too worried about what you fall for. I have truth on my side. You were there. How could you miss Millie?"

And there it was. Aunt Tillie was going to wear them down until they had no choice but to doubt any conclusion they came to.

"I think that you're playing games with us," Hodgins replied. I had to hand it to him, he had more balls than brains. If he was smarter, he would've figured out by now that pushing Aunt Tillie wasn't going to end well for him.

"How would I be playing games?" Aunt Tillie replied in innocent fashion. "According to you, I'm senile."

Oh, so this was also payback for calling her senile. *Well played, Aunt Tillie, well played.*

"I think you convinced someone to create that entry for you," Hodgins said. "I think perhaps it was someone in this room."

I dropped the rib I'd been gnawing. "Are you accusing Landon and Chief Terry of something?" I demanded.

Landon held up his hand to quiet me. "It's okay, Bay. I understand why Zach is suspicious. If I've ever been in that record—which I have not—you'll see. Go ahead and check."

Hodgins was haughty as he started working on his phone again. "Huh," he said after several seconds. "This record has not been accessed other than to upload a current driver's license photo in forty years."

"Which means Millie has likely been off the grid," I volunteered. What was I even saying? Millie wasn't real. Here I was embracing the lie. "If the record hasn't been accessed in forty years, Landon is definitely out."

"And Terry has no access to the FBI database," Landon added. "Someone else created the record."

"And it's been there for forty years," I pointed out. "How could we be using that for cover now if it was created forty years ago?"

Hodgins looked at a loss. "I guess I need to find Millie," he said.

"Good luck with that," Aunt Tillie offered. "She's a skulking skulker. I'm not sure you're smart enough."

Hodgins scowled at her. "I think I can find one little old lady."

"I guess we'll see, won't we?"

19
NINETEEN

Landon was eager to get out of the inn. I didn't blame him. He leashed his dog, took my hand, nodded at Hodgins, and then swept us to his truck. He gave me a warning look that suggested he didn't want to talk for the walk to his Explorer. On the road, he remained silent.

At home, he made sure Winchester did his business and then headed straight for the bedroom. I'd already changed into jogging pants and an oversized T-shirt before he left the bathroom, and I waited him out on the couch. When he appeared, in boxer shorts and a T-shirt, I knew he was ready to talk.

"Tell me about Millie," he ordered as he sat on the couch.

"It was a game," I replied. "Aunt Tillie used to tell Chief Terry that he couldn't blame her for things because Millie did it."

"That sounds like something she would do. I'm not even angry about it," he said. "What I want to know is how she managed to get Millie to show up in legitimate files."

I didn't have an answer for him. "Maybe Chief Terry..." I trailed off. There's no way Chief Terry would ever do anything of the sort.

"I see you're coming up against the same wall," Landon said. "Forty years ago, Aunt Tillie managed to make her imaginary friend real. And then she sat on this alibi for four decades."

"There's no way." I vehemently shook my head. "Just no freaking way."

"That is my feeling on the subject. Yet here we are." He leaned back on the couch and rested his hands on his knees. "What are we going to do?"

"Maybe we can get away with blaming it on Millie." I was hopeful, although wary.

"How would that work?"

"I don't think she expects it to work. I think she's just trying to punish the Feds for daring to venture onto her turf."

"How does distracting them from the true killer help us?"

"You'd have to ask her."

"She's even more belligerent than normal. I'm not asking her anything." Landon's lower lip came out to play. "She's being mean."

"Aw." I shifted closer to see if he would rebuff me. His arm automatically slid around me. "I thought maybe you were angry with me," I admitted.

"I'm not angry. I am ... confused ... and frustrated ... and annoyed with Aunt Tillie. You didn't do this."

"Seeing my father today, it got me to thinking. His nose is out of joint about Mom getting married."

Landon's face registered surprise. "Why? He's the one who left."

I lifted one shoulder. "I don't know why he's acting the way he is. I tried asking Warren, but he said I had to talk it out with my father."

"Which means there's actually something to talk out."

"Yeah." I rested my head against Landon's shoulder. "It's all very weird. I don't know what to make of any of it. I don't have time to deal with it now. He was upset about the Childs situation. I should've told him."

"You can't force your relationship with him. He made the choice to leave. You're doing your best. He has to understand that."

"I need to be better. I was technically being stalked. Shouldn't I have considered that Childs would go to him?"

"In hindsight, it seems like something that we should've considered," he agreed, "but it is what it is."

"I guess." I closed my eyes. "What about Spencer?" I asked after several seconds.

"Terry told me it's likely he saw something."

"At the very least he heard us talking. He was right behind us."

"I watched him at dinner. He kept looking at you." Landon didn't sound happy. "At first, I thought it was him being suspicious. Now I'm not so certain. Maybe he was turned on by you."

"I don't think that's it."

"Why not? You're hot."

I laughed, as I was certain he intended. "You're a funny guy, Landon Michaels."

"I'm serious. Some men fear powerful women. Some are turned on."

"I guess I got lucky that you're one of the latter."

He kissed my cheek. "In fact, I'm feeling a bit turned on right now."

I rolled my eyes. "My dinner is still digesting."

"You ate more than you usually do. I also find that a turn-on."

I choked on another laugh. "You're too much. If you wait for my dinner to digest, I might be able to help you out."

"It's a good thing I also enjoy sitting with you on the couch."

"That does work out well for me."

We sat in silence, content to just be together. Our moment of connection didn't last long, because we were jolted back to reality by a sharp knock on the door.

"Who is that?" Landon sat up straight and stared at the door. Very few people bothered to visit us at the guesthouse.

I was about to go find out when Landon extended his arm.

"I'll do it." He looked through the window to the left of the door before opening it. The grim set of his shoulders told me that whoever our visitor was, it wasn't good.

My heart plummeted to my stomach when Spencer entered our sanctuary.

"Nice place," the FBI agent announced as he looked around. "I don't know what I was expecting, but this is like a little house."

"It's called a guesthouse for a reason," Landon replied. He motioned to the chairs across from the couch. "Have a seat." He didn't bother asking why Spencer had tracked us down. "Would you like something to drink?"

"I could use a beer. I think this is the sort of conversation that requires alcohol."

Crap. He was about to blow our lives out of the water.

Landon walked into the kitchen and returned with three uncapped beers. He handed one to Spencer before sitting next to me on the couch.

Even though there was more room on my right, he sat to my left, essentially setting himself up as a protective barrier between Spencer and me.

"You're a real witch," Spencer announced, his eyes on me. He took a swig of his beer before continuing. "I wasn't certain when I met you. I'd heard the stories, of course, but this is the sort of town where stories get exaggerated. After this afternoon, I know you're the real deal."

I didn't deny it. I just waited.

Landon couldn't. "What do you want, Spencer?"

"We need to come to an understanding."

"Are you about to shake us down?" I blurted. "Are you going to try and blackmail us?"

Surprise registered on Spencer's face before he shook his head. "That's not why I'm here. Do you really think that's something I would do?" He almost seemed wounded.

"I don't really know you that well," Landon replied. "We could deny what you're saying—and if you bring it up in front of anyone else, we will—but I know you at least heard some of the truth of what went down this afternoon."

"You mean during the Great Clown Assault of 2024?" Spencer looked far too amused. When we didn't smile, he sobered. "I'm a shifter," he announced.

I straightened. "What?"

"You heard me." Spencer let loose a sigh. "It's a secret for obvious reasons, but you won't loosen up if I don't tell you my secret."

"Probably not," Landon agreed. "What kind of shifter?"

"The fact that you know there are different types suggests you're familiar with the paranormal world." Spencer tried another smile. Then he sighed. "Geez. Lighten up, guys. I'm not here to shake you down for money. I just want to understand."

"You still haven't told us what type of shifter you are," I pointed out.

"Bear."

I frowned. "You're not big enough to be a bear shifter."

"I'm considered a runt. Also, I have a hell of a time growing a beard. I'm an anomaly for my people, and that's why I moved from Minnesota. I don't fit in there so I'm trying to make a go of it in the human world."

Bear shifters were territorial. He wasn't big enough to protect any land,

and if he was considered a runt, even if he hit a late-life growth spurt he would never garner the respect needed to be considered a leader.

"I'm not sure what you want us to say," Landon hedged.

"Well, for starters, I want you to know that I was aware of the whispers about the Winchester witches before I took this position." Spencer leaned back in his chair. He was a bit more relaxed now. "You guys are famous in certain circles."

"That means you knew who we were before you were tapped for this case," I said.

He bobbed his head. "I kept my distance for obvious reasons. I was curious about Landon, and it wasn't just the deal he struck to not have to be in the office. He always came across as relaxed when he was present for meetings, but I figured he had to know what you were when he married you."

"We don't keep secrets," Landon said. "I've known what Bay was since the beginning."

I cocked a challenging eyebrow. That wasn't entirely true.

"Well, within a few weeks," Landon amended. "I was undercover when we met."

"When you got shot," Spencer pressed. "I heard the story."

"Bay didn't know who I was—not really—until that night," Landon explained. "I didn't find out who she was until a few weeks later."

"Then he broke up with me," I supplied.

Landon scowled at me. "Each and every time."

I laughed at his hangdog expression. "He wasn't gone long, but he needed time to think," I explained. "I wasn't angry. I'm glad he took that time. I wasn't certain he could handle this life."

"You're not regular witches," Spencer agreed. "You're more powerful than any witches I've ever met. I saw that firsthand when you went after that clown yesterday."

"That wasn't even a fraction of what they can do," Landon said. "They're amazing. They're also to be protected." He was stern. "If you tell someone what they can do, the wrong person, things could get very bad for my family."

"Why do you think I told you the truth about me?" Spencer challenged. "I don't want to make things more difficult for you. I just need to understand what we're dealing with."

"You mean the clowns?" I asked. "That's Aunt Tillie. She hexed them to torture Mrs. Little and then the spell got away from her."

"That happens a lot," Landon said.

Spencer chuckled. "Tillie is ... all kinds of interesting. What about Millie?"

"We don't know what to tell you about Millie," Landon replied. "We're still trying to figure that out."

"So she's not real?" Spencer pressed.

Landon and I exchanged looks.

"We don't really know," Landon replied. "Tillie is very careful about what she does and doesn't share sometimes. We're going to get to the bottom of that. In fact, we were just discussing that situation when you knocked."

Spencer didn't look convinced—it wasn't a very good response—but he nodded. "Millie likely doesn't matter, right? We're looking for an outsider who killed Brad Childs."

"We don't know the answer to that either," Landon replied. "I can tell you nobody in this family killed him. How he ended up at Margaret Little's house is beyond me."

"He was stalking you because he thought you could magically get him his job back?"

"That's it in a nutshell," I confirmed.

"How did he find out about your magic?"

"We don't know if he ever had confirmation on what we can do," I replied. "I helped Landon and Chief Terry track down some of the escaped convicts. Childs found that suspicious. He started making demands. I wouldn't do what he wanted. He kept showing up. We were in a standoff right up until the moment I found him in the ditch."

"And you don't find that suspicious?" Spencer pressed. "The man was found in the ditch of the woman you torture."

"We weren't lying when we said that Margaret and Tillie have a very long history," Landon said. "They've hated each other from long before they could drive. Margaret does sneaky stuff and upsets Aunt Tillie. In return, Aunt Tillie tortures Margaret in the most imaginative ways."

"For instance?" Spender prodded.

"For instance, Margaret's unicorns have been farting glitter and dancing for months now," Landon replied. "It's never anything major. It's all little things."

"The clowns don't seem all that little."

"Yes, well, the clowns are ... not good," I agreed. "I'm not sure what we're going to do about them. Burt is particularly troublesome."

"Is Burt the big clown?" Spencer asked. "The one with the butcher knife?"

I nodded. "He is indeed. He's ... not very nice."

"I happen to find all clowns creepy."

"Sane people do," Landon agreed.

"That clown is the stuff of nightmares." Spencer looked momentarily lost in thought. Then he shook his head. "The clowns are an issue I don't know how to fix. That's going to have to work itself out. Brad Childs is another thing entirely. Hodgins won't let it go."

"I wouldn't let it go in his shoes either," Landon said. "Childs may have lost his way, but at one time, he was a solid lawman. Somebody did kill him."

"He didn't fall and accidentally break his neck. The medical examiner confirmed that."

"But a broken neck was his cause of death?" Landon pressed.

Spencer hesitated, but only for a moment. "I'm not supposed to tell you that. I don't believe you guys are murderers. You had other options to deal with Childs. So, yeah, he died of a broken neck—manually broken."

"How can you know that?" I asked. "That seems like one of those things that's a gray area."

"I'm not a medical examiner. There are certain things they look for. I only know they determined Childs's neck was manually broken."

"There's something to do with rotational shift," Landon explained to me. "If the medical examiner has made that determination, he has a reason."

"Somebody took his head, jerked it, and snapped his neck?" I asked.

"In a nutshell," Spencer replied. "It would take someone with a lot of strength. I think that's one of the things stymying Hodgins. He wants to blame it on someone in your family, but none of you are big enough."

"And yet he's still going after us," I mused.

"He is," Spencer agreed. "He wants it to be one of you because it will reflect poorly on Landon. He wants to leapfrog Landon in the bureau hierarchy."

"I don't care if he leapfrogs me," Landon argued. "I'm where I want to be."

Spencer held up his hands to placate him. "I understand why you're happy here. You guys are fighting bigger fights behind the scenes. Hodgins doesn't—or rather can't—understand that. He's not paranormal. He's a black-and-white guy. This world would shake the very foundation on which he's built his belief system."

"Then we have to find who killed Childs, and it can't be a paranormal," I surmised.

"Pretty much." Spencer was grim. "If we are dealing with a paranormal and you get rid of him or her, Hodgins will likely never let it go."

"And he'll turn into another Brad Childs," Landon said. "He'll be forever changed by a world he doesn't understand."

"I don't think you realize how hard it is for an outsider to grasp what's going on in your witch's world," Spencer said. "She was raised with this stuff. It's not too much for her to accept. You shouldn't have come around as easily as you did."

Landon took my hand and cupped it between his. "I knew she was it for me almost from the start. I needed time to think—as she never lets me forget—but even when I was 'thinking,' I knew she was still the one. Once I came back and accepted this world, I never looked back.

"The things I've seen her do, the evils I've seen her vanquish, I know this is the world for me," he continued. "We fight the good fight but can't tell anyone.

"And that puts you in a rough spot," Spencer said. "What are you going to do about it?"

Landon sipped his beer, then shook his head. "I have no idea. We have to find Childs's killer. Once we know who did it, we'll be able to figure out the rest."

"You have to be careful." Spencer's tone was grave. "If you make the wrong move in front of Hodgins, he will nail you for it."

"No pressure," I said grimly.

Spencer smirked. "No pressure."

20

TWENTY

S pencer knew we were paranormal, but we weren't about to give him the keys to the Winchester information castle. He wanted to hear stories about the things we'd done. We kept them light. I could tell he wanted more, but he seemed to realize that we would collapse into a protective ball if he pressed too hard.

After he left, we took Winchester outside for another bathroom break. Neither of us said anything when we were outside. Once back inside, protected by wards, we got into bed and had the conversation that neither of us desired but knew needed to be had.

"What does it mean if he's a shifter?" Landon asked me. He spooned behind me, Winchester curled at his back.

"Bear shifters organize into packs, but not huge packs like wolf shifters."

"Like Gunner and Graham."

I nodded. "Gunner and Graham were pack at one time but aren't any longer. Gunner told me that while they are still listed as pack members, they don't take part in pack activities."

"Can we trust Spencer?"

It was the question I'd been struggling with myself. "He came to us," I said. "We could use someone on our side, but I'm naturally suspicious."

"Something tells me he doesn't want Hodgins to know the truth. He's comfortable with Hodgins being in the dark regarding the paranormal world."

"That doesn't mean he's on our side. We'll have to watch him."

Landon's lips moved to my neck. "I think we're safe for now."

"And here I thought you were putting romance on the back burner," I teased when his hands started wandering.

"I never put romance on the back burner. If I put romance on the back burner every time a magical threat descended on this town, I would never get any relief."

"Nice," I said on a laugh as he started tickling me. "You're obviously frisky."

"Oh, baby, you haven't seen anything yet."

I WAS IN A SURPRISINGLY GOOD MOOD when I woke the next morning. I took Winchester out after I showered, which allowed Landon to take his time in the bathroom. I dried my hair so it would look nice—I wanted to appear put together for Hodgins and the rest of the team. Then I offered to walk Winchester to the inn even though I knew Landon planned to drive.

"What aren't you telling me?" he asked as I clipped Winchester's leash on him.

"I want to talk to Aunt Tillie," I replied. "I think she might be more open to the conversation if it's just us."

"Do you really think she'll tell you the truth?"

"Probably not."

"Yeah." Landon sighed. "She is way too much work sometimes."

"I can handle her." Or maybe I just hoped that was true. "We'll figure it out. Just let me try."

"Fine. I'll head straight to the dining room. It's possible Hodgins will let something slip."

"I don't think he will."

"He might if he thinks he can trip me up."

"Does he really think we killed Brad Childs and then tattled on ourselves while torturing Mrs. Little?"

"He wants it to be that easy."

I gave him a kiss and headed for the door. "See you soon."

"I'll be the handsome one at the dining room table."

"That's Chief Terry."

Landon growled. "Don't push me. I haven't had my bacon yet."

I chuckled. "I'll try to hold off until after your first hit."

"That would be wise."

I talked to Winchester for the duration of the walk to the inn. He stopped a few times to sniff the bushes. Nothing was blooming yet—it wouldn't for weeks—but he seemed to be interested all the same. I let him off his leash once we entered through the back door and he immediately tore off looking for Peg. That left me to eye Aunt Tillie, who was watching her morning shows on the couch.

"How are things?" I asked in a wary voice.

"The world is going to hell in a handbasket," she replied, never looking in my direction. "There's war in the Middle East."

"There's always war in the Middle East."

"Religious wars are the worst," she said. Slowly, she tracked her eyes to me. "Do you have something you want to say?"

It wasn't a test and yet it felt like one. "How did you manage to get a police record for a woman who doesn't exist?" I asked. I had to attack directly. It was the only tactic she recognized and didn't disparage.

"I have no idea what you're talking about." Aunt Tillie's face was a blank chalkboard. "You're going to have to be more specific."

"Millie," I gritted out.

"Millie is real."

"Aunt Tillie—"

"Just because you haven't heard of her doesn't mean she isn't real," Aunt Tillie insisted. "You don't know everything, Bay."

"I know this." I wasn't having it. "You can't gaslight me into believing Millie is real. I'm not an outsider, and I'm not a kid any longer. You might've been able to pull it off when I was ten, but I'm an adult now."

Aunt Tillie snorted. "An adult who dresses in a bacon costume to amuse her husband."

"Says the woman who wears a cape."

"That's different."

"It's really not." I folded my arms over my chest. "Talk."

"I don't know what you want me to say." Aunt Tillie had an air of indifference about her, but inside I knew she was crowing. "Millie has been a stain on my life from the minute she was born."

"Conjoined with you."

"It was a terrible existence. She talked as much as Twila ... and about the same sort of inane things. Thankfully, medical advancements allowed us to be separated."

I leaned closer to her. "What happens when Hodgins questions the people in town who grew up with you?"

"You mean Margaret?" Aunt Tillie's smile was evil. "She's busy babbling about things that nobody believes. She's not a solid source."

"Aunt Tillie—"

"I've got this, Bay." Her eyes glittered with warning when they locked with mine. "Don't get in my way."

I could've pushed her harder—part of me knew I should have—but I didn't. In truth, I was curious how it would all play out. If Hodgins was busy trying to prove Millie didn't exist, that would allow us some wiggle room—at least for today—to figure out who killed Childs.

"Be careful," I said in a low voice. "They won't believe it. No matter how far you push, they'll know you're lying."

"Good luck proving it." Aunt Tillie almost looked gleeful now. "I kind of hope he does arrest me. My day in court will be glorious."

All I could do was shake my head. "You'd better tread lightly," I said as I headed for the kitchen.

"I've got everything under control, Bay. All you need to worry about is finding a murderer. Leave the rest to me."

My mother and aunts were putting the finishing touches on breakfast. "That smells good." I smiled at them, but there was enough tension in the room that none of them smiled back. "Do I even want to know?" I complained.

"That was going to be my opening line," Mom replied. "Did you ask Aunt Tillie about Millie?"

It was only then that I realized what was really bothering her. "Is she trying to gaslight you into believing her?" I was incredulous. "That's ballsy, even for her."

"It's annoying is what it is," Mom replied.

"We tried sitting her down to tell us the plan," Marnie said. "She just kept apologizing for not having a serious talk about Millie with us when we were younger."

I was amused. "You have to hand it to her. She does commit."

"She should be committed," Mom huffed. "She's making things worse."

"I don't think so," I replied.

"What?" Mom's eyebrows seemed somehow bigger that close to her hairline. "Terry is beside himself."

"That's because Chief Terry can't see the big picture. He's worried about whoever helped her do this."

"Aren't you worried about that?" Mom challenged.

"No, because I think I know."

Mom waited.

"She spends a lot of time in Hawthorne Hollow," I explained. "Her and Whistler are doing things I don't want to think about. Scout told me Whistler used to be pretty good with a computer. He supposedly hacked into the FBI computer system when he was younger."

"And you think he somehow knew to create Millie forty years ago?" Mom was dumbfounded. "Bay, that makes no sense."

"I don't think he did it forty years ago. I think he did it yesterday ... or the day before."

"But the date said..." Mom broke off, realization dawning. "Magic. She used magic."

"She probably had some help from Mama Moon or Scout. I mean ... Scout hasn't popped up here even though she likely knows about the clowns from Evan. I'm guessing she's feeling guilty."

"Oh, I'm going to hurt Scout when I see her." Mom shook her head. "I can't believe she helped Aunt Tillie do this."

I could. Scout would get a little thrill from pulling one over on the Feds. "It's done. Now we have to see it through."

"Why aren't you more upset about it?" Marnie asked.

"Honestly? I'm curious how it's all going to play out."

"And if they prove there is no Millie?" Mom challenged.

I shrugged. "Good luck proving that Aunt Tillie got a bartender and a bike gang member to do her dirty work."

I left them to ponder it and walked into the dining room. I expected the FBI agents to be there—and they were—but there was a face at the table I didn't expect. "Dad?"

My father sat in the chair Chief Terry normally claimed, his hands resting on the table. "Hello." His smile was ... well, it was odd. I'd never seen that smile before.

"What are you doing here?" Bewildered, I looked around the room to see if Warren and Teddy were with him. It appeared he was alone.

"Can't I want to have breakfast with my daughter?"

"Sure." I glanced at Landon, who was standing at the juice bar, looking as confused as I felt. "You never come here for meals. Does Mom know you're here?"

"Your mother won't mind." Dad looked around before his eyes landed on Hodgins. "You must be the FBI agents investigating my daughter."

Hodgins took it upon himself to introduce everyone. Dad smiled at them all in turn. I was still staring at him like an idiot when Chief Terry strolled into the room. He did a double take when he saw my father.

"Jack," he said stiffly.

"Terry," Dad replied darkly.

Chief Terry shifted from one foot to the other. Dad was in his chair, so he took the chair at Dad's right. "How are you?" he asked as he sat.

Chief Terry was a good six inches taller than Dad. He also had a good forty pounds on him. Most of it was muscle, although that muscle had softened a bit. Still, my father almost looked like a little boy sitting next to my surrogate father.

"I'm great," Dad replied. "Couldn't be better."

"I didn't realize you were coming to breakfast." Chief Terry accepted the mug of coffee Landon handed him.

"I'll take one of those," Dad said to Landon, who nodded.

I felt multiple sets of eyes on me as I tried to wrap my brain around what we were dealing with. Why was my father here? Was he going to allow his jealousy to make things weird with the FBI? He'd seemed fine when I left him the previous afternoon. The man sitting next to my usual chair did not look fine in the least.

"It's a nice surprise," I said finally and forced myself to move to my chair. "I just wasn't expecting it."

"That's why it's called a surprise." Dad beamed at me, then sent a dirty look to Chief Terry. "A father can surprise his daughter whenever he wishes."

I figured I should say something, and yet there were no words to express what I was feeling.

Unfortunately, Aunt Tillie didn't feel the same way. Her reaction upon seeing Dad at the table when she emerged through the swinging doors was to make an exaggerated face. "Ah, it must be deadbeat morning."

Dad glared at her. "Tillie," he growled.

"Jack," Aunt Tillie replied. Her smile was sunny when she aimed it at the opposite end of the table. "I see 'The Man' is still here."

"Where would we go?" Hodgins asked. "We are in the middle of a murder investigation."

"Whatever sparks your wand." Aunt Tillie looked torn. It was rare she had so many people to mess with in such a small space. "What's the plan for today?" she asked me.

"Yes, what is the plan?" Dad asked. "I figured we could spend the day together."

"You want to spend the day with me?" The question came out as a squeal.

"Don't act like that's out of the ordinary," Dad said. "Fathers love spending time with their daughters."

"But..." I had no idea how to tackle this situation. All I knew with any certainty was that I couldn't question Dad about his presence in front of the agents. "You know what? If you want to come to the office with me today, that sounds great."

"Lovely." Dad's smile stretched across his face, and he directed it at Mom as she walked out of the kitchen with a huge bowl of scrambled eggs. "Hello, Winnie."

Mom almost threw the eggs into the air she was so surprised to see him. "Jack," she said once she'd recovered. She looked between him, Chief Terry, and then me. "It's nice to see you."

"Especially when he wasn't invited," Aunt Tillie added.

Mom gave her a dirty look. "It's fine. We have more than enough food."

Landon slid a mug of coffee in front of me as he sat on my left. "I looked for some bourbon to slip in it but there isn't any."

"Bummer," was all I could say.

"So, how is your investigation going?" Dad asked as he dished eggs onto his plate. He put the spoon back in the bowl rather than hand it to Chief Terry, and then grabbed the bacon platter.

"We're making progress," Hodgins replied. "We can't go into specifics, but we're hopeful that we'll be able to make some headway today."

"We're getting the final autopsy report today," Cam volunteered.

Confused, I knit my eyebrows together. "I would've thought that you already have that." I had to force myself not to look at Spencer. Didn't he say they already had the cause of death?

"We're waiting for the toxicology results," Hodgins replied. "They put a rush on them for us. We know how he died. We need to make sure there weren't contributing causes."

"Oh, sure." I nodded and filled my plate full of food. "Well, hopefully you'll come up with answers soon. Everyone in town is eager to put this behind us."

"I'm sure that everyone wants that to happen as fast as humanly possible," Hodgins agreed, "but it's better to be right than fast." His gaze was clear when it locked with mine. "What will you be doing today?"

"Oh, a little of this," I replied. "A little of that. I do have a business to run."

"Right. The newspaper. Perhaps I'll stop by later to check out the operation."

He didn't care about the newspaper. He wanted to make certain he could unnerve me. Well, better men had tried. "That's fine. I don't know if I'll be there all afternoon—there might be a story to go out on—but you're more than welcome to stop by."

"I'm looking forward to it."

That made one of us.

21
TWENTY-ONE

I managed to hold it together until breakfast was finished. The agents excused themselves shortly after. Landon made sure they left, and when he gave me the "all clear" nod I exploded.

"Can you not be you?" I demanded of Aunt Tillie.

"I have no idea what you're talking about."

"You asked Agent Hodgins if he had to join a special club for teeny weenies."

"I was curious. Since when is it a crime to be curious?"

"You then asked him if the doctors had determined he could have children with a unit that small."

"Again, I was curious."

"Then you asked Cam if she was in heat given the way she kept looking at Landon."

"That was a legitimate question," Aunt Tillie insisted. "I can feel the heat rolling off the girl whenever she looks at your husband."

I was at the end of my rope. "You were mean to Dad."

"I'm fine with it," Dad said. "It was actually nice to see her be mean to someone else for a change. It didn't feel as pointed today."

"You were low on my list of targets," Aunt Tillie confirmed. "Still, what the hell are you doing here?"

"Aunt Tillie," I growled.

She ignored me. "You keep trying to pretend that this is all normal, when it is so not normal."

"I don't think I should be mercilessly grilled simply because I want to spend time with my daughter." Dad looked to Chief Terry for support. "Am I right?"

"I'm not getting involved in this." Chief Terry leaned back in his seat. Then he readjusted. "You are in my chair."

"I didn't see your name on it." Dad was being awfully belligerent for a guy who had essentially invited himself for breakfast.

"Can I talk to you?" I used my sweetest voice when addressing my father. I didn't want to make things worse ... if that was even possible.

"I'm having a conversation with your future stepfather," Dad replied. "You can wait." His gaze was deadly when he fixed it on Chief Terry. "I didn't realize that there was assigned seating at The Overlook. I apologize."

Nobody could've mistaken his words for an actual apology.

"Yeah, let's talk." I grabbed his arm and dragged him to his feet. "We'll be in the library."

"We'll be here." Landon, his attention firmly on his phone, waved me off.

I slowed a bit before leaving the room. "What are you doing?"

"Trying to see if the autopsy report on Brad Childs is in the system."

"Will you be able to see it if it is?"

"Hopefully." He flashed me a tight smile. "It's going to take a few minutes. Talk to your father."

"Definitely talk to your father," Mom agreed. She looked confused more than anything.

"Don't you go anywhere," I warned Aunt Tillie. "I'm not done talking to you. That Teeny Weenie Society business went too far."

Aunt Tillie waved me off. "You have a terrible personality sometimes," she complained. "You're a whiner. I didn't raise you to be a whiner. I would expect something like this from Clove, but not you."

"Just stay there." I tried to maintain a calm veneer as I led Dad to the library. "I'm trying to remain calm," I said once I'd shut the door. "I just don't understand."

"What don't you understand?" Dad appeared to be having trouble deciding what to do with his arms. First, he crossed them over his chest.

Then he planted his hands on his hips. Then he crossed them again. "I'm just trying to spend time with you."

His declaration rang false. "Dad—"

"I'm your father, Bay. I have a right to have breakfast with you."

"Is that in the Constitution or something?"

"You don't want to have breakfast with me?"

The question chafed. "Of course I do, but you've never shown a burning desire to eat breakfast here before."

"I didn't really think about it until yesterday. You're here every morning for breakfast. It's out of your way to come to the Dragonfly. I thought I'd come to you."

His words were perfectly reasonable, but there was a storm brewing in his eyes. "Dad, are you jealous?" I asked finally. Warren had suggested that I take up the matter with my father. It appeared I had no choice.

"Jealous?" Dad sputtered. "Why would I be jealous?"

"Maybe you have some residual feelings for Mom."

"Ridiculous."

"Well, you didn't start acting this way until you found out she was engaged." I was at a loss. "If you're not jealous, what's going on?"

"I ... you..." Dad threw his hands in the air. "I'm not jealous because your mother is remarrying. I want her to be happy. Do I wish things could've played out differently? Yes. No matter how I look at things, though, I know that we weren't compatible. We were never going to make it."

"Then why are you acting this way?"

"How can you not know?"

"I'm not a mind reader."

"Are you certain? You can do everything else. You talk to ghosts. You wipe memories. You accrue stalkers without telling me."

I frowned. "I said I was sorry about that. I didn't mean to cut you out."

Instead of accepting my apology—which would've made us both feel better—he shook his head. "I don't want to have this conversation." He pulled open the door.

"I thought you were coming to work with me."

"I changed my mind."

"You changed your mind?"

"That's allowed."

"You're allowed to do whatever you want to do," I agreed. "I just don't understand why you're doing this."

"And that's the problem." With that, he stormed through the door.

I trailed behind him, watching as he disappeared into the lobby. I heard that door open and then slam shut. I waited for what felt like a long time. In reality, it was probably only thirty seconds. When he didn't return, I trudged back to the dining room.

"That didn't sound like it went well," Mom said. She almost looked happy.

"Don't you start," I warned her. "I can only take so much." My eyes moved to Aunt Tillie's empty chair. "I told her to stay here."

"She had to go to the bathroom," Landon said. "If you have to go, you have to go."

"You fell for that?" I was disappointed. "You're a duly sworn officer of the law."

"She's going to do what she's going to do," Landon replied. "Plus, she threatened to make the stinky smell come back if I didn't get out of her way. When your own wife won't smell you, there's a problem."

I sank back into my regular chair. It hadn't escaped my attention that Chief Terry had moved over a seat and was back in his. "Dad is acting strange."

"Your father *is* strange," Mom said. "You shouldn't be surprised."

"I don't ever remember him acting this way. I think he's jealous."

Mom smiled. "It *does* seem that way, doesn't it?"

I narrowed my eyes. "Are you happy that he's jealous?"

"Of course not." She answered a little too fast.

"Mother—"

"Why would I want something like that?" Mom demanded.

"Probably because it's good for your ego," Marnie suggested. "You were happy when you were the only one dating someone. Now I'm dating someone, and you have two guys interested in you. It's typical that you would have to get one over on us."

"You're making that up," Mom complained, her smile still in place. "If you're asking if I'm happy that your father is pining for me, I'm not. I don't want him to be unhappy."

"Are you buying this?" I asked Landon.

"Oh, I'm not answering that question." Landon shook his head. "She's my bacon supplier. There's no way I'm risking being cut off ... especially with a wife who has suggested she's traded out my bacon for the fake stuff."

It shouldn't have been possible, and yet Mom's smile grew even wider.

"Unbelievable." I pressed the heel of my hand to my forehead. I was starting to get a headache. "I don't know what to do."

"Your father will work things out," Mom said. "He'll eventually find someone to fill the obviously big hole in his heart."

I darted a look to Chief Terry to see if he was bothered by Mom's glee. He looked the same as he always did. "Let's talk about something else," I suggested. I could no longer worry about Dad. He was a problem that had to be solved, but it would have to wait. "Did you find the autopsy report?"

"I did," Landon confirmed. His mouth was a tight line. "It seems Spencer left a few things out last night."

Chief Terry's shoulders jolted. "When did you see Spencer last night?"

"He came to the guesthouse."

"You failed to mention that." Chief Terry's voice boomed. "Why wouldn't you bring that up right away?"

"Because it was nowhere near as dire as you seem to think," I replied. "He's a bear shifter. He did see what we thought he saw, but he's not spreading the news because he has his own secret to keep."

"Are you sure about that?" Chief Terry asked. "He could've been yanking your chain."

"Or testing you," Mom interjected. "He might've wanted to gauge your reaction."

"He could've been testing us," I replied. "But he came across as sincere. If he lied about the autopsy report, perhaps it was a mistake to trust him."

"I don't know if 'lie' is the right word," Landon said. "He did leave a few things out."

"Meaning?"

"Brad Childs definitely had a broken neck. He also had two strange puncture wounds on the back of his neck."

"He was stabbed?"

"They weren't knife wounds. There is no weapon on record that's a match. They're still looking for whatever made them."

"Do they have a photo of the wounds?"

"Yup." Landon angled his phone so I could see what we were dealing with. The wounds were deep, but they didn't look like knife wounds.

I angled my head. "I've never seen anything like that before either."

"It almost looks like a snake bite," Chief Terry noted. "That would have to be a pretty big snake."

"Does it say anything about fluids?" I asked.

Landon's upper lip wrinkled. "What sort of fluids? Like ... sexy fluids?"

I made a face. "Not sexy fluids. Those bite marks are deep enough that someone might've sucked something out of him."

Realization dawned on Landon's face. "Blood?"

I held out my hands. "That would be my first guess."

"It was a vampire?" Chief Terry asked.

"I've never seen vampire marks like that," I countered. "Those marks are at least five inches apart. Vampire fangs are two inches apart tops. Try to imagine getting your mouth over those marks."

"I don't see how a human mouth could manage that," Landon said.

"We're likely not dealing with a human." I was grim as I looked at Aunt Tillie's empty chair yet again. "The one time we could actually use her, and she takes off."

"Aunt Tillie didn't do that," Mom argued.

"I'm not saying she did. I'm not saying Millie did it either, for the record. And we really should talk about Millie at some point. Aunt Tillie might recognize the wound pattern."

"Did she see it when you were on the scene?" Marnie asked.

I shook my head. "He was on his back when we found him. We didn't move the body. We couldn't risk it."

"I didn't want Bay's DNA all over him," Landon volunteered.

"I'm not blaming you," I assured him. "You did what needed to be done. We probably should've known about those marks, though."

"Spencer didn't mention them for a reason," Landon said. "He was trying to feel us out to see if we'd suggest something that explained them."

"Probably," Chief Terry agreed. "It's better that we didn't know, because then we would've tried to fill in some gaps."

I thought for several seconds, then leaned back in my chair. "Whatever we're dealing with, it's not human."

"Did you think we were dealing with a human at any point since this happened?" Landon asked.

"Maybe I was hoping." I was rueful.

"I kind of knew from the start that we were dealing with something paranormal. It's the only thing that makes sense."

"What sort of creature would leave those types of marks?" Mom asked.

"It could be a giant vampire," Twila suggested. She always came up with the most off-the-wall suggestions.

"It's not a vampire." That was the only thing I knew for certain. "It's some sort of creature that sucks blood, but not like a vampire. I bet Childs's blood volume was low."

"Let me check." Landon went back to looking at his phone. "You're right," he said after a beat. "His blood volume was down almost a gallon."

"How much blood does the human body hold?" Mom asked.

"Usually between 1.2 and 1.5 gallons," Chief Terry replied. "Childs was a big man. He was probably in the 1.4-gallon realm."

"Two-thirds of his blood was gone," I said.

"Someone fed off him," Marnie realized. "Then broke his neck. Was that cover?"

"Or maybe Childs fought with his attacker," Landon suggested. "The creature—or whatever it was—could've snuck up behind him. He fought and his neck was broken during the sucking."

"It's a possibility," Chief Terry agreed. "What could suck the life out of a person?"

"There are any number of paranormals capable of that," Mom replied. "Ghouls. Vampires. Demons."

"Changelings," I added. "A succubus or incubus could do it too."

"Most of those creatures avoid this area," Mom continued. "They don't want to take us on. Ghouls sometimes show up, but you can't count them among the great thinkers of the paranormal world. They act on pure instinct."

"They also wrestle humans to the ground, suck them dry, and then eat the husk," I replied. "We're not dealing with ghouls."

"You're saying there's a paranormal creature out there that ate Brad Childs for dinner," Landon said.

"Drank him, but close enough," I confirmed.

"How do we find this creature?"

I'd already figured out our next step, and I wasn't happy about it. "We need to talk to Mrs. Little."

Chief Terry balked. "That's the worst idea you've ever had. She is not in a good headspace right now."

I couldn't argue with that. "This happened outside her house. We know she was in contact with Childs. She might've seen something."

"Wouldn't she have mentioned it?" Marnie challenged. "She's not the sharpest tack in the corkboard, but she still sticks to it."

"Maybe that's the answer to the riddle," I suggested.

Chief Terry looked baffled. "What riddle?"

"We thought she was off in the diner. Even that night, it's not normally her way to go straight to the shotgun. What if Childs wasn't the only one being fed on?"

Revulsion had Chief Terry shivering. "Are you saying something has been feeding on Margaret and that's why she's acting even worse than normal?"

"It's possible."

"How do we find out?"

I could think of only one way. "We need to talk to her. We have to get a look at the back of her neck. If there are no marks, then maybe Aunt Tillie really has pushed her too far."

"If there are marks, we have to save her," Landon said.

I nodded. "We'd have no choice."

"We wouldn't let her die no matter how annoying she is," Mom argued. "That's not our way."

I couldn't argue with the sentiment, although part of me wanted to. "We have to save her. Again. This time, she'll thank us."

"Right," Landon scoffed. "She'll never thank us."

"Oh, she's going to thank us." I was determined to get something worthwhile out of that woman. "She won't have a choice."

"We'll head to her house," Chief Terry said. "I'll take the lead. You're not to push her unless I give the okay." There was no give to his tone, so I knew he was serious.

"You're in charge," I agreed.

22
TWENTY-TWO

I didn't want to take Aunt Tillie to Mrs. Little's house, but I didn't have a choice. I needed backup in case she started throwing knives.

"Where do you think you're going?" I asked Landon when I realized he was still in the lobby.

"I can't believe you're asking that." Landon let loose a laugh.

"Well, I am." I folded my arms over my chest. "You don't think you're going with us, do you?"

"I *know* I'm going." Landon was matter of fact. "You're not giving me grief about it either."

"It's as if you don't even know me."

He smirked. "You need me with you in case the other FBI agents see you at Mrs. Little's house. You need someone to serve as an alibi."

"What if that gets you into more trouble? Landon, if you ever want to leave this place..." I trailed off, frustrated.

The look Landon shot me said he was frustrated too. "Bay, we've been over this."

I held out my hands. "I just ... well ... I don't want you to ever regret me."

"That's not possible."

"I know. I just want us to live happily ever after." I flapped my hands and shifted from one foot to the other.

Frustration lined his face. "What makes you think that we won't?"

"Look around. The men in this family don't stay. They voluntarily leave or die."

"I should've taken that worry into consideration," he acknowledged, surprising me. "I never really thought about it. Your father acting weird probably has you thinking that. I need you to consider something else.

"You left because you thought you wanted something else and came back." He held up a finger to silence me when I opened my mouth to argue. "Your father and uncles left for the same reason. Guess what?"

I already knew where he was going with this. "We all changed our minds."

"Yes." He nodded. "So, knowing that, why isn't it possible I already realize this is where I want to be?"

I hated that he had a point. "I guess it's possible," I hedged.

"Just possible?" He appeared to be fighting back a chuckle. "You're a pessimist, Bay. You always expect the worst. Knock it off."

Did he think that was the end of the conversation? Because—loath as I was to admit it—he'd won. He was right. I was being a pessimist. Fear was an unholy beast sometimes. Fear of monsters was one thing. Emotional fear was another.

"I'll stop," I said.

He pulled me in for a hug. "Good."

"That's it? You're not going to give me more grief?"

"No, because you're going to stop monitoring my bacon intake for a full week as penance."

"Funny how that works out for both of us, huh?"

He kissed the top of my head, then pulled back. "I'm going with you to Mrs. Little's."

"*We're* going with you to Margaret's," Chief Terry announced as he joined us. "Don't argue, Bay," he instructed. "If the others catch us there, we need an excuse."

"What excuse can you cover for that I can't?" I asked.

"Well, for starters, if it's just you and Tillie they'll assume you're torturing Margaret again. They'll be less likely to assume that if I'm with you."

"And second?" I prodded.

"I can say I've had conversations with concerned townspeople, and we all decided to stop in together. You and Tillie want to apologize for all the torturing."

"No, we don't."

"Yes, you do." Chief Terry was firm. "If we get questioned, that's the story. I don't want to hear another word about it."

I grumbled something contrary under my breath but nodded. "Fine. If it comes to a magic fight, though—which is entirely possible—you're going to back off and let us do what needs to be done."

Chief Terry didn't look happy with the declaration but didn't argue. "We'll take two vehicles. You and Tillie can head off together when we're done."

"That's my punishment for being a pessimist, isn't it?" I whined.

Landon grinned. "You know it."

AUNT TILLIE WASN'T ANY HAPPIER ABOUT CHECKING on Mrs. Little than I was. Still, she looked intrigued when we parked in the driveway, studying the garbage strewn across the front lawn.

"We didn't do this," I said when I joined Landon and Chief Terry at the porch.

"It's weird," a concerned Chief Terry said.

I started up the stairs, but Landon caught me at the top to allow Chief Terry to knock.

"It's just better this way," Landon argued.

I made a face but didn't complain.

Chief Terry knocked, waited, then knocked again. He checked the driveway, his gaze moving to Mrs. Little's vehicle. Then he knocked a third time. I was about to suggest he let me handle entry when he did the unthinkable and opened the door himself.

"Margaret?" he called inside, pushing the door open so we could see the mess exploding from every corner of Mrs. Little's house. Mrs. Little was a fussy individual. There was no way she'd leave a pair of underwear directly next to the front door, let alone the takeout bags and pizza boxes strewn about the room.

"We have to go in," I said to Chief Terry.

"I've got this." Aunt Tillie pushed her way to the front of the group. "You stay here. I'll smite her, and we'll be done."

Landon snagged her by the back of the shirt, shaking his head. "We're doing this by the book."

I stood rooted as I surveyed the mess. Mrs. Little wouldn't live like this. Even if she'd shaken loose of her grip on sanity, this was too much.

"She might be dead," I said. "Maybe whatever creature we're looking for killed her."

Landon shot me a dubious look. "Is this you being an optimist?"

"I'm just saying."

He shook his head. "It doesn't smell like death in here, Bay."

"What bodies have you been hanging around?" Aunt Tillie challenged. "It smells exactly like death."

Landon ignored her. "She's not dead." The words were barely out of his mouth when Mrs. Little shuffled into view, and he let out the sort of breath that told me he was relieved he'd been right.

"You didn't know," I snapped when he sent me a triumphant look.

"But I did." Landon exhaled again to regulate his breathing. "See. She's fine."

Dressed in a 1970s housecoat, Mrs. Little was not the picture of health. Her hair was wrapped in curlers, but none of them were straight, and her eyes were bloodshot to the point it hurt just to look at them.

"Yes, she's the poster child for mental stability," I agreed dryly.

"She's halfway to dead," Aunt Tillie noted. She moved closer to Mrs. Little, who didn't look as if she recognized Aunt Tillie. In fact, Mrs. Little appeared to be lost in some sort of haze.

"Hold on." I moved behind Mrs. Little. Her hair was in curlers, so it was easy to see the festering wound on the back of her neck. Up close, it did smell like death no matter what Landon said. "Look at that," I said on a breathy exhale.

Landon moved closer and jolted at the wound. "We have to call an ambulance." He moved to pull his phone out of his pocket, but I stopped him. His eyebrow raised in surprise. "I know you don't like her, Bay, but she needs medical attention."

Now it was my turn to give him a dark look. "I'm not a monster," I snapped. "A hospital can't do anything for her. Something has been feeding on her."

"And it's not a vampire," Aunt Tillie said as she studied the wound. "It's something with one of those hidden tongues that swoops out and latches on so they can drink."

Chief Terry looked dubious. "A hidden tongue?"

"A proboscis," I volunteered. "It's quite normal in some demons and succubi. That's obviously what we're dealing with here. Whatever this creature is, it's been feeding from her."

"For how long?" Landon asked.

"I don't know. She hides her neck with high collars and those weird buns. For all we know it could've been going on for weeks."

"But?" Landon prodded when I didn't continue.

"She's been going downhill fast. I guess it's possible the creature only took small nips here and there and has been ramping it up, but to what end?"

"So it's only in the last few days," Landon surmised.

"Obviously, I don't know for certain, but that seems likely." I pulled my phone out of my pocket.

"What are you doing?" Landon asked.

"We can help her." I gestured to Mrs. Little. "We can help heal the wound and get some magic into her to help her rebound. We need some stuff from the medicinal stash at the inn. I'm going to have Mom bring it."

"Okay."

"Then, while we're fixing her, we're going to question her. We need to know who we're dealing with."

Landon nodded. "I'll start cleaning up while we're waiting for your mom to get here. We don't want her having a heart attack when she wakes up and sees the mess."

"That would not be good," I agreed, darting a look to Aunt Tillie, who was oddly quiet. "Do you agree this is the best plan?" I asked.

She nodded after a few seconds of silent contemplation. "Yeah. We need to fix her."

"I'm surprised you care so much," I teased.

"It's no fun to torture her if she can't fight back."

"Yes, well, there is that." I turned back to Landon. "We'll get some potions here and go from there."

He bobbed his head. "Sounds like a plan."

. . .

MOM WAS CURIOUS WHEN SHE showed up with the items I'd requested. She looked around in disbelief as Chief Terry and Landon cleaned Mrs. Little's house. They'd already filled two garbage bags and were working on two more.

"This is gross," she announced.

I nodded. "I guarantee she didn't do this herself. At least not willingly."

Mom made a face. "Who did it?"

I took the bag from her and motioned to the living room. We'd gotten Mrs. Little settled on the couch, where she sat staring blankly at the ceiling.

"What's that smell?" Mom asked as she grew closer.

"That would be Mrs. Little." I sat on the floor and started rooting through the bag as Mom stared at Mrs. Little.

"What did this?" she asked.

"Some sort of monster. There's a weird mark on the back of her neck." I paused with a potion bottle clutched in my hand. "I think whatever has been feeding on her has done so for at least a few days. She's been getting takeout in an effort to recoup her strength."

"My goddess!" Mom shook her head. "This is not good."

"Definitely not," Chief Terry agreed. "Bay says not to call an ambulance." The way he said it suggested he thought Mom might have a different response.

"Bay is right," Mom said without hesitation. "They can't help her. We have to fix this."

I started with the mark on the back of Mrs. Little's neck, dabbing a healing salve on it. Mom studied the mark for a long time, shaking her head.

"That's more than one feeding," Mom said. "I'm guessing Margaret wouldn't have survived more than one or two more feedings." Her eyes moved to me. "Is this what we think happened to Brad Childs?"

I shrugged at the question. "I think it's more likely he was out here doing something and whatever it is decided that small doses of Mrs. Little weren't as good as a big dose of him."

"What was he doing here?"

"He wanted me to help him," Mrs. Little said, her voice thin and reedy. "He came to me, said he needed help getting you to do something for him. I told him to let it go. He wouldn't listen.

"He's like me," she continued. Her eyes were closed, and her skin so pale I saw the veins underneath. She looked half dead already. "He just can't let it go."

"Why didn't you mention him coming here?" Chief Terry asked. "When I asked if you'd seen him, you said you didn't know why he was here."

"He approached me days before he died," Mrs. Little replied. "I didn't know he was here that night."

"You still could've mentioned his visit," Chief Terry growled.

"I didn't want him to get in trouble."

"You didn't want us to think you were conspiring with him," I countered. "You were afraid we would come after you."

"You come after me regardless."

"Yes, well, perhaps you should stop trying to buy up the town so you can pretend to be queen," I suggested. "That might stop us from coming after you." It was only then that I realized Aunt Tillie was missing. She'd disappeared right after I'd called my mother, and I hadn't seen her since. I raised my chin and scanned the space. She was nowhere to be found.

"I'm on it," Landon said, correctly reading my expression. "She's probably going through Mrs. Little's things because she's a busybody." He started down the hallway.

I took the purple potion from the bag and uncorked it. "You need to take this," I said to Mrs. Little. "You can take it voluntarily, or I can force it down your throat. You decide."

There was no wariness in Mrs. Little's eyes. With a shaking hand, she accepted the potion and downed it in one gulp.

"You must be feeling pretty rotten," I noted as I took the empty bottle and tossed it into the bag. "You didn't even ask if we were going to turn you into a frog."

"If you were going to turn me into a frog you would've done it a long time ago," Mrs. Little replied dully. "Anything is better than her."

"Aunt Tillie? I'm definitely the better option," I agreed.

"Not Tillie." Mrs. Little's eyes were closed again.

"If not Aunt Tillie..." I trailed off, realization dawning. "It's a woman. Whoever has been doing this to you is a woman."

"A bad woman," Mrs. Little added.

"Who is she?"

"I don't know."

"What does she look like?"

"It's never the same, but I know it's her whenever she shows up. I can't … be me. She won't allow it. She's going to kill me."

"No." Mom made a clucking sound with her tongue. "We won't let that happen. I promise you that."

"I'm tired." Mrs. Little closed her eyes. "If she comes again, that's it. I'll be gone. Then Tillie will get what she's always wanted."

I had bad news for Mrs. Little. "Aunt Tillie doesn't want you dead. She'll be bored without you to torture. She wants you alive." I looked up when Landon returned from checking the bedrooms. He was alone. "What is she doing?"

Landon's expression was stark. "She's not back there, Bay."

"What do you mean? She was here."

"She's not here now."

Reality was a mean bitch that smacked me across the face. "She's going out hunting," I realized.

"Do you think she knows what it is?" Mom asked.

"I don't know. It's possible she doesn't care. We need to figure it out."

"We can't keep Margaret here," Chief Terry said. "We need to move her to the inn so we can keep an eye on her."

Mom nodded. "We'll take her to the inn, get her settled, and find Aunt Tillie. She's probably there loading for bear hunting even as we speak."

That was a frightening, although likely accurate, assumption. "We'll pack up some stuff for Mrs. Little and you guys will take her."

"Just what do you plan on doing?" Landon demanded.

"I'm going to set a trap. If this thing comes back to Mrs. Little's house, it won't like what it finds."

Landon opened his mouth, then shut it. "I'm with you."

"You can't do anything to help," I argued.

"I can watch your back so it doesn't get sucked on, and that's exactly what I plan to do."

There was no give to his tone, so I nodded. I needed to work fast. If Aunt Tillie went hunting on her own, we were all going to regret it.

23
TWENTY-THREE

I was careful when laying the trap. It was deadly, but not foolproof. Still, I was diligent in laying down ward lines. If this creature returned, it was going to get quite the jolt.

"What happens if a human crosses the ward lines?" Landon asked as he watched me work.

"There are allowances for humans," I replied. "Don't worry, I was careful."

"I know you were. I'm just trying to understand."

I continued working "Allowances are made for humans," I assured him. "But that means if any hybrid or half-demon comes through, they'll be spared. A full-on succubus or incubus is a goner."

"How can you be certain that's what we're dealing with?"

"I can't. In fact, it's likely we're not dealing with either, because there's almost always a sexual component to their killings."

"How does that work?"

"There's a lot of sucking while they ... you know."

Landon made a face. "I could've gone my whole life without knowing that."

He wasn't the only one.

"If Hodgins brings his team here to check on Mrs. Little..." Landon prodded.

"They'll be fine," I assured him as I dropped my hands. The wards were handled.

"That's something at least." Landon forced a smile for my benefit, but he didn't look happy. I didn't blame him. "What about the clowns? Will it kill them if they come back?"

I hadn't been thinking about the clowns when I'd erected the wards, but I nodded. "Yup. They'll be toast too."

"Can't we set the wards everywhere in town so we can end it all right now?"

"Sure." I bobbed my head amiably. "If you want to kill me."

Horror washed over Landon's face. "What?"

"If I were to try to expend that much energy, I would die," I explained. "You might think I'm unstoppable, but I have limitations."

Landon moved his hand to my cheek. "I can't live without you, so I guess that's out of the question."

I nodded in agreement. "Definitely."

"Are we done here?"

"We are."

"Then come here." He pulled me in for a hug and kiss, holding me tight for a few seconds before releasing me. It was a moment we both needed to center ourselves. Something told me we wouldn't get another like it for a long time. "Let's go," he said. "We have a monster to hunt."

"And a great-aunt to find."

MOM, MARNIE, AND TWILA WERE BUZZING WHEN we got back to the inn. They'd gotten Mrs. Little settled in one of the guest rooms and were happy as they put together a tray to feed Mrs. Little in bed.

"I've never seen her this nice," Twila enthused when she saw me. "I think we're going to become friends."

"You don't think that," I argued.

"I do. It will irritate everybody here, and that's worth it alone."

"Lovely." I shook my head and focused on Mom. "Have you seen her?"

Mom's smile wavered. "She was in her greenhouse when we got back."

I headed in that direction, but Mom stopped me. "What?" I demanded.

"She was packing a bag," Marnie volunteered when Mom didn't immediately answer. "She was throwing weapons and potions in it. Then she took off on her four-wheeler before we could stop her."

"She didn't say anything?"

Mom shook her head. "She was dressed for battle."

"Let's not panic," Landon chided when everybody looked at one another. "She knows what she's doing."

"Or she purposely went out alone because she didn't want to put the rest of us at risk," I countered.

Landon huffed, then looked around. "Can you cast a locator spell?" His knowledge of magic was limited, but he'd picked up a few things over the years.

"No," I replied. "She's made herself untraceable."

"I was about to call Evan," Mom said. "He has a better chance of tracking her."

I nodded. "Definitely do that." I tapped my fingers on the countertop. "I'll be back."

"Where are you going?" Landon called out. He looked as if he wanted to follow but was perhaps worried that would overstep his boundaries.

"The Dragonfly. They have wards, but they aren't strong enough. While Evan is looking for Aunt Tillie, I'll take care of that."

"And perhaps talk to your father about his jealousy?" Mom asked, her eyes sparkling.

"How can you think him being jealous is a good thing?" I demanded.

"I didn't say it was a good thing." Mom was suddenly cagey. "It's just ... it hurts my heart that he's never gotten over me. You need to talk him down. My heart belongs to Terry."

"Oh, look at you." I rolled my eyes. "You're eating this up. You want him to pine for you."

"A little jealousy is good for the ego," Mom replied. "I don't want him to pine for me, but if he's a little jealous ... there are worse things. I guess I was too much woman for him."

She looked far too impressed with herself. "You are unbelievable." I shook my head. "As for you ..." I focused on Landon. "I can handle the wards myself. You need to keep in contact with Evan. If he finds Aunt Tillie, call me. We'll converge on her together."

"If you're worried that thing is going to be out there, I don't want you going alone," Landon said. "It could sneak up on you."

"It won't," I assured him. "I'll handle it. I can't cut Dad out of this one. Not again. I have to talk to him, and something tells me the conversation won't go over well if you're there. I have to make sure they're protected and not melting down."

Landon sighed. "Fine. But I don't like it."

I didn't blame him. "I don't like it either, but it's where we're at."

"Just take care of my witch."

I smiled. "Always." I started for the door. "No more than three cookies for a snack," I called over my shoulder.

Landon groaned. "What happened to you paying penance for being a pessimist?"

"My penance is bacon, not cookies."

WARREN WAS GOING OVER THE LOBBY WITH A feather-duster when I walked through the front door. He didn't look surprised to see me.

"I wondered how long it would take," he said.

"Did you miss me that much?" I teased.

"I figured you would eventually come to talk to your dad about what happened this morning."

Guilt wormed through my stomach. If I hadn't been worried about a strange monster coming after him, I wouldn't have bothered with his feelings for at least a day. "Where is he?"

"Out back working in the garden."

"It's not warm enough for gardening yet."

"He's just looking for something to do, so he's messing with mulch and weeds."

"You haven't seen Aunt Tillie, have you?" I asked, internally cringing when Warren's gaze sharpened. "What? It was just a question."

"Is that why you're really here?" Warren's disappointment was palpable. "Your father made an ass out of himself this morning, stormed away, and you're worried about Tillie. Why am I not surprised?"

I was caught between annoyance at myself and him. "My father wasn't an ass this morning. He did make a weird spectacle of himself. He's not my only problem, though. We just came from Margaret Little's house and some magical creature has been feeding on her. We also have an army of clowns on the loose and the Feds are looking at me as a murderer.

"So, yeah, I'm kind of a jerk, Warren," I said. "I also have a lot going on."

Warren looked taken aback by my vehemence. "Okay, well, just so you know."

I adjusted my tone. "I'm going to talk to him right now. I'm also going to strengthen the wards around this place because I don't want whatever monster is out there sucking on you guys. I did come here for him, but I need to find Aunt Tillie, too."

"What is she doing?"

"Nothing good, but don't worry about her." I waved my hand. "Evan is on the hunt for her. I need to talk to Dad."

Warren grabbed my wrist before I could move too far away. "Really talk to him, Bay. He needs it."

"I will. I promise."

The sun was bright as I left the inn. My father was on his knees, vigorously using a rake to turn the mulch.

"Hey, Dad," I called out.

His body went rigid at the sound of my voice.

"We need to talk," I said.

When he looked up at me, I saw shame. I didn't like it.

"Don't," I chided, shaking my head. "You didn't do anything more embarrassing this morning than we do every single morning. Nobody is holding what happened against you."

"I shouldn't have done it." Dad sat back on his haunches and stared at the tree line. "I don't know what I was thinking. I lost my head."

I lowered myself to the ground next to him. It was still cold. "You can't hold onto the past," I started. "We can't go back. We can only move forward. If you still have feelings for Mom..."

The odd look on his face stilled me.

"Is that what you think this is about?" Dad asked.

"It's natural to be jealous. Mom is actually excited that you're jealous, if you want to know the truth." I realized how that sounded too late. "Not that she wants you to act on it," I added quickly.

He sighed. "Bay, there is a part of me that still loves your mother. I'll always love her. She's the mother of my child, and that makes her one of the most important people in my life."

There was a but coming. I knew it.

"But I'm not jealous because your mother is getting married," he continued. "I'm jealous because you're finally getting the father you always wanted."

"Oh."

"Oh," he agreed. "I'm being a big, fat baby because Terry is going to have more meals with you. He'll be there if you need something fixed. He's always there."

I had no idea what I was supposed to say to that. "I don't ... you..."

"I understand that I'm being unreasonable," he said. "You don't have to trip over yourself not to hurt my feelings. Terry has always been there for you. *Always.* He is your father. I'm the spare. I just wish it were different."

There was only so much I could do to make him feel better. Chief Terry was my father. "I can have two fathers," I said. "There was a whole show about a girl having two dads back in the 1980s. I saw it on Tubi over the winter. It was pretty cute."

Dad chuckled. "I appreciate you trying to make me feel better. I know this is my problem. Of course you love Terry. He fixed your bike chain when you were a kid."

"That was Aunt Tillie. She also souped up our bikes with magic so they went really fast. We had e-bikes before they were a thing."

"You know what I mean. It was one thing when he was dating your mother. Now he's actually going to be your father. Legally."

"You do realize he's not adopting me?"

"Close enough."

I sighed. "Dad, you can't hold a grudge against Chief Terry." As much as I wanted to make my father feel better, I wasn't about to give Chief Terry short shrift in the process. "He was there when I was a kid. He was always there. I don't hold what happened against you."

"How can you not?" Dad's eyes flashed with annoyance. "I wasn't there for you, Bay. Now, as an adult, you don't need me. I feel like a burden."

"You're not a burden. You're a good man, but I can't have the same relationship with you that I have with Chief Terry."

"Why not?" Dad looked so forlorn.

"Because he was there when we got our Christmas puppy. When Lila Stevens was mean to me in elementary school ... and middle school ... and high school, he took me out for hot chocolate and doughnuts. He never tried to fix the problem. He just listened.

"When we were kids and Mrs. Little called the cops on us for helping

Aunt Tillie terrorize her, he sat us down and explained why it was a bad idea to vandalize Mrs. Little's house. Then, in the same breath, he explained the importance of standing up for ourselves.

"Hell, he was there the day I got my first period." I smiled at the memory. "He was horrified, of course. Thistle spent the entire morning throwing sanitary napkins at me. He took me out for hot chocolate that day, and he explained that no matter how embarrassed I was—I was wearing light pants that day—that one day I would get over it and laugh at the memory. I didn't believe him, but he was there."

"He was there for all the things I should've been there for," Dad lamented.

"You're here for new things. I won't trade the relationship I have with Chief Terry for anything. That doesn't mean we can't have a relationship."

Out of the corner of my eye, I saw the bushes move. The clown-red shoes poking from beneath the bush were all the hint I needed. I kept my eyes on Dad so the clown wouldn't run away.

"I just ... want to go back in time." Dad's eyes were sad. "I don't want to share you."

"You have to get over that. I'm not letting Chief Terry go. I'm not letting you go either."

"I know. I'll be better about it."

"Good." I exhaled heavily. The clown was still in the bush, trying to edge closer. "I am here for another reason. I planned to come here to talk to you regardless, but we have a few things going on."

Dad's eyes narrowed. "Why do I think this is going to be bad news?"

"Because it is. In a nutshell, there's a monster in town feeding on people. We found Mrs. Little near death. The FBI thinks I killed Brad Childs. Aunt Tillie has another spell running amok. She's gone AWOL, so if you see her, call me. I'm here to ward your property so you don't die."

Dad's eyes were the size of saucers.

"Why can't you guys ever have a normal week?"

I held out my hands. "That's not how we roll. In fact..." I jerked out my hand and caught the encroaching clown doll around the neck and yanked it out of the bush.

"Get off me!" it screeched, hitting at my wrist with its inefficient doll hands. "I'll sue," it yelled. "I'll take you for everything you're worth."

"What is that?" Dad's revulsion needed its own ZIP code.

"This is one of our problems." I glared at the doll. "Where are your friends?"

"I'm not telling you," the clown hissed defiantly.

"You will tell me."

The clown sneered. "Let. Me. Go."

I stared hard.

He stared back.

I shook my head. "Fine. We'll do it the hard way." I turned to Dad. "I need something to lock this little terror in. A wooden box or something."

"You monster," the clown yelled. "You are a freaking monster."

I ignored him. "Then I need to up your wards. I'm not sure what we're dealing with, but I want to make certain you guys are protected."

"Sure." Dad looked unsteady. "Are we in danger?"

"I hope not. I'm going to fix whatever this is today. You have my word."

Dad grinned. "Okay, I can find a box. What are you going to do with that thing?"

"We're going to have a little chat. Then he's going to help me, whether he wants to or not."

"I'll die first," the clown declared. "I will fight for my right to clown around and you can't stop me!"

"We'll just see about that."

24
TWENTY-FOUR

Dad insisted on returning to The Overlook with me. He said he wanted to apologize to Mom. I wasn't certain that was a good idea because she was having such a good time believing he was jealous of her relationship with Chief Terry. Dad also wanted to make sure the clown didn't claw his way out and attack while I was driving.

"Where are we going?" Dad asked as we carried the locked chest from the parking lot past the inn. "I thought we were going inside."

"I thought about it," I replied grimly. "With the FBI agents staying here, we don't really have that option."

"Ah." Realization dawned on Dad's face. "Are we taking it to the guest-house? We could've just driven there."

"We can't take it to the guesthouse." I tried to picture Landon's face if he came home and found a possessed clown doll strapped to a chair in our living room.

"Then where are we taking it?" Dad asked.

"To a magical world," I replied.

He was dubious but game. He wanted to be part of this world. I'd made a mistake trying to keep him at arm's length. Part of it had been because I wanted to protect him. Part of it was because I feared if he saw the wrong thing he would take off running again.

I had to stop living in fear. If he wanted to leave again, he would do so. I couldn't modify my behavior to make sure it didn't happen. I had to be myself and trust that I was enough.

The same was true for Landon, although I already knew I was enough for him. He showed me every single day. I had to let it go.

Feeling lighter, I let myself breathe and directed the walk away from the sidewalk. Dad seemed confused when I led him to Aunt Tillie's pot field. The field was glamoured beneath a dome, so he had no idea what he was seeing.

"I don't understand what we're doing," he said.

"It's okay," I assured him. "Just take a breath."

Dad went stiff and sucked in a breath. The world around us shimmered, causing his eyes to widen. Then we emerged in Aunt Tillie's glorious utopia.

Dad's mouth fell open. "Is that a big field of pot?" he asked.

"It is indeed."

"But it's not warm enough yet to grow anything."

"There's a spell on the dome," I explained. "It stays this warm year-round."

Dad looked flabbergasted. "Why have you been keeping this place secret?" His tone was accusatory.

"Because it's not her dome, sparky," Aunt Tillie replied as she appeared along the end of the nearest row of plants. "What are you doing here, Jack?"

To his credit, Dad managed not to jolt out of his skin. He paled two shades at the sight of my great-aunt, though. She was terrifying when she wanted to be, and Dad had been at the wrong end of her wrath more than once.

"He's with me," I replied when Dad couldn't seem to find words. "I was at the Dragonfly when one of your pet clowns decided to attack."

Interest piqued in Aunt Tillie's eyes as she regarded the chest. "Huh."

"Is that all you have to say?" Irritation spiked through me. "You have to say more than that," I insisted. "You created them."

"I might have created them," Aunt Tillie replied grimly, "but that doesn't mean I have control over them any longer."

That was exactly what I was afraid of. "Does anyone have control over them?"

Aunt Tillie gave me a dubious look. "Is there something you want to say, Bay? Are you getting at something specific?"

Was she kidding? "I want to know if it's possible that whatever tried to kill Mrs. Little is controlling your clowns."

"Why would you just jump to that conclusion?" Aunt Tillie demanded.

"That wasn't a denial," I noted.

"I don't have a denial to give you, Bay." Aunt Tillie's tone was brittle. "I don't exactly know what's going on."

"But you suspect something," I insisted.

"I..." Aunt Tillie held my gaze for an extended beat, then shook her head. "I don't know." When she turned her back to me, I saw what I'd initially missed. Her shoulders were slumped. Her gait was slow.

I decided to take a different tack. "Why did you leave Mrs. Little's house the way you did? We went looking for you. We thought maybe you'd gone on a monster hunt."

"I did." Aunt Tillie's hands were on her hips when she turned back. "I couldn't find anything."

"Did you see anything?"

"Like the vampire you sent to spy on me?" Aunt Tillie's eyes narrowed in fury. It wasn't because we'd called Evan. It wasn't even because she couldn't find the monster. She was angry because of something else.

"Why did you leave Mrs. Little's house without telling us?" I demanded.

Next to me, Dad shifted from one foot to the other. He was going to have to suck it up. Being involved in my life meant dealing with Aunt Tillie. I didn't always like it either.

"I had things to do," Aunt Tillie replied, avoiding eye contact. "You had Margaret under control. I'm sure she's still alive."

"She's at the inn."

Aunt Tillie's eyes widened, and her mouth dropped open.

"What did you expect us to do?" I asked. "We couldn't leave her. If you don't want her here—"

"I didn't say I didn't want her here," Aunt Tillie snapped. "Of course she should be here. She's a sitting duck until we figure this out."

"Then what's the problem?" I pressed.

Aunt Tillie's eyes fired. "You're the one with the problem."

"I *do* have a problem," I agreed. "You're being a real pain in the ass. That's my problem."

Dad's sharp intake of breath betrayed his shock at my back talk to Aunt Tillie.

"Well, welcome to my world, Bay," Aunt Tillie shot back. "You're always a pain in my ass."

"Stop whining."

Aunt Tillie gripped her hands into fists at her sides. "You're on my list."

"Yeah, yeah, yeah." I wasn't in the mood. "You've been nothing but a complete and total monster the past few days. I get that the FBI agents being here cramps your style—"

"FBI agents that are here because of you!"

Now it was my turn to be furious. "I didn't ask Brad Childs to stalk me," I said. "We were at Mrs. Little's house because of you."

"Don't pretend you weren't having a good time. You wanted to do it as much as me. She's your enemy as much as she's mine now."

My dislike for Mrs. Little had grown into a beast. "I don't like that she seems to be trying to take over my town." I chose my words carefully. "I don't like her as a person. That doesn't mean I wanted anything like this to happen to her."

Frustration exploded across Aunt Tillie's face. "Of course not, Bay. I didn't want this to happen to her either. It's only fun when I torture her."

And that's when the truth behind Aunt Tillie's actions became apparent. Realization was a hard ball of sadness in the pit of my stomach. "You actually feel bad for her."

Aunt Tillie's sparse eyebrows flew toward her hairline. "I didn't say that."

"You didn't have to. I see it. I feel it too."

Aunt Tillie worked her jaw but remained silent.

"It's one thing for us to mess with Mrs. Little—make her unicorns fart glitter and send the Christmas decorations to her house to sing until she wants to scream—but it's another for some sort of monster to suck her dry," I continued.

Aunt Tillie nodded. "She's my nemesis. I'm the one who gets to mess with her."

"There's something out there that thought otherwise and now we have to deal with it. You can't take off on your own, even if you do fancy yourself a one-woman killing squad."

Aunt Tillie sighed. "I went all around the town. I can't sense anything out of whack. I don't know what we're dealing with."

I considered it for several seconds. "Then maybe we're not dealing with something magical."

"Oh, right," Aunt Tillie said dryly, her eyes rolling. "A human sucked Margaret dry."

"I didn't say a human. I said something not magical. We could still be dealing with something paranormal."

Confusion knit Aunt Tillie's eyebrows, then she straightened. "We're talking about a monster, but not something that has the sort of powers that can be detected."

"Exactly."

"I need to come up with a different locator spell." She wriggled her fingers. "That's good. I can work with that." She turned to walk away but I stopped her with a growl.

"Before you run off to fight the ultimate evil alone, I was thinking we could do something together."

When Aunt Tillie turned, she looked confused.

I shook the handle of the chest for emphasis. "The clowns have been out in the wild. We know they haven't been doing what you want them to."

"Don't rub it in," Aunt Tillie warned.

"I'm just saying, maybe they're following orders from somebody else."

Dad cleared his throat. "Didn't you just say this thing isn't magical?" he asked. "If it isn't magical, how is it controlling them?"

"Well, in her infinite wisdom, Aunt Tillie made the clowns sentient," I started.

"I didn't know I was going to do that," Aunt Tillie fired back.

"They're not listening to you. That means someone else has managed to get them working under a different banner."

"To what end?" Dad asked.

That was a very good question. "I'm guessing they're being offered some sort of freedom. The clowns know it's only a matter of time before we end them or Aunt Tillie regains control. If this creature—whatever it may be—takes us out of the equation, they'll be free to keep on clowning."

"What does that look like?" Dad seemed as horrified as I imagined Landon would be upon hearing the news.

"It probably looks like a reality star who gets told he has to get a real job," I replied. "It will be an ugly situation." I ran my tongue over my teeth and pinned Aunt Tillie with a serious look. "You can't do this alone. We need to work together."

"I thought that if I could find it and end it..."

"You thought you could avenge Mrs. Little," I filled in. "I get it."

"I don't want to avenge her." Aunt Tillie made a face. "I don't want anyone else having the power to mess with her."

I didn't believe her. Deep down—somewhere very deep down—Aunt Tillie had marked Mrs. Little as belonging to her. Sure, it was in a negative way, but she was feeling protective regardless.

"We'll figure it out. Starting with this clown." Dad and I lowered the chest to the ground and flicked the locks on either side. "Ready?" I asked Aunt Tillie.

She nodded.

The clown slowly peeked its head over the edge of the chest and looked between us. "I don't suppose you would take a song in exchange for my freedom?" he asked. "I have an excellent singing voice."

"Nobody wants to hear you sing," Aunt Tillie growled. "Get out of there, Crusty."

My upper lip wrinkled. "Crusty?"

"He looks like a Crusty," Aunt Tillie insisted.

"Did you name all of them?"

"Yes, and if I was tired at the time, some of the names are ... not good."

"That must have been hard for you to admit. You named the pig Peg. If it's worse than that, I'm almost afraid to hear them."

"You shouldn't have to hear them," Aunt Tillie replied. "We're going to get that situation under control today too." She sounded sure of herself. I wasn't certain I believed her.

"We don't want songs," I said to Crusty. "And if you run, you should know there's nowhere to go. You're trapped in here. You can only leave if we say you can leave."

"You're no fun at a party, are you?" Crusty complained. "Zero freaking fun."

"I happen to think I'm tons of fun," I shot back. I looked to Aunt Tillie for confirmation. "Tell him."

"She's okay," Aunt Tillie said to Crusty. "She's better than Thistle, but that's not saying much."

The clown nodded sagely. "She looks like a whiner."

"Oh, totally," Aunt Tillie agreed.

"I can't believe you're ganging up on me with an evil clown doll," I complained. "This is completely unacceptable."

"Blah, blah, blah." Aunt Tillie shook her head. "Tell me about your new master," she instructed Crusty.

The clown—all seventeen inches of him—feigned innocence. "I have no idea what you're talking about."

Aunt Tillie extended a warning finger. "We don't have time for games. Tell me or we'll kill you."

"Oh, come on," Crusty whined. "There must be some wiggle room in there. I don't want to die ... but even if I survive you, that doesn't mean I'll survive her. She has a bad, bad attitude."

"I have a worse attitude," Aunt Tillie insisted.

"Not really." Crusty shook his head. "You act tough, but deep down you're a big softie."

It was the meanest thing he could've said to Aunt Tillie. She was furious —and then some.

"You take that back," she hissed.

"I can't." Crusty held out his hands and shrugged. "It's the truth. You have a big, soft core."

I grabbed Aunt Tillie's wrist before she could bop Crusty over the head with her fist. "We need him," I said.

"We don't need him for anything," Aunt Tillie countered. "He won't help us. He's a clown, for crying out loud. That makes him a sociopath by nature."

"And you gave him sentience," I muttered.

"How many times must I tell you I didn't mean to do that?" Aunt Tillie's rage was palpable. "It was an accident."

"That accident has come back to bite us now."

"Shh." Aunt Tillie pressed her finger to her lips. "It's quiet time. You need to stop talking."

I wasn't about to do that. I focused on Crusty. "Where is the creature? Actually, *what* is she?"

Crusty shook his head. "I have no idea what she is. That's mostly because I have no basis for comparison. It's not as if I have access to the whole of human knowledge. We only know a few facts."

"Where is she?" I repeated.

"Last time I saw her, she was downtown. She doesn't always look the same."

"A glamour?" Aunt Tillie asked me.

I shrugged. "That would suggest she's a witch and does have access to magic. Your locator spell didn't work, so that can't be right."

"Unless she knew to protect herself from a locator spell," Aunt Tillie said.

I considered it, then shook my head. "If she's strong enough to block us she's going to be a bigger problem."

"If you can't tell us where or what she is, what can you tell us?" Aunt Tillie demanded.

"Last time I saw her she was talking to you," Crusty replied, his eyes leveling on me.

I was caught off guard. "Me? When?"

"Outside your office. She was picking at the mulch when you walked up on her."

Realization dawned. "Tricia Childs."

"Childs's wife?" Aunt Tillie looked dumbfounded. "But..."

"Maybe she's been fooling us this whole time." I pointed at Crusty. "Keep him in here. Don't let him leave."

"I've got it," Aunt Tillie said. "Where are you going?"

"Where do you think?"

"You shouldn't go there alone," Dad called out. "It isn't safe."

"I'll take Evan."

"Will I see you later?" Dad sounded hopeful.

"Count on it," I called back. "Thank you for helping me."

"That's my job."

"I'll talk to you soon."

Dad and Aunt Tillie were eyeing each other darkly. "Yes, yes you will."

25
TWENTY-FIVE

I only had to go as far as the kitchen to find Evan. He was sitting in Aunt Tillie's recliner, Winchester on his lap, gossiping with my mother and aunts.

"I found her," he said to me when I walked through the back door.

"So did I," I said. "She's with my father and Crusty in her dome right now."

"Do I even want to know who Crusty is?" Mom asked with a whine.

"He's one of the clowns. He moved on me at the Dragonfly."

"He tried to kill you?" Mom looked appalled.

"I'm not sure what he was trying to do. Right now, he's contained, though I have a feeling Aunt Tillie will mess with him. She's feeling a bit out of sorts."

"I don't understand why," Mom complained. "It's not as if she could've known this creature was out there."

"I think it's because it messed with Mrs. Little."

Mom made a face. "Aunt Tillie spends half her day messing with Margaret. You would think she'd want to high-five the monster and do a little dance."

"She definitely doesn't want to do that."

"It's an ownership thing," Evan volunteered. "Tillie can mess with Margaret. Nobody else can. That's simply the way she thinks."

"Pretty much," I confirmed. "Speaking of, how is Mrs. Little?"

"Asleep," Mom replied. "She needs a lot of rest. This whole ordeal traumatized her."

"Well, she's going to have to get in line. We're all traumatized." I tapped my fingers on the counter. "Where did Landon and Chief Terry go?"

"To town," Marnie replied. "They figured it was best to show themselves because the other agents are down there asking questions."

I nodded, briefly wondering if I should call them before setting out with Evan. Ultimately, I opted against it. "We have a mission," I said to the vampire.

He cocked an eyebrow. "Are we hunting clowns? I have to say, they're getting irritating."

"The clowns are a concern. They're no longer under Aunt Tillie's control, and there's going to be a reckoning on that front. But they're not my major concern right now."

"What is your major concern?" Mom asked.

"Crusty said he'd seen the creature. He also said he saw it talking to me."

Mom straightened. "How is that possible? Wouldn't you have realized you were talking to a monster?"

"It seems this creature can change appearance. That suggests a glamour of some sort. Aunt Tillie cast a locator spell to find it this morning but came up empty."

"What are our options?" Mom asked.

"The individual Crusty described is Tricia Childs, so I figured I would go have a chat with her."

"Tricia Childs?" Mom looked flabbergasted. "You don't think she was feeding off Brad?"

It was a question I hadn't really considered, though it made sense. "It could've led to his mental instability. It also could've glommed on to Tricia because she was in town and it decided to use her image because nobody would question her presence."

Evan bobbed his head. "You met Tricia. If the creature made itself look like her, it would be able to get close to you without you saying anything."

"It makes an odd sort of sense," I agreed. "Our biggest problem is that we don't know what this thing is or what it hopes to do. That's why I need you with me. If this thing doesn't have a lot of magic at its disposal, we can probably beat it."

"Ah, to be wanted because I'm manly," Evan teased.

I rolled my eyes. "Normally I would handle something like this alone. But I'm guessing this thing can paralyze people with its proboscis, so I don't want to take any chances."

Evan climbed out of the chair and placed a sleeping Winchester in the spot he'd been sitting. "Let's do it. Do you know where she lives?"

"I googled and found an address."

"Then, let's go."

Mom, who had been listening to the conversation with rapt attention, started shaking her head. "Wait. Don't you think you should take Landon and Terry? They're at least an official presence."

"The address is not in Hemlock Cove," I countered. "It's in Bellaire."

"Landon still has jurisdiction." Mom looked distinctly uncomfortable.

"And if Tricia Childs is a monster?" I asked.

"You'll have to kill her," Mom said on a sigh.

"Yes, and I don't want Landon and Chief Terry to have to see that or watch as we break the law to hide a body."

"I suppose." Mom didn't appear to be swayed by my argument, but she nodded all the same. "Okay, I guess you know what you're doing."

"We shouldn't be gone long," I said. "If Landon and Chief Terry ask if you've seen me, I don't expect you to lie."

"Good, because I won't lie for you, Bay." Mom was stern. "Terry and I are getting married. I won't lie to his face."

"You won't have to. I've got this."

"Just be careful. We don't want you ending up dead in a ditch."

"I won't let that happen," Evan promised. "I'll keep her safe."

I hated—*absolutely loathed*—how smug he sounded. "You're kind of a tool when you want to be."

"I'm really coming into my own as Tillie's sidekick," he agreed.

I didn't want to laugh. It would only encourage him. But I couldn't stop myself. "Your personality is definitely growing more colorful."

"You love me, and you know it."

. . .

THE CHILDS RESIDENCE WAS A NONDESCRIPT RANCH house set about a half a mile back from the road two miles outside Bellaire. It was surrounded by trees, which hid our approach. We parked around the bend from the house and went in on foot. There was a vehicle in the driveway, but the house was quiet.

My plan was to stroll up to the door and knock. Evan shook his head when I started for the door. He turned and went to a window on the side of the house.

"What if she's naked?" I whispered. "You could be invading her privacy."

"Do you really care about me invading a monster's privacy?" he challenged.

"What if she's not a monster?" I pressed. "What if the monster only borrowed her face for a bit?"

Evan looked taken aback. "Well ... then I'll apologize." He went back to staring through the window.

Even though I was against it, I stood next to him and looked. If he was already stepping all over her privacy rights, it couldn't hurt to join him. I had to shade my eyes to see through the window, and it took my eyes a moment to adjust. I saw something of concern immediately.

"Is that...?"

Evan was grim. "If you mean a body, then yes."

My heart lodged in my throat. "It's not a child's body, is it?"

He shook his head. "It is a woman's body. If the shoes are any indication."

I didn't know what to do or say. For a moment, I remained frozen. Then I dug for my phone.

"What are you doing?" Evan pinned me with an alarmed look.

"The kids could be in there."

"Aren't Childs's kids teenagers?"

"Yes, but if this creature has been feeding off them..." I trailed off as understanding sparked in his eyes.

"You're right." He was resigned. "Call him."

Landon answered on the first ring. "I've only had two cookies," he said. "I swear you have radar when I'm thinking about food."

"You can have as many cookies as you want," I said. He was going to need a peace offering.

"What did you do?" Landon growled.

"That's a terrible assumption. You don't know that I've done anything."

"Bay."

"You need to come to the Childs residence." I rattled off the address from memory. "We've found something."

"What?"

"I'm pretty sure it's a body. We have not entered the house. We peeped from outside."

"I thought you were with your father."

"He should still be at the inn. He was with Aunt Tillie last time I saw him."

"It seems I'm behind." He didn't sound happy about it. "I'm on my way."

"Thank you."

"Bay, don't enter that house. I know you want to, but don't do it."

"I promise not to go in unless we have a good reason."

"What reason could you possibly have?"

"Childs has kids. We haven't seen them. If one of them were to scream or do something to suggest they need help, I would have no choice but to go in."

Landon sighed. "I'll be there in thirty minutes."

BECAUSE WE WERE BOTH ANTSY, EVAN AND I walked the perimeter surrounding the house. He pointed out something I initially missed when kneeling to get a better look at the dirt beneath a pine tree.

"Little clown shoes," I realized as I stared at the now familiar prints. "So they were out here."

"The question is, what were they doing?"

"Crusty doesn't seem keen to spill his guts."

"Crusty will do what I say. And what a stupid name that is."

"Crusty fits a clown. Burt less so."

True to his word, Landon arrived exactly a half hour after our call. To my surprise, he'd brought Chief Terry.

"You don't have jurisdiction here," I blurted.

"He does if I say he does," Landon replied. He strode to me, looked me up and down, and then ran his hands over my shoulders. "Are you okay?"

"I've been better."

"Show me the body."

Evan led him to the window, where Landon stared for thirty seconds. Then he viciously swore under his breath. "I have to enter," he said.

"I can kick the door down if you want," Evan offered. "It doesn't take much effort."

Landon glared at him. "I can kick in my own door."

Chief Terry cleared his throat.

"Not that we're doing that," Landon amended. "We'll try for a soft entry first."

"Okay, but that doesn't sound like any fun at all," Evan complained.

Landon snapped on a pair of rubber gloves before testing the doorknob. To all of our disappointment, it turned. It seemed nobody would be kicking in any doors.

"Wow." Landon waved his hand in front of his face as the scent of decomposition hit us. "That is not good."

"And that's from a professional," Chief Terry said dryly. He was grim as he aimed his gaze into the house. "You guys stay here."

"I think *you* should stay here," I replied.

"Excuse me?" Chief Terry's tone ratcheted up a notch. "Last time I checked, I was in charge."

"Technically, I'm in charge," Landon countered. "I brought you as backup."

Evan slipped around us and strode into the house as we continued to argue. I glared at his back—he was definitely getting bolder—and pushed through Landon and Chief Terry to follow.

"I'm pretty sure you're not following protocol," Landon complained to Evan.

"You'll survive," Evan replied. He cocked his head as he listened for noises from deep inside the house. He shook his head when he looked at me. "There's nobody else here, and I don't smell any other bodies."

"Then where are the kids?" I asked.

"It's possible they're with their grandparents," Chief Terry said. "They're teenagers. One of them is eighteen. She might not even live here."

I nodded. "We need to track them down."

"We will," Landon promised. He dropped to his knees next to the body. Even though I'd only briefly talked to her, I recognized it as belonging to

Tricia Childs. She looked almost nothing like I remembered her. "She's almost been mummified," he mused.

"No." I shook my head. "I mean ... yes, but she's not a normal mummy."

"I love that I married into a family that can say 'it's not a normal mummy' and it's totally true," Landon complained.

I would've laughed under different circumstances, but there was nothing funny about this situation. "I meant that her fluids have been drained."

A muscle worked in Landon's jaw. "Our monster sucked her dry."

"Yeah."

"This didn't happen today, Bay," Landon said. "Even if she wasn't hollowed out the same way a normal mummy would have been, the body would react the same way. She died at least a week ago. We have to get the medical examiner here to make a determination."

My heart sank. "Are you sure?"

"We're dealing with the paranormal, so occasionally the rules go out the window, but I would bet money on it under different circumstances."

I gripped my hands into fists at my sides, digging my fingernails in until it hurt.

"What are you thinking, Bay?" Chief Terry asked after a few seconds of my mind buzzing with possibilities.

"I don't think I met Tricia Childs," I said. "It was the other thing."

"What did she say to you? Were there any hints to suggest what we're dealing with?"

That's what I kept going over in my head. "No. I believed everything she told me. She seemed like a sad woman who lost her husband months ago but hadn't come to terms with it yet. She played me."

"Bay." Landon's tone was full of warning. "Don't blame yourself for this."

He was right, but I still was bothered that I hadn't seen anything. Shouldn't I have seen a glimmer of the paranormal in the woman? To be fair, I hadn't been looking at her that hard. I sat down with her out of obligation. My mind had already been on the FBI agents at that point.

Wait ... the FBI agents.

I straightened. "We need to talk to Spencer."

Landon's brow furrowed. "Why?"

"I think he knows more than he's letting on."

"You think he's part of this?" Chief Terry challenged. "If so, we have to come up with a plan before taking him out. We can't kill an FBI agent under the noses of other agents."

"We're not going to kill him," I reassured him. "I don't think he's involved. I do think he knows more than he's letting on. He knew I was a witch before he came. He essentially said so. I think he came here to check me out because he has other plans."

"Like … sexy plans?" Landon looked as if he was about to Hulk out.

"Not sexy plans." I rolled my eyes. "He wants to see if I'm a friend or a foe. He's testing me. He also knew there was a paranormal explanation to what happened to Childs. He was trying to tip us off without coming right out and telling us."

"Bay, I didn't see anything in his demeanor to suggest that," Landon said. Even as he said it, he didn't look certain. "I guess it can't hurt to talk to him."

"That's the plan." I motioned for Evan to follow me. "We're going to talk to him."

"Hold up." All of the softness went out of Landon's eyes. "Why are the two of you going to talk to him?"

"Because you have to call this in, and I can't be here. Plus, we need to work fast. I don't know much, but I do know that."

Landon looked as if he wanted to argue, but Chief Terry sent him a subtle headshake.

"Let her go," Chief Terry said. "She won't rest until she figures this out. She's our best shot."

Landon's exhale was long and drawn out. "Fine. Be careful."

"I'm always careful."

"Be way more careful than that."

26

TWENTY-SIX

You wouldn't think finding a specific FBI agent in a town the size of Hemlock Cove would be all that difficult. You would be wrong.

Two hours after returning, Evan and I were still looking. We finally found Spencer in the last place we thought to look.

"What are you doing here?" I asked the FBI agent as Evan and I slipped inside the Unicorn Emporium, which was not supposed to be open today.

"I think the better question is what are you doing here?" Spencer challenged. His gaze moved to Evan. "And what in the hell are you?"

Evan didn't take offense at the way Spencer phrased the question. "Vampire."

Spencer did a big stretch toward the window and gestured to the sun.

"I'm not that kind of vampire," Evan replied evenly.

"What other kinds of vampires are there?" Spencer demanded.

"You would be surprised." Evan moved to the huge porcelain unicorn situated on the table in the center of the store. "I think this might be worse than the clowns," he remarked.

"Nothing is worse than the clowns," I replied. I folded my arms over my chest as I eyed Spencer. "We have a problem."

"You and the vampire who is not your husband have a problem?" Spencer was a little too full of himself, and that was on full display as he glanced between us. "Does Landon know about this ... situation?"

I didn't like the insinuation.

"My boyfriend knows about it," Evan replied before I could muster an answer.

"Oh." Spencer nodded in understanding.

I couldn't let the opening go. "Boyfriend? Is that what you're calling Easton now?"

"Oh, that was a mistake." Evan squinched up his face into one of pain. "I shouldn't have said that."

"You really shouldn't have," I agreed. "I won't be able to let it go."

"You can never let things go as it is. This was just providing you with ammunition after I'd already hobbled myself with a leg shot during the zombie apocalypse."

"We're going to talk about this." Something else occurred to me. "Does Scout know about you having a boyfriend? You're going to be in big trouble."

"Unbelievable," Evan muttered.

"As for you, don't worry about my relationship with Evan," I said to Spencer. "He's a good guy, and he's not interested in stealing Landon's bacon. He never would. I never would either, for that matter."

"Are you the bacon in that comparison?" Spencer asked.

"Yes. I even have a costume."

Spencer took us all by surprise—including himself if his expression was any indication—when he burst out laughing. "I always knew Michaels was a kinky guy. You can kind of tell sometimes. That's way more than I was anticipating."

"It's not kinky," I argued. "It's sweet."

"If you say so."

"We're not here to talk about Landon."

"You'd better be here to talk about a life-or-death situation, because if Hodgins or Cam see you in here with me, they're going to have questions. I don't want to answer those sorts of questions."

I didn't blame him. Those were the sorts of questions I avoided too. "I glamoured us on the way in. Evan will see them if they get close."

"Oh, right." Evan turned quickly. "I'm supposed to be watching for them."

I gave his back a dirty look, then turned back to Spencer. "Tricia Childs is dead." I could've tried to soften the blow, but we didn't have time.

"Tricia Childs is who again?" Spencer asked.

I gave him a dirty look. "Brad Childs's widow."

Realization dawned on Spencer's face. "Man, that is a bummer for that family. How did she die?"

I narrowed my eyes. If he was putting on an act, he was good at it. "A magical creature sucked her dry of all her fluids. You know, the same thing that was happening to Margaret Little."

Now Spencer did react. "Margaret Little is dead? Oh, you guys are going to be in so much trouble."

"She's not dead," I replied. "We went to talk to her earlier because we had some information about her interactions with Brad Childs. We found her ... well, in a very weakened state."

"But not dead?"

I shook my head. "We gave her a few potions, got a healing salve on her wound, and then moved her to the inn to sleep."

Spencer blinked twice. "How exactly are you going to explain why your mortal enemy is now sleeping under the family roof?"

"We really didn't have a choice. We couldn't leave her at her house to be attacked again."

"I get that, but you guys are acting like..."

"Like we have nothing to hide," I finished for him. "There's a reason. We don't have anything to hide."

"Okay, but this is still a big pile of crap we need to find a specific fly in."

"So gross," Evan complained.

Spencer shrugged. "How hard was it for you guys to stay out of trouble? I did warn you."

"Yes, and I want to talk about why you warned me the way you did," I said.

Spencer had relaxed some but became suspicious in a heartbeat. "I'm terrified of whatever story you're spinning in that busy brain of yours. I guarantee it's wrong."

"I'll take that bet." I folded my arms over my chest. "I think you know what we're up against."

"What makes you think that?"

He was a good liar. Given the fact that he lied every single day when doing his job, that was a given. Still, he wasn't raised with Aunt Tillie. He didn't get lying lessons from the best. "I don't have time to screw around. Just tell us what we're fighting so we can plan accordingly."

"Why not send Millie out to do your dirty work?"

"Stop your obsession with Millie. That situation will work itself out."

"She's made up. How is that going to work out?"

"Please." I waved off the comment. "Aunt Tillie has come up with far more elaborate lies. That's not even in the top ten. Tell me what we're up against. We cannot track it unless we know what it is."

Spencer looked caught. "I..."

"Do you want to know what I think, Bay?" Evan asked.

"Always," I replied without hesitation.

"I think you're right about him testing you. I also think he didn't decide to do it himself. I'm guessing the order came from above."

That statement—right on target, as always—cleared things up for me. "Oh, geez." There were no mental gymnastics involved in sticking this landing. "Steve sent you here because he wanted you to decide if we're open to whatever he's planning."

"Who is Steve?" Evan asked.

"Landon's boss. He's been here before. He's seen a few things, but he's been careful not to delve too deep. That's why Spencer is here."

"I volunteered for this case because I was interested," Spencer countered.

"I'm not talking about the case. I'm talking about the office."

He looked as if I'd hit him in the face with a sledgehammer.

"There it is." I nodded. "Now you understand what I'm talking about."

"And I finally understand what you're talking about," Evan said. "Landon's boss knows about the paranormal. He knows Spencer is a shifter. He's trying to build some sort of paranormal team."

Spencer let loose a sputtering laugh. "That's quite the leap."

"She's right." Evan's tone was no-nonsense. "It's the reason Landon was allowed to make his base here. The boss said the position was different, but it's not. They wanted to make sure his bond was strong with the resident witches."

Spencer cocked his head. "I'm not sure I'm allowed to talk about this. In fact, I know I'm not."

"Well, you're going to." I refused to be used as some sort of pawn in a game I didn't even know I was playing. "When Steve approaches us—and

I'm sure that will happen soon thanks to this little adventure—I'll pretend I don't know what's going on. Right now, you're going to tell me exactly what's going on."

Spencer looked out the window, then back at me, his frustration was evident. "I could lose everything if I talk to you."

"Tricia and Brad Childs have already lost everything," I pointed out.

"There's nothing I could've done to stop that."

I jutted out my chin. Spencer stared back, his agitation growing. Finally, he shook his head. "Unbelievable." His hands moved to his hips. "Steve warned me you guys couldn't be controlled or manipulated. He said I should be as straightforward as possible.

"All I saw when I first got here was three older witches who liked to cook, three younger ones caught up in their love lives, and one crazy old witch who enjoyed torturing people," he continued. "Obviously, looks can be deceiving."

I waited.

"You're basically right," Spencer said. "Given the level of paranormal activity in this area—murders and disappearances that have no explanation—Steve has decided a paranormal unit is in order. He wants to partner with the Spells Angels group in Hawthorne Hollow."

It was hard to keep a straight face and not dart a look toward Evan. I managed, but only barely. "Really."

"Have you heard of them?" Spencer reminded me of an earnest kid now. "They ride motorcycles and are supposed to be amazing. Apparently, they got a huge power boost in the last year."

"Huh," was all I could say. I wasn't about to out my friends.

"Fire magic is on an uptick in this area too," he continued. "We're still trying to track the source of that." He lowered his voice to a conspiratorial whisper. "There might be a hellcat in the area. They were thought to be extinct. How amazing is that?"

"Totally amazing," I replied. Apparently, my response was a bit too fast, though, because Spencer narrowed his eyes.

"You already knew all of this," he realized. "You know who I'm talking about."

"I'm not getting into that," I replied.

"You're making me talk."

"I'm nowhere near as weak willed as you." I shot him a smile that was anything but friendly. "Finish it."

"How can I share information with you if you won't share with me?"

"Because if you don't, I'll eat you for lunch," Evan replied. "Suffice it to say that we're familiar with the other paranormals in the area. We might even be able to make you look really good in front of your boss at some point. Today we're talking about what killed Brad and Tricia Childs."

"And took over Tricia's identity," I added.

Spencer's spine snapped straight. "How do you know?"

"We found Tricia's body three hours ago. She's been dead for more than a week, and I just had a conversation with her a few days ago."

"How did you know to look for her?"

I couldn't tell him about Scout and Stormy, but I could tell him this. It was just a little something to bolster his faith in me. "Crusty told me."

"Crusty?"

"One of the clowns. I captured him today. Apparently, they've switched allegiance because they want to keep their sentience. Whatever is doing the killing has convinced them to go after us."

"Oh, geez." Spencer glanced around the store. "There aren't any in here, are there?"

"Not that I know of, but they'll be coming. That's why you have to tell me what you know."

"Technically, I don't know anything," he hedged. "I do have a theory."

"What's your theory?"

"Changeling." Spencer seemed resigned to giving me all the information. "I think we're dealing with a changeling, because the mark that was on the back of Brad Childs's neck makes me believe he was fed on before his death."

And there it was. Confirmation that I was on the right track. "What sort of changeling?"

Spencer's face went momentarily blank. "I didn't actually know there was more than one kind."

"There are several," I replied. "Most prefer desert climates. Some slip into the skin of their intended victims. That's obviously not what we're dealing with here."

"Obviously not," Spencer agreed dryly.

"If you know there's something paranormal about Childs's death, why are you still looking at me?" I demanded. It wasn't his fault, but that didn't change the fact that my annoyance had teeth.

"Hodgins doesn't know about the paranormal," he replied. He almost looked amused. "That's not something he can swallow. All he knows is that you were out there in the middle of the night with your crazy great-aunt and mouthy cousin. He's seen the body. He gets that all the fluids were removed. He knows that Childs's neck was broken. He does not, however, understand how all those pieces fit together."

"You said there was a mark on the back of Childs's neck," Evan said. "Isn't he questioning where that mark came from?"

"Yeah, but if you don't believe in the paranormal, you're going to look for a human explanation. He thinks some sort of weapon was used to draw the fluids from the neck. The medical examiner keeps telling him that's not possible. That doesn't stop him from pursuing that line of thought."

"What about the others?" I asked. "Cam? Patrice?"

"Patrice doesn't believe in the paranormal," Spencer replied. "She would like to, because she reads a lot of vampire romance novels—she would love you, Evan—but she just can't open her mind to the possibilities. As for Cam..." He took a moment to really consider it. "She's shrewder than anyone wants to give her credit for. She's smart and can figure things out. She doesn't have a lot of imagination, though."

"You have to be able to open your mind to possibilities," I said.

"Yes."

"She's still playing a game with me. She wants me to believe she's interested in Landon. She made sure to tell me that all the women in the office were brokenhearted when we married. She doesn't really care about that."

"Actually, I believe she does, just not for the reason you think. Cam wants upward momentum. She believes Landon is Steve's favorite, and he is. It's because he doesn't give Steve a lot of grief. He does his job and keeps to himself. The rest of us are in a gossip pressure cooker from day to day."

"Steve also wants Landon to be the point man of his new paranormal unit," Evan pointed out.

Spencer hesitated. "He's never said that."

"It's what he wants," Evan insisted. "Trust me, Landon is going to be the go-to guy for whatever's coming. He knows all the players, after all."

"Meaning there are more players than just you guys," Spencer realized.

"You're way behind," I acknowledged. An idea was starting to niggle the back of my brain. Landon might get his upward momentum, only here, after all. That was tomorrow's problem—or, rather, opportunity—though. Today, we needed to deal with the changeling. "We're going to help you with whatever machinations you've got going. I need to know what you know about the changeling."

"I've gotten a whiff a few times," Spencer replied. "I haven't seen it up close. I think it can change its appearance at will. No buildup."

"Always women?" I asked.

"I don't know."

"Can you scent the changeling because you're a shifter?"

"Yes. If I were a wolf shifter, I think it would be even easier. You don't happen to have one of those you can tap? I bet one could lead you right to your prey."

"As a matter of fact, we do," I said grimly, my eyes going to Evan. "Do you want to call in the cavalry?"

Evan nodded. "Shall we meet in Tillie's special spot so we don't risk the Feds stumbling over us? It's going to be hard to explain Gunner and Scout to outsiders."

"Especially since we already have to explain Mrs. Little's presence at the inn," I said. "Aunt Tillie's special spot is good."

"Where is Aunt Tillie's special spot?" Spencer asked. "You can't just leave me hanging."

I patted his shoulder like a teacher might a child's. "Thank you for the information. We'll be in touch when we're finished."

"By finished, you mean you're going to kill this thing, right?"

"Do you see another way around it?"

"No, but without someone to blame, Hodgins will keep coming after you."

There was no fixing that problem. At least not today. "We'll deal with that when we can. The changeling is our biggest problem. We have to get to her before she gets to another innocent person."

"What can I do?"

"Keep your team away from the inn for as long as possible. We'll handle the rest."

27
TWENTY-SEVEN

Everybody converged under Aunt Tillie's garden dome within the hour. Gunner and Scout were the last to arrive. They both had big smiles on their faces ... right up until they saw Crusty.

"What the hell is that?" Gunner jumped into Evan's arms to keep the clown from getting anywhere near his feet.

Evan effortlessly lifted Gunner. "Seriously? You're supposed to be a big, bad shifter."

Gunner didn't climb out of Evan's grip. "That thing is not natural."

Crusty, who had not stopped complaining his entire stay, smiled and waved at Gunner in irritating fashion. I found the move mildly entertaining —almost endearing in a weird way—but Gunner didn't like it.

"Make him stop that," the shifter hissed.

For her part, Scout didn't seem afraid of the clown as much as curious. "What's your deal?" She hunkered down to get a good look at the doll. "Do you talk?"

"Do you?" Crusty fired back.

"Don't get testy," Scout chided. "It was just a question. You are a doll."

"Perhaps I should ask if you're capable of thought," Crusty sneered. "It's entirely possible all that bleach in your hair seeped in and killed brain cells."

Scout narrowed her eyes, and for a moment I thought she would tear him in half. But she grinned. "I like him," she announced. "I kind of want to keep him."

"You can't keep him," Aunt Tillie said. "He's mine."

Gunner, who was still in Evan's arms, finally put his feet back on the ground. He smiled at the clown, although there was no warmth to it, and offered up a lame finger wave. "Hey, little guy."

Crusty hissed at him.

"I don't like him," Gunner said. "We're not taking him home."

"I already told you he's staying with me," Aunt Tillie said. "Can you hear? I thought shifters were supposed to be able to hear."

"Nobody is keeping him," Mom announced. She'd left Mrs. Little with Marnie and Twila, insisting on being present for the conversation. Her mood was dark. "He's going back into whatever box he came out of."

Crusty didn't look all that worried. He piled on the charm. "It's sad that a woman of your beauty—and obvious heart—doesn't see that I can be a fully-functioning member of society. Just because I started as a doll doesn't mean I have nothing to contribute. I have feelings, too."

Mom looked taken aback. "Oh, well..."

"Don't fall for it," Dad said. "He'll attack your ankle if you turn your back to him. He's a vicious little monster."

Mom darted a look to Dad. They'd been talking when I walked into the dome, and neither were bloodied or crying. I took that to signify that Dad had explained to Mom that his meltdown was about me and not her. She appeared to have taken the news better than I expected. Of course, we had bigger worries, and she might be holding off on complaining until we were done.

"Thank you for the tip," Mom said to Dad.

"You're welcome," Dad replied.

Chief Terry, sitting on one of Mom's garden chairs, narrowed his eyes as he took in the interaction.

"Don't worry, big guy," Gunner said as he slapped Chief Terry's shoulder. "That's not a sex look. It's a 'we used to have sex but now we have to put up with each other for the sake of our grown daughter' look. You have nothing to fear."

The look Chief Terry shot Gunner was withering. "Thank you, Gunner."

Gunner beamed. "You're welcome."

Crusty waved at him again, which made Gunner's smile slip.

"Seriously, what sick mind thought of this thing?" Gunner demanded.

"That would be me," Aunt Tillie replied. "He's awesome."

"What about Burt?" Thistle challenged. She'd been quiet since my arrival, her attention on Aunt Tillie more than anything else, but it was clear she'd spent her time during the intermission plotting against Aunt Tillie rather than contemplating the problem hanging over us.

"Burt is misunderstood," Aunt Tillie replied. "All I need is a few minutes to reason with him, and he'll be right back in the fold."

I snorted.

Aunt Tillie pinned me with a death glare. "I've got this."

"Who is Burt?" Scout asked.

"The four-foot-tall Pennywise replica that is wandering around town with a butcher knife," I replied.

Scout's nose wrinkled. "Pennywise? The clown from *It*?"

"The replica is of the recent movie version, not the vastly superior Tim Curry version," I offered.

"That's creepy." Scout shuddered. "And he's four feet tall?"

"With a butcher knife," I confirmed.

"I don't want to see him," Gunner announced. "Wherever you send me, he'd better not be there."

"We don't know where we're going yet." It was time to get down to the nitty-gritty. "According to Spencer, who had a lot to say even though he was annoyed about having to say it, we're dealing with a changeling."

"What sort of changeling?" Scout asked. "Are we talking about a succubus?"

"There's no sexual component I can find," I replied. "I think it's just a regular changeling."

"What's it want?" Scout was all business.

"I don't know." That was the question I kept running through my mind. "I have no idea what it wants."

"What do we know?"

"We know that it pretended to be Tricia Childs. We know that Brad Childs was fed on before his death. We have no idea why he was targeted."

"Maybe because of the jailbreak," Evan suggested. "Maybe he caught this creature's attention because he was in the news."

It was possible. It had been a paranormal jailbreak. The people who helped were gone. "Maybe it's payback for killing some of them," I mused.

"Does it matter?" Mom asked. "The why of this creature being here isn't as important as getting rid of it."

I didn't disagree. Still, I liked knowing the hows and whys before I dealt a death blow.

"Whoever it is, they went after Childs but came here after the fact," Landon said. "It's interested in Bay. Why else would it have gone after Mrs. Little? She doesn't make an enticing target other than her proximity to this family."

"It could be after me," Aunt Tillie said. "I'm the wickedest witch in the Midwest. I'm totally awesome. Who wouldn't want to go after me?"

Landon smirked. "If you're the overall target, why hasn't it gone after you? You're out all the time."

"Because I'm too powerful."

"Or Bay is always surrounded by other people and it hasn't had a chance to get to her," Landon said. "It would have to get by me to get to her."

"Oh, like that's some hard feat," Aunt Tillie muttered.

"I'm just saying that she's never alone."

"You two are tragically codependent," Thistle agreed. She hadn't put up a fight when I called. We both agreed to leave Clove out of it because of the baby. They'd shut down the store early and Clove was home with Sam and baby Calvin until this was over.

"Thank you, Thistle," I sneered. "I don't know what I would do without your opinion on my marriage."

Thistle's lips twitched—it was a victory for her because she'd managed to irritate me—but she didn't push things further.

"What exactly did Spencer say?" Landon asked.

"He said a lot of things." This was a conversation I wanted to have with Landon in private, but Scout and Gunner were going to be included in things and had a right to know. "He also owned up to the fact that Steve is looking to put together a paranormal team."

Landon's eyes went wide.

Scout's forehead creased in confusion. "Who is Steve?"

"Landon's boss," I replied. "He's been here a few times. He's seen a few things. He seems to know about the paranormal world but doesn't want to talk about it much."

Landon found his voice. "I don't know how much he knows. He has at least a little knowledge." He turned to me. "What makes you think that he wants a paranormal team?"

"Because it makes sense."

"And because Spencer basically confirmed it for us," Evan added. "They know about certain things. They don't know I'm a member of the Hawthorne Hollow group, but they know about the group as an entity. They've heard about Scout. They don't seem to realize that we're all working together."

"They likely wouldn't just jump to that conclusion," Landon agreed. "My first reaction is shock, but I guess it makes sense. Steve has been making noise about wanting to know more about this family. I guess I know why." His eyes were clear when they locked with mine. "I'm sorry."

I was thrown off guard. "Why are you sorry?"

"I'm supposed to protect you from exposure and now my people are coming after you."

"It's not like they're hunting us," I replied. "They want to work with us. We've done enough to expose ourselves over the past year so it makes sense he would be the one looking."

"Did he recruit Spencer because he was paranormal?"

I shrugged. "We didn't get that in depth on it, but I believe so. We'll have to talk to him about it. I don't see that we have a choice because once we kill this thing, we'll have to tell him what happened if we don't want Hodgins and Cam hunkering down in the inn for the foreseeable future."

Landon nodded in agreement. "I hadn't considered it, but that makes sense." He dragged a hand through his dark hair. "We're going to have a hard enough time explaining what Mrs. Little is doing here. They're going to assume you guys are trying to poison her."

"Oh, if only," Aunt Tillie lamented.

I shot her a dirty look. "Don't take it to a weird place," I ordered. "We need to focus on the changeling. It can look like anyone. It does seem to prefer to take on the identities of females."

"It did approach you as Tricia Childs," Landon pointed out.

"It did," I agreed. "It's a dangerous creature. It killed Childs and almost killed Mrs. Little. We don't know if anyone else has fallen victim to it. Mrs. Little referred to 'her,' so that's what we're dealing with."

"What about a locator spell?" Gunner asked. He was still giving Crusty a wide berth.

"I tried that and got nowhere," Aunt Tillie replied. "That suggests this thing can shield itself."

I turned to Crusty. "You need to help us. You're the one with the information."

He didn't look happy with the suggestion. "What did I say?" The small clown planted his hands on his hips. "I can't tell you. She'll kill me."

"We'll kill you," Scout countered. "What makes you think we won't rip you to shreds right here?"

"Because you're the good guys." Crusty looked smug. "The good guys don't rip dolls to shreds, especially if they're screaming and begging you to stop."

Well, that was a visual I wouldn't be able to get out of my head.

"You're a creepy little dude," Scout said. "I like it, though." She showed Crusty her teeth when she smiled. "What if we make a deal with you?"

I didn't like her tone. I wanted to stop her before she made a deal we would have to honor, but it was already too late.

"What sort of deal?" Crusty cocked his head.

"The sort of deal where we put the other clowns to sleep and let you stay awake," Scout replied.

Was she really going there? "We can't have a sentient clown doll running around," I hissed.

She waved me off. "You can come to Hawthorne Hollow if it's a problem. We'll let you stay awake—under certain guidelines, of course—and in exchange you'll tell us what we need to know about the changeling."

Despite his best efforts to look uninterested, Crusty leaned forward. "How do I know you'll honor your promise?"

"Because we're the good guys. You already said it yourself."

Crusty hesitated, wringing his white-gloved hands. "Deal." He jutted out his small hand.

"Don't touch him," Gunner growled. "He might give you clown cooties."

"There's no such thing," Crusty replied.

Scout readily took the clown's hand. "Deal."

"The changeling is here for payback," Crusty said. "Apparently, one of the prisoners killed during the escape—I don't know which one, so don't ask—was her brother. She's angry and wants to make the witches who took him down pay."

I ran the information through my head. "It doesn't really matter which prisoner. That explains why she went through Childs to exact her revenge."

"She can look like anyone," Crusty explained. "She can't maintain the illusion unless she takes some of the essence from the individual."

Something occurred to me. "So she's been wandering around town looking like Mrs. Little?"

Crusty scratched under his hat. "I don't know about that. I only know what I've heard her say. She and Burt have come to an arrangement."

"Of course they have." My annoyance knew no bounds.

"He's her soldier. He's the one who convinced us to join the team. She's made promises to him."

"The sort of promises she can keep?" Scout asked. "How much magic does she have?"

"Enough that she can hide her identity from you. She was crowing about that. She said the old witch couldn't find her."

"Who is she calling old?" Aunt Tillie demanded. "I'm middle aged."

Crusty snorted. "Anyway, she can emulate anyone she wants but only if she has a bit of them to fuel her. She goes for women because they're smaller and don't take as much magic. She says it's harder to pretend to be a man because they stand a different way and carry themselves with more swagger."

"Who does she look like now? Tricia Childs is dead. Mrs. Little is out of her reach."

"I saw her new identity," Crusty said. "I saw her downtown this morning before I went to find you. She sent me on a spying mission. She's probably wondering where I am even as we speak."

He sat there and waited.

"Don't keep us in suspense," Landon prodded after several seconds. "Who is it?"

Crusty looked smug. "She's staying at the inn."

It took me several seconds to figure it out. "It's either Patrice or Cam."

Crusty just kept smiling.

"It has to be Patrice," Landon said, his voice low and grave. "I saw Cam this morning. She's wearing her hair up today. If she had a mark on the back of her neck, I would've seen it."

"But you would've seen the changeling," I argued. "You wouldn't have actually seen Cam."

"Where would the real Cam be?" Landon's face rippled with alarm.

"Oh, crap," I said as reality hit me in the face.

"Would she be here?" Scout asked. She could essentially read my mind.

"She would have to be," Landon said.

"We need to split up and search the grounds," I said. "Did either Patrice or Cam go on the grounds alone last night?" I asked Mom.

"Patrice did," Chief Terry replied. "She went out after dinner. Said she wanted to take a look at the greenhouse and bluff."

"That's when it likely happened."

"And that means Patrice is dead." Chief Terry said.

"Not necessarily." I shook my head. "She could be incapacitated like Mrs. Little. We have to find her."

"Come on." Evan slapped Gunner's arm. "We have the best sniffers. Let's find her."

They took off together without another word. The rest of us—other than Aunt Tillie, who showed no interest in going anywhere because she was busy gathering herbs—went out to join them.

It didn't take long to find what we were looking for. Gunner emerged from the storage shed with an unconscious Patrice in his arms less than ten minutes after he set out.

"Is she alive?" Landon hurried to him.

Gunner nodded. "She's unconscious but breathing."

"We need to get some potions in her," Mom said. "We'll take her up to her room and get to it." Her eyes moved to me. "What are you going to do?"

I could think of only one thing. "We need to set a trap. That means Spencer might have to get her out here for us."

"We have to keep the others away from the inn while we're working on this," Chief Terry said. "We can't risk them walking in when we're killing a monster that looks like one of her co-workers."

"Call Cam and Hodgins to a meeting at your office," I said. "Sit them down and talk to them about Tricia Childs. Keep them busy. I'll have Spencer lure Patrice here. We'll come up with a story."

"What if she doesn't fall for it?" Landon asked.

"Then we'll have to go to her. It's better she comes here."

He nodded. "Well, let's get Patrice upstairs. We need her to get better."

"Yeah." I sighed. "We're not out of the woods yet."

28
TWENTY-EIGHT

Spencer didn't like the plan at all, but he agreed to it without too much prodding. He seemed to understand that the changeling getting access to FBI information was bad news. He told her that he wanted to come to the inn for lunch—he was keen on the hot beef sandwiches he'd been promised—and the fake Patrice wasn't included in the meeting with Chief Terry, so she had no good reason not to accompany him to lunch.

We took over the main floor of the inn to deal with her.

The changeling's expression was sour when Spencer led her into the lobby.

"How can you not be excited for hot beef?" Spencer asked. "I mean … there's gravy. Have I ever mentioned how much I love gravy?" Outwardly he appeared calm, but I picked up the undercurrent of his jangling nerves.

"I've never met anyone who gets this excited for gravy," she complained as she followed him. Gunner and Scout had positioned themselves in the bushes outside and would close off the front door as an escape route once they were certain the changeling was inside.

I crouched behind the front desk, Landon on one side of me and Thistle on the other, waiting for Spencer to say the right words to spring the trap.

"It's as if you don't know me at all," Spencer lamented in a wounded voice. "We've had some big conversations about gravy, Patrice. How can you not remember?"

The changeling must've realized she made a mistake, because she stopped moving. I saw from shadows under the desk, and when her feet stopped clopping on the hardwood floors the shadows halted. "I ... must have forgotten."

"I don't know." Spencer clucked his tongue. "They were very memorable conversations. Are you sure you haven't been taken over by a body snatcher?"

It wasn't the exact phrasing I told him to use, but it was close enough. I pushed myself to a standing position behind the desk and fixed the fake Patrice with a sunny smile. "Nice day, huh?"

Patrice's shoulders jerked. Even though I knew it wasn't really her, looking at her now, seeing her up close like this, was uncanny. I wouldn't have been able to ascertain I wasn't dealing with the real deal if we hadn't just carried the real Patrice upstairs. Even now, my mother and aunts were tending to her. She would be okay.

As long as we put an end to this.

"You gave me a fright," the changeling said, her hand going to the spot over her heart as her eyes narrowed. She'd figured out that something was going on. She was still trying to gauge exactly what.

"Sorry." I said the word, but my eyes told her I wasn't sorry in the least. "I thought you saw me standing here."

The changeling eyed me, considered her situation, and scowled. "You weren't standing there. You were hiding behind the desk like a big freak."

I didn't deny it. There was no point. "Well, since you've figured it out..." I motioned for Landon and Thistle to stand.

Slowly, the creature's eyes moved over Landon and my cousin before landing on Spencer. "You set me up." It wasn't a question. It was resignation.

"You are pretending to be a friend of mine," Spencer replied. "It seemed like a fair tradeoff."

She swore under her breath, then straightened. "How did you figure it out?"

I appreciated she wasn't trying to deny it. That would've made things worse. "Once we found the real Tricia Childs dead, it wasn't difficult to get to this place. I never met the real Tricia."

"Definitely not," the changeling agreed. She folded her arms over her chest. "Why did you go to the Childs house?"

I thought about Crusty, who had led us there. He hadn't decided if he could trust us yet, but he was testing us to work out his own plan. "Let's just say we had inside information."

The changeling's scowl broadened. "The clown. I knew I should've sent Burt."

"Where is Burt?" I figured if we were going to have a conversation I might as well get some actionable information out of it.

"Oh, he's around." The changeling's smile turned bemused. "He's quite interesting." She looked at Aunt Tillie, who had appeared in the opening that led to the hallway. "You're quite gifted. I wouldn't mind getting a few pointers from you."

Aunt Tillie screwed up her face. "I think I'll pass. I don't like sharing my gift with monsters."

"That's pretty rich coming from the woman who spends all her free time torturing another old woman to the point of mental illness."

"You said 'another,'" Aunt Tillie prodded. "Who is the other old woman? You'd better not be talking about me."

"Oh, but I am." The changeling's smile was evil.

"I'm going to give her ten-pound hemorrhoids for life," Aunt Tillie announced. "Be forewarned. It's coming."

The changeling rolled her eyes until they landed on me. "What's your plan? Are you actually going to kill an FBI agent when you're already under investigation for another murder? That's stupid, even for you."

"You're not an FBI agent," I countered.

"I have credentials that say otherwise. Without me, you have no chance of finding the real Patrice."

I could see why she used the tactic. It was her only chance to navigate an escape.

"The real Patrice was in the shed. We found her."

The changeling's eyes narrowed. "How?"

Gunner and Evan raised their hands as they swaggered through the door behind the changeling, Scout between them.

"We have super-sensitive noses," Gunner replied. "It wasn't that hard once we figured out what we should be looking for."

"How did you figure that out?" The question was barely out of the creature's mouth before reality struck her across the face. "Where is that clown?"

"Don't worry about it," I replied. "We've struck our own deal with him. As for Burt and the others, they're on our to-do list as soon as we're finished with you."

"The clowns won't roll over and accept whatever you throw at them. They've had a taste of freedom. They won't give it up."

"Probably not," I confirmed, "but they won't have a choice."

"It sounds as if you've got it all figured out." The changeling allowed her eyes to bounce around the room. I recognized the moment she realized she was surrounded. "It seems as if you've won. Why haven't you finished it?"

"I have some questions."

"Of course you do. Your type always has questions."

"I know you'll answer the questions because you're still looking for an out, a way to talk your way to freedom. We're giving you time you wouldn't otherwise get."

"Just ask your questions," the changeling snapped.

"Which prisoner was it?" I folded my arms over my chest and waited.

"Which prisoner was what?"

"You had a tie to one of the prisoners, one of the ones who died. This is payback for his death. Which one was it?"

If looks could kill, I would be dead. The changeling knew that launching herself at me would only bring the end sooner. She really was looking for any edge to make her escape. "Craig Archer," she finally spat.

The name didn't stand out.

"One of those in the warehouse," Landon replied. He'd memorized all the names. "One of those we took out early."

"Oh, right." I nodded. "Sorry about that."

"No, you're not," the changeling spat. "You don't regret what you did in the least."

She was right. "Fine. I don't regret it. They were a threat."

"It wasn't their fault. They were under a spell."

"That's true," I conceded. "We still didn't have a choice. It was us or them. Don't pretend you wouldn't have made the same choice."

"I have made that choice," she replied. "I've made it a hundred times over."

I bobbed my head. "Several times in my own town."

"Why is it okay for you to make that choice and not me?"

"I killed people trying to kill me. You're killing people to avenge an individual who was already in prison."

"He was sorry for what he did," she fired back. "He deserved a second chance."

"Then take it up with the people who hexed him into becoming an assassin."

"I can't. You handled those individuals."

"Then you should be thanking me, not trying to kill me."

"I wasn't going to kill you." The smile the changeling unleashed was chilling. "I was going to kill everything you love and leave you alone ... just as you did to me. I was going to start with her." She pointed at Aunt Tillie.

"I told you she was coming for me," Aunt Tillie said smugly.

"Then I was going to go for the other aunts," the changeling continued. "I was going to take your husband last. I was going to let you know I was coming, make you desperate to protect him, and then I was going to suck him dry in front of you."

"That didn't work out very well for you, did it?" I challenged.

"It would've worked if it hadn't been for the clown."

I shook my head. "You never would've gotten that far. Aunt Tillie might come across as crazy and distracted, but you never would've gotten one over on her."

"Besides," Evan added. "You would've had to get through me, and that wasn't going to happen."

The changeling's lips curved down. "You have more friends than I realized." She darted a glare to Spencer. "That was my mistake. You still can't kill me." She almost sang it. "You can't kill me because you'll never be able to explain what happened here. You'll always be suspects in Childs's death if you don't hand over the real culprit." She puffed out her chest as if she'd somehow just won her freedom.

"It won't be easy," I agreed. "Hodgins and Cam are unlikely to believe us simply because we want to play nice. Unfortunately for you, it appears the FBI is working on starting a paranormal team."

"And guess who they want on it," Scout taunted.

The changeling's face froze in disbelief. "They can't," she insisted. "They can't do that. They don't believe."

"Not everyone has a limited imagination," I said. "So, yeah, we're not going to be able to slip around Hodgins and Cam, but we can go over their heads."

"But..." The changeling vehemently shook her head. "That's not the plan."

Before I could tell her what she could do with her plan, movement outside the front window caught my attention. I darted my eyes in that direction and found Burt lurking with his butcher knife.

"How many are here?" I asked her when she allowed her gaze to move with mine.

Her smile told me that she was feeling better about her odds than she had been only seconds before. "Enough," she replied.

"Take them out," I said to Scout.

She nodded, a twisted smile on her face. "Gladly."

Evan was close on her heels. Gunner remained rooted to his spot.

"I'll stay here," the shifter called out. "I'll watch the door just in case she tries to make a run for it."

Scout laughed. "Okay, honey," she drawled. "I'll handle the fighting. You can feed me grapes in bed when I'm done."

Gunner wasn't smiling. "You're not funny," he complained.

"I have it on good authority that I'm downright hilarious," Scout replied.

"I'll watch her back," Evan promised.

"Watch for Burt," I reminded them. "He's wily."

"I've got Burt." Evan almost sounded eager to take on the clown. "Don't worry about him."

I turned my grin to the changeling. "Now, where were we?"

"You think you've won." The creature's fury was palpable. "You haven't. I'm nowhere near done."

The words were barely out of her mouth before a ravaged doll body flew through the open door and hit the grandfather clock with a heavy thunk.

"Sorry," Scout called from beyond the threshold. "I got a little too excited with that one."

The changeling stared down at the ruined doll. "You won't win," she said. "You can't beat me."

"I already have," I countered.

"You'll be arrested." The changeling was grasping now. "You'll be thrown behind bars. You'll have to live your life away from him anyway, and it will ruin you."

"That will never happen," Landon countered. "I won't let it."

"You can't explain it all away." The changeling was talking to herself more than me now. "There's too much. You're going down for the warden's death."

"You might have been able to pin that on me if you hadn't gotten greedy and gone after Mrs. Little," I said. "The fact that she has the same mark on the back of her neck—and the medical examiner is going to make note of the mark on the back of Tricia Childs's neck—means they're going to realize that it's bigger than what they thought."

"That doesn't mean you didn't do it."

I glanced at Landon and mustered a smile for his benefit. "I think I'm covered."

"You're definitely covered," he agreed.

Before I could say anything else, another clown doll came barreling into the room, skidding across the floor. It was bigger than the others ... and it had a knife.

Burt had another hole through his chest and yet he somehow managed to stagger to his feet.

"Kill them!" the changeling shrieked. "Do it now!"

Before Burt could respond, Gunner grabbed the clown's head and ripped it off. Then he used it like a bowling ball and threw it through the door as Burt's body crumpled to the floor.

"Stop throwing clowns at me!" he ordered Scout and Evan.

Evan apologized this time. "Sorry. He got away from me."

"You did it on purpose," Gunner insisted.

"It was an accident. I swear it."

Gunner growled something under his breath.

"Finish it," Landon whispered. He'd moved up behind me, his body close enough that I could feel his warmth pressed against my back. "End it. We still have cleanup. Don't drag it out."

He was right. This was my least favorite part of the job—endings were always hard—but it had to be done. "It's time to say goodbye," I said to the changeling.

"No." She fervently shook her head. "We can work together. I can help you get one over on the FBI."

"I don't want to get one over on the FBI."

"They'll never let you live in peace. Once they know what you are—"

"They already know."

"They don't." The changeling almost wailed the words. "They have no idea about our world."

"Is that true?" I asked Spencer.

To show her how wrong she was, he allowed his hands to shift into claws and held them up for her view.

The fake Patricia's face, already pale, whitened two shades. "I don't want this."

She almost sounded pathetic enough to give me pause. Then I remembered Brad Childs being thrown away in the ditch. I remembered Mrs. Little's confusion. I remembered Tricia Childs's body, and even though I'd never really met her, I felt pity for what could have been.

"I think we're done here." I took a step toward the changeling, grimacing when Evan appeared and grabbed her from behind. He lifted her by her neck and held her high enough that her toes dangled three inches above the ground.

"Do it," he ordered. His eyes were lit with adrenaline, the fight from outside fueling him. "Finish her."

Dragging things out was just cruel at this point. I sent my magic into the changeling and watched her grow rigid as she tried to fight it off. In the grand scheme of things, she wasn't that powerful. Within seconds, the fight was over and her body began to turn to ash and flake away.

"Well, that's going to be messy," Thistle said as she took in the ash flying around the room. "Our mothers won't like that."

"What about the yard?" I asked.

"It looks as if a *Toy Story* war erupted," Evan replied as he dusted off his hands. It was as if the changeling had never been here. Mrs. Little and the real Patrice would always carry the scars, though, so it wasn't easily forgotten for everybody. "We can have it picked up in no time."

"We should do it now." I lifted my eyes to the ceiling, where Mom and my aunts were tending to Patrice and Mrs. Little. "We're not quite done yet."

"Let's finish it." Landon's hand landed on my back. "Bay is right. There's more, and we're not ready to deal with it."

"We'd better get ready," I said. "I'm pretty sure it's coming to a head today."

Landon looked as if he wanted it to be otherwise, but he nodded. "Yeah. Let's get ready."

"Then can we get something to eat?" Gunner asked. "All the clown fear has made me hungry."

I laughed despite myself. "You came to the right house. I'm sure we can take care of your needs."

He managed a smile. "That's exactly what I wanted to hear."

29
TWENTY-NINE

I had no idea Landon had called Steve to the inn until the man walked through the door. He was dressed in a nice suit, his hair perfectly slicked back, and a smile at the ready.

I paused, a broom clutched in one hand and the dustpan in the other and stared like an idiot. "Hey."

Steve looked around the lobby, toed Burt's headless body, then grinned. "Looks like I missed something fun."

That was not how I would've described things. Still, this felt somehow fortuitous. "I wasn't expecting you." I shot Landon a questioning look.

"I didn't call him," Landon said.

That's when the truth of it hit me. "Where is Spencer?"

"He's eating cookies in the dining room," Chief Terry replied as he appeared in the hallway. He looked worried. Despite that, he marched forward and extended his hand. "Steve."

"Terry." Steve nodded in greeting.

"Don't hurt my family," Chief Terry blurted.

"I'm not here to hurt your family," Steve assured him. He glanced around. "Where are Cam and Hodgins?"

"Downtown," Chief Terry replied. "Dinner is in two hours, so I expect them here in about half that time."

"And Patrice?" Steve's expression was grave.

"Upstairs resting," Mom replied. She'd descended the stairs without me realizing. "She should be okay. She wasn't subjected to a long drain like Mrs. Little. In twenty-four hours, she'll be back to normal."

"Then we have time to talk."

Mom gestured for Steve to follow her. "We can have a nice afternoon snack."

I remained frozen as Steve and Chief Terry followed my mother. I didn't move until Landon slid next to me and took my hand.

"It will be okay," he said in a low voice.

I wanted to believe him. Heck, right up until I'd seen Steve I felt everything was going to be okay. Now I wasn't so certain. I fell into step with Landon, and we walked into the dining room.

Steve was seated in Aunt Tillie's usual chair—I had no idea where she'd disappeared to, but I had a feeling she was trying to figure out if there were more clowns to deal with—and he smiled indulgently at Mom as she poured him a glass of iced tea.

"Sit," Steve ordered.

My stomach constricted. He meant business. "What do you want to talk about?" I asked as I sat in my usual chair.

Landon took his spot, which was to Steve's right, and then Chief Terry sat on the other side of me. This was the normal configuration. Today it felt as if they were standing as shields. I appreciated the effort but didn't know if it was wise.

"Spencer has filled me in," Steve began. "I had hoped to broach the subject of a new team—under Landon's watchful eye, of course—on a day we didn't have reality breathing down our necks. It appears that is not the case."

I glanced at the end of the table, where Spencer sat with a plate of cookies in front of him. He looked as shell shocked as I felt.

"Let's cut to the chase." Steve rested both of his hands on the table. "I know you're witches. We've had ... *interesting* ... conversations before. We haven't gotten into too many details. After meeting you, I started researching the world you live in."

"Hemlock Cove?" I asked.

Steve sighed. "I know you want to protect your family, Bay, but it's really not necessary. I've gotten a crash course on the paranormal world in the past year. I've been made aware of a great number of things. I also realize that I know very little. I want you to help me bridge that gap."

I felt sick to my stomach. All of this was really happening. It was like a freight train barreling toward me and there was no stopping it.

"I don't expect you to sign on today," Steve continued. "I do hope that you'll consider helping us on certain cases going forward."

"What would that look like?" Landon asked. He leaned back, giving the appearance of being relaxed, and slipped his arm around the back of my chair. His message was clear: *Hurt my family and you'll pay.*

"I don't actually know the answer to that. I'm just getting started."

"Just getting started with what?" I asked.

"There's a lot out there besides the human world, Bay." His tone was serious. "I know that. I recognize that I'm behind and will need experts to teach me. I'm hoping you will be one of those experts."

I didn't respond. Mostly because I had no idea what to say.

"Landon is in a unique position to bridge the gap between two worlds," Steve continued. "Terry is also in a position to help. I don't expect you to come work for me."

I let loose the breath I didn't even know I was holding.

"You're not going to be an FBI agent," he said. "There aren't enough cases to warrant that."

"But?"

"But there are enough cases to warrant utilizing your skills," Steve replied. "It was the prison break that really got me thinking. I'd been pondering a few ideas before then, but the prison situation made me realize that your skills could be helpful in a lot of cases."

"What do you want her to do?" Mom, looking skeptical, asked. "She's not a witch for hire. You can't just call her and point her at an enemy and ask her to smite it."

"I have no intention of doing that," Steve assured her. "When we have a case that we think we need some help with, I will contact Landon. He will talk to you—and whatever friends you think might be necessary—and we'll go from there.

"It would be a test to start," he continued. "I don't know how it's going to go because, to my knowledge, it's never been done. We'll be learning as we go."

It didn't sound bad when he said it like that, but I wasn't certain I could trust him. "What about Patrice? What about Hodgins and Cam? How are you going to handle what happened here?"

"I'm not actually sure what happened." Steve scratched his jaw. "Spencer gave me a rundown, but I kind of got confused when he mentioned possessed clowns."

"Yes, well, welcome to our world." Landon laughed, but it was hollow.

"I don't expect you to tell me everything." Steve's gaze was pointed directly at me. "I know you have your own things to deal with and it has no bearing on what I might need your help with. I'm not your father."

"She has enough of those," Chief Terry muttered.

"I want to take small steps on the sort of partnership that will allow our world and your world to overlap," Steve said. "I don't know what that will look like. I only know I want it to work."

It was an interesting offer. "I have to think about it," I said.

Aunt Tillie picked that moment to insert herself into the conversation. She came barreling into the room, eyes wide. "I'm in." She stuck out her hand. "Sign me up."

I was floored. "Aunt Tillie," I hissed.

"You want to be part of the team?" Steve raised one skeptical eyebrow.

"I want to lead the team," Aunt Tillie replied.

"Oh, um..." Steve shifted on his chair, his discomfort eliciting a smirk from just about everybody gathered around the table.

"I watch all the detective shows," Aunt Tillie replied. "I've conducted my own investigations over the years. I had my own detective agency once."

"I don't believe that's in your records," Steve replied. Thankfully, he didn't bring up the Millie record. I'd warned Scout that we would be talking about it later. She neither denied "helping" Aunt Tillie falsify the record, nor seemed worried about how the ultimate conversation would go. Instead, she'd just smiled.

"It's true." Aunt Tillie was solemn. "I was born to solve crimes. I could do it professionally. That's lucky, since that's what you're asking us to do."

"Yes, well..." Steve flicked his eyes to me.

"I'll need a badge," Aunt Tillie continued. "And a gun. Oh, and I would love a taser. Winnie was supposed to get me one for Christmas two years ago but flaked out."

"That was never going to happen," Mom growled.

Aunt Tillie ignored her. "I'll need cuffs, too. And a direct line to the president."

Amusement flitted over Steve's features. "Anything else?"

"That should do it."

"Well, I can certainly make some of that happen."

"Not the taser," Mom hissed.

"Not the taser," Steve agreed. "Nor the gun. I might be able to come up with some sort of badge."

"We'll talk." Aunt Tillie winked at him.

"What about you?" Steve asked me.

I hated being put on the spot before I could have a private conversation with Landon. "I need to talk it out a bit," I replied. "I think, maybe, we can work something out."

Steve beamed at me. "Great. That's exactly what I want."

"You have to deal with Hodgins and Cam," Landon said. "We want them out of the inn. There's too much going on ... and they're looking at Bay for reasons other than they believe her to be guilty."

Steve was quiet for several seconds, a wealth of silent conversation taking place between him and Landon. Then he nodded. "I'm sure I can handle that."

I would believe it when I saw it. Still, I smiled. "We're having pot roast for dinner. Do you want to stay?"

Steve leaned back in his chair. "I don't mind if I do. That sounds delicious."

"Oh, it is," Aunt Tillie said. "You're going to need to get out of my chair if you want to live to taste it, though."

Steve looked taken aback. "Come again?"

"Get up, or I'll hex you."

Steve laughed as if it was all some big joke. When none of us laughed with him, he rose quickly. "Absolutely. Are there any other chairs I need to worry about?"

"No," I replied. "If you see a two-foot clown walking around, though, lift your feet. He acts friendly, but bites when you're not looking."

Steve's face went blank. "Something tells me this is going to be an interesting experiment."

Made in the USA
Las Vegas, NV
25 November 2024

12641200R00143